CW01665159

SPECIAL MESSAGE TO READERS

This book is published by

THE ULVERSCROFT FOUNDATION

a registered charity in the U.K., No. 264873

The Foundation was established in 1974 to provide funds to help towards research, diagnosis and treatment of eye diseases. Below are a few examples of contributions made by THE ULVERSCROFT FOUNDATION:

A new Children's Assessment Unit at Moorfield's Hospital, London.

•

Twin operating theatres at the Western Ophthalmic Hospital, London.

•

The Frederick Thorpe Ulverscroft Chair of Ophthalmology at the University of Leicester.

•

Eye Laser equipment to various eye hospitals.

If you would like to help further the work of the Foundation by making a donation or leaving a legacy, every contribution, no matter how small, is received with gratitude. Please write for details to:

THE ULVERSCROFT FOUNDATION,
The Green, Bradgate Road, Anstey,
Leicester LE7 7FU. England

Telephone: (0533)364325

I've travelled the world twice over,
Met the famous: saints and sinners,
Poets and artists, kings and queens,
Old stars and hopeful beginners,
I've been where no-one's been before,
Learned secrets from writers and cooks
All with one library ticket
To the wonderful world of books.

© JANICE JAMES.

A PLACE TO STAND

Noel's sister, Ethel, is dying, and for the first time since they were children, he spends a week in her company. As the old lady — a formidable fighter for women's rights in education — drifts in and out of consciousness, Noel discovers more about her struggles, both professional and intimate, and in the process he reassesses his own life. Buried in Ethel's past is a secret infatuation for a man who reappears in her story, and that of her daughter, in a most unexpected way.

Books by Stanley Middleton
in the Ulverscroft Large Print Series:

AN AFTER-DINNER'S SLEEP
RECOVERY

STANLEY MIDDLETON

A PLACE TO STAND

Complete and Unabridged

ULVERSCROFT
Leicester

First published in Great Britain in 1992 by
Hutchinson
Random Century Group Limited
London

First Large Print Edition
published January 1994
by arrangement with
Random House (UK) Limited
London

The right of Stanley Middleton to be identified
as the author of this work has been asserted
by him in accordance with the
Copyright, Designs and Patents Act, 1988

Copyright © 1994 by Stanley Middleton
All rights reserved

British Library CIP Data

Middleton, Stanley
A place to stand.—Large print ed.—
Ulverscroft large print series: general fiction
I. Title
823.914 [F]

ISBN 0–7089–3012–3

Published by
F. A. Thorpe (Publishing) Ltd.
Anstey, Leicestershire

Set by Words & Graphics Ltd.
Anstey, Leicestershire
Printed and bound in Great Britain by
T. J. Press (Padstow) Ltd., Padstow, Cornwall

This book is printed on acid-free paper

For Bill Kerr and Frank Pinion

. . . and permit
A place to stand and love in for a day,
With darkness and the death-hour rounding it.

Elizabeth Barrett Browning
Sonnets from the Portuguese

Dear, beauteous death, the jewel of the just.

Henry Vaughan, 'They are all gone'

Our little systems have their day;
They have their day and cease to be.

Alfred Tennyson, 'In Memoriam'

Of all the trees in England
Her sweet three corners in
Only the Ash, the bonnie Ash
Burns fierce while it is green.

Walter de la Mare, 'Trees'

The last of life, for which the first was made.

Robert Browning, 'Rabbi Ben Ezra'

1

THE old man looked out of his window.

He often stood there these days staring over his garden. Too often, he thought. Time was when he'd have been outside, busy, dominating the ground, writing his personality and knowledge over the showy beds, the borders, the trees. Alexander Pope had advised variety, surprise and a hiding of the limits. He'd achieved the last; his garden merged into those of his neighbours so that the huge sycamores and ash trees of the house three doors away always seemed to belong to him.

Summer light blazed, and though it was not yet eleven in the morning the temperature on his hall thermometer touched 79°F. He'd looked carefully at the centigrade scale, 26°; he had no reaction to this. He knew what 32° or 50° or 75° meant in the old style, but not centigrade numbers. The weathermen even called it Celsius these days on the television forecasts. Determined not be beaten he read both scales and tried to remember the second; living, he told himself ironically, in hope.

It had not rained for a fortnight and his lawn looked bare, hay-yellow. He ought to use the sprinkler, but the media reported water shortages all over the country, bans on the use of hose-pipes. The leaves on his trees and shrubs still shone green, their roots deep down in the thin sandy soil. Out there in the open spaces, on the patio, the paths, the front drive, the street it would be like a furnace, in the nineties, making the first step indoors a temperate pleasure.

> 'Or wallow naked in December snow
> By thinking on fantastic summer's
>   heat,'

he quoted to himself, pulling a wry face at this use of literature.

Noel Smith tapped the sill. It was too early to think about the preparation of lunch, and besides he was not hungry on these dog days. A cup of coffee, a few dry biscuits and a piece of Lancashire or Stilton cheese sufficed. But today he had energy of sorts and his obstinacy would therefore force him to the peeling of potatoes, the washing and slicing of runner beans and the selection of a piece of beef or pork from his cooler. Old men grow into habits of idleness; he did himself; on his better days he fought off languor and spent an hour in the kitchen preparing to be gluttonous to allay his puritan urge towards duty.

Butterflies fluttered on the huge buddleia next door which towered over his drive. His neighbours never pruned it (they had better things to do), and in this case were rewarded. Peacocks and cabbage whites darted and settled; there had been a red admiral on the path this morning, wings widespread. He'd stamped his foot for he did not want his cat to catch and eat the beautiful creature and it had obligingly taken off and he had nodded, thankful that sense existed somewhere. A black and white cat now leapt on to the sill and began to butt him, purring loudly. He hoisted it up and laid it over his left shoulder, burying his face in the fur.

"More food, eh? Come on, then."

He put the pet down and they made together for the kitchen.

On the table where he'd breakfasted his morning newspaper lay unopened and uncreased, reproaching him. What was the main item on the eight o'clock news? He could not remember.

He stood still, angry with himself, willing himself to recall. He succeeded. It was something about the foreign secretary and Hong Kong. Satisfied he bent to touch his cat to indicate their mission had not been forgotten.

"Come on, fellow."

Noel Smith, N. S. P. Smith, emeritus professor of English literature, did not give up, or in, easily. He spooned out the cat's meat from its tin; it smelt revolting. He'd mop the kitchen floor once Tib had fed himself. The animal bent with application to the dish.

Smith looked about.

The place seemed clean enough. He dusted, used the hoover, washed up religiously after every meal while his wife was away spending August with her relatives in France. He ought to join her; the family would make him welcome, feed him like a milord, take him into their confidence, treat him as an honorary Frenchman. When he was younger he had revelled in the sunshine, the welcome, the wine, his wife's obvious glowing pleasure at their efforts, but now he was in his seventy-fifth year he could not rouse himself. He drew in his stomach, looked at his face in the large mirror over the mantelpiece. He touched the polished wooden frame, with its small inlaid squares of black and white. It had stood on the mantelpiece over the firegrate in his mother's living room when he was a boy, fly-spotted then, now brilliant with new glass. He edged his gold-rimmed spectacles up his nose, snatched them off to allow them to dangle on a cord. His face had not sagged. Without his spectacles it had a youthful smoothness, a tan, an undented oval shape. The glasses were put sternly back into place, and the wrinkles, the pouches, the unevenness, the discolorations became apparent. Justified he turned away.

He could remember when he was a child not tall enough to look into the mirror, and how he'd stand on his toes, holding on to the fire-guard, craning his neck. His brothers, thirteen and twelve years older, combed their brilliantined hair, before college or cricket matches, and his sister, Ethel, nearly fifteen years his senior, powdered her nose in front of the mirror last thing before she set out for a social or concert or lecture, while he, preparing for school or bed, watched with an appraising eye.

His brothers were both dead, and his sister, almost ninety and lively until recently, he now understood to be dying. Noel Smith wondered if she minded; by far the strongest, the most forceful, always ready to set anyone, parents, siblings, neighbours, superiors, her own husband or children, right and to back her opinion by appropriate action, she might by this age have had enough of life, willing to lie in the churchyard with few to correct, and with no possibility of intervening on the behalf of this or that minority.

In the last few weeks Ethel, the powerful woman, had been sent back from the hospital to the home of her daughter, Imogen, to die. The daughter, an unmarried retired headmistress, knew her duty, prepared a bed in her specially bought bungalow, and wrote to Noel that her mother only had a week or two to live. That was two months ago. In the meantime he and Irène had spent a week in the Yorkshire Dales, and now she was on her annual summer month in France. Irène also was mindful of family responsibility, and had offered to stay back until the funeral was over, but he had demurred, saying she'd miss the best weather.

"It's just an excuse. You get rid of me for a month, and you don't have the trouble of going to France yourself."

"You may well be right," he answered drily.

"Are you growing old, or merely idle?" she asked.

Her English was perfect, but her sentence still held French intonational patterns, small, but distinctive and thoroughly attractive. He remembered the first time he had seen her, with her dark hair, parted in the middle, combed down puritanically straight and tied into a bun at the back, like his mother's. A lecturer at the time, he had been 'slumming' at a student 'crush' and had danced with this pale, neat Frenchwoman with violet eyes. She was shy, said little, but was not afraid of him. "You kicked me," she had said. "Not intentionally," he answered. "Are you a student?" she asked. Thirty-four years of age, he had felt flattered. "I am sorry," she continued when he had put her right. "You do not look your age. And besides many of the students are demobilized from the army and have served in the war, and so seem older." He smiled at her, attracted by the pert expression which complemented her self-contained calm. She was nineteen, but looked older. "Were you in the forces?" she asked. He had served in anti-aircraft. "Did you go abroad?" "No, I defended the east coast and then London." "Were you sorry? Not to travel, I mean?" "Oh, yes and no." In fact, though bored out of his mind, he had been pleased to stay; he did not know how it happened as most of his fellow subalterns had been posted overseas, but always without him. Luck? He supposed so.

He had danced once more with Irène Dalsaux, and later in the month had invited her to lunch. By the end of the year they were engaged, and Irène, having consulted her family, had decided not to complete her studies at the Sorbonne, but to marry her Englishman. By the time that he had achieved a chair at the age of thirty-nine, she had borne him a son and had taken a degree in English and French. Like his sister she knew, or that was his impression, much more clearly what life was about than he did. Never hectoring, always sane, she made her own way. When he sometimes asked her, mischievously, whether she regretted marrying an Englishman she replied slowly, smiling, "There are drawbacks to everything, as well you should know."

Noel Smith forced himself to concentrate on the leaves of a large flowering cherry tree. They pointed downwards, bright but dusty-dry, sometimes half-shadowed. This year they were free from blackfly in spite of the mild winter and the recent hot weather. He admired the tree in spring, in its short season of blossom, though the garden round it would soon be covered, he knew, with brown, lumpy remains of the flowers, littering ground, shrubs, grass. There were drawbacks to everything. The telephone rang, and he started, but did not move. He would wait, letting it burr on, to see if the caller was serious.

In the end he picked up the phone, announced himself.

"This is Imogen." The smart, incisive voice of his niece, Ethel's daughter. He licked his lips. Her mother must have died. She inquired after his health, commenting on his reply before asking about Irène in France. Imogen was a year or so younger than her aunt-by-marriage. This social conversation suggested that Ethel was still alive. He asked plainly, drily. "She is much the same. Sinking, I suppose. Losing weight, but not violently. Bedridden."

"Is she in pain?"

"Discomfort is perhaps nearer. But you know Ethel. She doesn't make a fuss." Imogen drew in her breath. "Of course, from time to time she drifts away."

"What does that mean?" He could not connect drifting with his sister.

"Well, though she is clear in her mind much of the time, she is very seriously ill and so weak that there are periods when she seems unsure where she is or what is happening."

"In what way?"

"Well, she sometimes seems to think that my father's still alive, and needs looking after." William Wagstaffe, the father, had been a Manchester solicitor, respected and successful but, rumour had it, much under the thumb of his wife. "Only yesterday she said, 'Imogen, look at the collars of Daddy's shirts. He doesn't notice if they've begun to fray'." Wagstaffe had been dead for sixteen years.

"Does she seem unhappy?"

"It's difficult to say. She knows she's not in control even of herself and needs a lot of help, but I'd say she comes to terms with it most of the time. She was always a realist."

Noel doubted it. Ethel Wagstaffe saw the world as she wanted it, or was trying to make it, but he said nothing. He felt sorry for Imogen, a handsome woman, full of certainties like her mother, but who never married. He wondered why; perhaps the combination of so formidable a mother and daughter had repelled suitors. He doubted that also.

"The reason I'm ringing is that she would like to see you."

"For any specific reason?" That sounded mean-minded as soon as he'd said it.

"Not really. She dwells in the past. She has for some time, even before she was really ill." That was the first he had heard of it. "And last night she said, 'I would like to see our Noel again.' I explained that Irène was back in France, and that you didn't much like travelling on your own, but she snapped back at me in quite her old manner, 'Imogen, you will argue. Just ring him up and ask and see what he says.' So here I am carrying out my instructions."

He listened. 'Our Noel.' The possessive adjective harked back to their childhood. Ethel Wagstaffe, ex-Principal of the Kay-Shuttleworth College of Education, spoke standard English. 'I'd like to see Noel again.' The intrusive word indicated recession or affection revived; he dreaded both. He and his niece discussed dates, made up their minds. He would travel up tomorrow, stay overnight. Imogen would meet him at the station.

"Can you leave your mother?"

"Yes. Provided British Rail aren't too late delivering you. I can always ask a neighbour to look in." Imogen seemed in no hurry to ring off. "Are you doing anything interesting now?"

"Not really. It's too hot to go out for any length of time. I'm reviewing three books on Shakespeare for the *Times Higher Educational Supplement*."

"Are they good?"

"Two of them are. Of their kind. Scholarly."

"You don't sound very enthusiastic." Imogen could be as sharp as her mother.

"No, I'm not. But that's a comment on me rather than the books. I don't feel the excitement I did once. When I was younger critics seemed to be making important discoveries, demonstrating critical insights, opening eyes to substantial subtleties in the texts. It made me excited even when I disagreed. Now, I'm interested, but it doesn't seem to matter."

"And do you feel the same about

Shakespeare himself?"

"I often read a scene or two. And he's still marvellous. But there are gaps. I've never come to terms with *Othello*."

"Do you go to the theatre to see performances?"

"When Irène forces me to. I'm a sticker, no, a stuck-in-the-mud? Past. Passive."

"I'll see you tomorrow afternoon, then."

He promised to call her again when he had contacted the station and chosen his train. He did not want to go. He'd have to ring Irène in France so that she wouldn't be worried when her calls went unanswered; he'd have to ask his neighbour to feed his cat, keep an eye on the house. He telephoned the inquiry office; engaged, as he expected. He dragged himself sullenly about the place, mocking himself. He was going away one day and returning the next; he could now put off the writing of his review for three days. That was idleness. He knew what he wanted to say. Groaning, he pushed out into the burning heat to see Mrs Strangeways, his neighbour, who would pull sympathetic faces, invite him in for coffee, question him closely about his sister's illness, his own readiness or fitness to travel. He sighed. A taxi to the station, though a pound to a penny Helen Strangeways would insist on driving him there herself, an hour or two on a comfortable train through the Pennines, beautiful and scorched, then a short drive in Imogen's Granada. She'd be grateful for the opportunity to get out of the house to pick up her distinguished uncle. His door did not close easily; he wrestled with it, slammed it to, walked the drive in melancholy. He turned in next door between the high laurel hedges, rang his neighbour's bell, depressed, not expecting an answer though he'd heard Helen drive home not twenty minutes ago.

At least he was alive, not unwell. The last enemy had not put the finger on him as on his sister. That did nothing to cheer him. He saw Helen Strangeways' blue-white hair through the stained-glass panel, heard her unclasp the chain, unfasten the lock.

He prepared his face, the introductory words to his suit.

2

NOEL SMITH'S train drew in on time, and his niece stood handsomely in the foyer. They kissed in an embarrassed scuffle, he stooping hugely. For a few minutes they sat in her car while she described her mother's final cancer, the prognostications of the doctors, their treatment about which she was scathing, and the deterioration of the last weeks. Her mother had up to this time been herself, looking disease and death in the face, fighting it off, if weakly, but now since her last stay in hospital her strength had evaporated, her spirit lost.

"She looks awful," Imogen warned. "There's nothing of her but skin and bone. The doctor doesn't know how she's lasted so long."

"Can she eat?"

"Pap. She has difficulty in swallowing."

"And pain?"

"She's drugged. I don't think she's

. . . I don't know. She's not happy."

Noel thought how like her mother Imogen was; she was preparing him for his ordeal, a good teacher.

"Will she know me?"

"Oh yes. I think so. She's looking forward to seeing you again."

He had not visited Imogen at home, but knew the street well for his sister had lived there. Tree-lined, it consisted of spacious semi-detached villas, the Gothic front doors approached by wide steps, the gardens dark with cherry trees, lilacs, holly, weigela, berberis, laurels. A few of the houses, to judge by the banks of lists and bells, were now divided into flats, but the street had not gone down far in the world, was almost as respectable as when William Wagstaffe had brought his wife here sixty years ago. When Noel had last visited his sister, two years back he remembered with regret, she had occupied number 4, under high ceilings, behind plate-glass windows large as shop-fronts, with a garden broad enough to need a gardener three times a week. Ethel had lived with a companion, Deirdre Commons, formerly head of the department of home economics at the training college where Ethel had been principal. These two lively old ladies had both continued to drive, cook, clean and set surburban Manchester right in their different forthright ways. Deirdre was ten years younger than her mentor, had died unexpectedly nearly eight years ago soon after Noel's last prolonged visit, and from that time Ethel's decline had begun. He recalled the four days there, the arguments about education, the giggling fits that he and his sister had succumbed to when they recalled incidents from his childhood. It must have been much this time of year; Irène, he recalled, was in France. The three had spent a day at a cricket match at Old Trafford, and he had been surprised at the paucity of the spectators. The old ladies had been much at home, coddling him, tempting him to eat, and obviously expecting him to enjoy every ball bowled. He did his best for them. Three months later Deirdre had died suddenly, walking the wide garden. Ethel, already successfully treated for cancer, found herself ill and alone again, and was admitted to hospital.

He and Irène had driven up twice while Ethel was in dock, but had no call to visit 4 Staines Avenue.

Imogen lived in a modern bungalow built in the garden of the corner villa, once the sole detached building, at the far end of the street from her mother's house. She had flatly refused to move in with her parent when she first began to consider retirement, but then, typically, Noel thought, had compromised by buying this expensive place in the avenue where she had been brought up as a child. Her mother's house had been let furnished to a family of American academics.

An admirable driver, the niece talked in short, informative sentences all the way. The sun burnt strongly in an air humid and unmoving as she parked on her gravel drive. Leaves on the lime trees in the avenue were already turning yellow. A peacock butterfly dodged past Noel's head. Somewhere in the gardens along the street youngsters squealed before a shrill, authoritative voice issued orders to the screaming children.

"I'm stiff," he said. "Sitting doesn't suit me."

"I'll carry your case."
"No, you won't."
Imogen introduced him to Mrs Stubbs, the neighbour, who was sitting in.
"How is she?" the daughter asked. "Has she been all right?"
"She was restless for a start, but I told her you wouldn't be long, and she soon dropped off. I looked in a couple of times, and kept the door open, but she was dozing."
The woman edged out, and Imogen led her uncle to the kitchen. "I'll put the kettle on and go in to Mother first. We won't disturb her if she's asleep. If she's awake, she'll want me to smarten her up before you see her." She whispered and smiled, tiptoed away to leave Noel to stare once more out of a window.
A line of three bungalows had been built in the garden of the corner house which towered, fortunately to the west, over them. Each plot was divided from the next by a rustic fence, and all seemed equally neat. An old lime and a sycamore remained in place and at the end of Imogen's thin lawn a massive hawthorn struggled

and bushed, a survivor presumably from the time when this was farm land. He gained the impression of a spick and span, well-cared-for estate, labour-saving but not cramped, of comfort, lassitude on this scorching afternoon, of money well spent. He turned round; the kitchen was ample, more convenient than his own, and modern, with machinery hidden behind matching woodwork, large work spaces, Scandinavian elegance.

Imogen crept back, closing the door.

"Well away," she said. She made tea, produced a jam sponge. "We'll eat later, when it's cooler, if it is cooler."

As they drank the Earl Grey Imogen told him of the circumstances under which she had bought her bungalow. "All three of us here had at some earlier period lived along the road. Mr Cooper, who lives in the big house, was in no hurry to sell; he's a builder, and he mentioned his scheme to my mother who thought of me. She knew she'd have to give that house of hers up sooner or later, but didn't really want to move. Neither did she want to take this bungalow herself at that time, as

Cooper suggested; she wanted to stay in number 4 as long as she could."

"These weren't built when I was last over here. That must be two years ago."

"No, but they were planned. One was intended for Mrs Cooper's sister, and one for Miss Spondon, a relative — she lived nearly opposite us when I was a child — and the third was for some suitably qualified buyer such as my mother. In the end I was found worthy." Imogen laughed.

She looked in again on her mother, still asleep, and then invited her uncle to take a turn down the pastel-shaded flagstones that ran the length of the garden. Outside the heat was overpowering. No one else anywhere risked the burning air.

"'The heavens are as brass,'" he said. "It's more like Timbuctoo than Manchester." He wiped his brow with a large, clean handkerchief. "Are you pleased to be back here?"

"No. The place is convenient. And I can give my mother care in the last weeks of her life. So I consider I've done the right thing. But when she dies I shall look round. In the country somewhere."

They were standing under the shade of two aged apple trees, part of the old garden.

"You don't mind living on your own?"

"I'm used to it. I prefer it, if anything. My mother liked somebody to dominate, hence Deirdre Commons. There are flashes of it still. Only yesterday she looked at me, and her voice was so weak I could barely make out what she was saying, 'Imogen, you came into this room like an old woman.' I couldn't help smiling. Here she is, nearly in the next world, and yet sufficiently the old-fashioned pedagogue to want to make last-minute improvements in this."

When nearly an hour later they had just started on a delicious vegetable soup, much apologized for by Imogen as unsuitable for tropical weather, the bell rang from the bedroom.

"Ah, ah, trouble," Imogen said. "She's woken up. You finish your soup."

It must have been fifteen minutes later when the daughter emerged, rubbing her hands.

"Sorry about that."

"How is she?"

"Oh, so so. She'd like to see you. Before I feed her. I'll just finish this." She pointed at her bowl.

"It will be cold."

"Just right for this heat."

She tiptoed towards the door, opened it and called in a strong, school-hall voice, "Here's Noel come to see you, Mother."

She ushered him forward, stood back to observe.

"Ethel," he said. "How are you?"

A smile cracked his sister's wrinkled face. He would not have recognized her. The forehead and cheeks were sallow, deeply lined and thin, stretched to the bone. Ethel had been round-faced, bonny, full-fleshed, large. Now she looked more like the skeleton of a child, some small skull half-cleaned at an archaeological dig. He took one of the claw-like hands, repeated his question. Her bony palm was warm. He bent to kiss her dry lips.

"It's Noel, Mother," Imogen said, from behind him.

"I know. I know." Ethel closed her eyes, opened them again. "I would recognize that voice anywhere." She murmured a short, incomprehensible phrase.

"What does she say?" he asked.

"What was that, Mother?"

Again the mumble. Noel held on to the hand.

"'Linden Lea'?" Imogen's interpretative query.

"'Linden Lea'," Noel confirmed. "I sang it at a concert when I was a boy. She liked to hear me sing it."

"I see. Just sit with her for a moment, will you? While I fetch her soup." Imogen marched smartly away.

"How are you, then, Ethel?" He tried again.

This time she rolled her head to look at him with wide-open eyes. She was not wearing her glasses so that the eyes pinched small, pig-like. Though she did not speak, the weak stare announced the absence of hope. The set of the poor, withered face conveyed an ironical approval of this: you see now to what I am reduced.

"Are you all right?" Her real voice croaked, almost unintelligibly.

"Quite well."

"Is Irène here with you?"

"No, she's in France."

"Is she?" The voice took on an ephemeral strength, as if she were indignant at Irène's defection.

"She's staying with her mother and sister." He gave a short, clear account of his wife's itinerary. When his sister did not answer, he gave a slow, brief account of his journey. "It's really very hot. It's roasting," he concluded. Ethel spoke, not clearly, a mumble which he suddenly understood half way through.

"Who can behold the blazing light?
Who can approach consuming flame?"

A hymn. The dull eyes watched his. Their father quoted hymns, but he was a pillar of pious nonconformity. Ethel was, if anything, an Anglican atheist, willing to take her part in such religious observances that her position of college principal demanded, but once she had decided intellectually that she could no longer believe in the existence of God, showed no further interest in forms of prayer, worship, ceremonial, music, even theological scholarship. Now near death, she harked back to and aped the father she had both admired and despised so that Noel's mention of the summer heat had dredged up a not very apposite quotation from the hymn book. How long was it since she had last recalled, or spoken, these lines? In her childhood, probably.

"Who wrote that?" he asked. He could remember no more of the hymn, not the first line nor the author. Isaac Watts? He did not know. Ethel made no attempt to reply, lay still, breathing heavily, hands flat on the counterpane. The brother was rescued from silence by the arrival of Imogen with a bowl on a tray.

"Do you mind going out?" she whispered, back to her mother. Noel left, occupied his uncleared place at the dining table; his niece, he noticed, had not touched her soup.

Twenty minutes later Imogen returned, grimly smiling. "Sorry to keep you waiting. This is what it's like."

"Did she eat anything?"

"Yes. Not bad. But it's a messy

business. She wouldn't like you to see the operation. And I've cleaned her up and potted her. The nurse will be coming in to give her an injection."

"That's a good service you have. I mean at this time of the evening."

"She lives close by. Comes in. She likes a chat. Does it in mufti."

She served out prepared salad, a delicious home-made cold meat pie with an egg in the middle.

"I haven't done potatoes," she apologized. "I'm trying to keep my weight down."

Both ate heartily, relieved that they were not required to talk. Imogen offered her uncle three choices of pudding, but he refused them all. She said that excused her from overindulgence, and both had settled to black coffee when the nurse arrived. Introductions were made; the title 'professor' impressed, was used twice a minute. Imogen suggested that Noel spent ten minutes with his sister while Mrs Jones prepared her equipment. He obeyed, fortified by a second cup of coffee which he carried in with him.

His sister was awake, acknowledging

him with a feeble, skewed movement of the head.

"How are you?" He leaned over. Ethel did not answer. "The nurse is here." No sign. He asked, for no good reason, if she remembered the nurse who lived next door to them when he was small. Ethel might well have left home to go to the university at that time, he couldn't be sure.

"Cousins," he said. "Elsie Cousins. I think that was her name."

Ethel murmured. He bent over.

"Constance," she said. "Elsie was the mother."

"That's right. Connie Cousins." It seemed a triumph that his sister had accurately called up the name from seventy years ago; she could barely articulate it, but it was ready for reference. Not that Nurse Cousins had played any great part in their lives. Ethel was speaking again.

"A beautiful head of red, curly hair." He made this out from the breathy, gasping syllables.

"I don't remember her appearance at all."

"She went to Canada. Married a wounded officer she'd looked after in the war. He came back to fetch her."

The effort, reflected by a new clarity of delivery, seemed to satisfy Ethel so that she closed her eyes. She had played her due part in the social round. Why she had answered his question about Constance, and not about her own health, he could not understand. He mentioned other neighbours, then notabilities at their father's Wesleyan chapel, trustees, poor stewards, Sunday School superintendants, ministers, one of whom, the young Rev. J. Gordon Stallworthy, B.A., was thought to be 'sweet on her'. His trawl brought no catch. Ethel's eyes were firmly closed. He took her hand, thought he recognized a returned pressure, could not be certain. The arrival of the nurse, with a quiet but firm greeting, addressing the patient as 'we', relieved him.

"We've had a nice chat with your brother, have we, Mrs Wagstaffe?"

Mrs Jones prepared her syringe from the bag she had placed on the dressing table.

"Perhaps you'd like to say good night,

Professor," she volunteered. "We usually settle down after this."

He bent and kissed his sister on the lips. She opened her eyes wide, those faded, grey-green eyes that were once steely. He stroked her hand. The nurse, almost ready, motioned him out.

"Your brother will see you tomorrow. Say good night."

Imogen entered; he left, closing the door. He wandered to the french window, looked out on the garden, now faintly darkening. "The nights are beginning to draw in," he said aloud. He approved of phatic communion, even with himself. From behind the door, across the hall, he could hear movements from the sickroom, the nurse's mild, firm, incomprehensible utterances, Imogen's "Oh, isn't that good?" in a youthful beauty of clarity. He watched unmoving, dusty leaves.

When the women returned he asked the nurse, comfortably at coffee and digestive biscuits, how long his sister had to live. Imogen, busy round the room, stood still for the verdict.

"I don't know, Professor. Nobody knows. My impression is that they expected her to go while she was in the hospital."

"So it might be weeks?"

"I don't like to put a time on it. She's strong for her age and her illness."

3

NEXT morning at seven fifteen Noel Smith, shaved and dressed, walked the coloured flagstones with his niece.

"This is the best time of the day," she said. "Before it's too hot." Not a wisp of cloud marred the blue sky. "I couldn't sleep last night."

"Did your mother sleep well?"

"Yes. I went in several times. I usually do. She wakes, but she doesn't make a fuss. Well, not always." Imogen grimaced. "She'll be asleep now. Dozing."

They sat on the small teak garden seat.

"It must be hard work for you," he said.

"I feel cramped. I can't leave her for more than half an hour while I go shopping, and yet I look forward to, I long for these little expeditions. They're life-savers. Every morning and afternoon. Thirty minutes' freedom."

"You leave her?"

"Yes. If it's longer, as yesterday, when I'd no idea whether your train would be on time, then I ask a neighbour to sit in. Two of them are very good." She sighed. "And a nurse comes in twice a day, and a home help. To bath her."

"What about the doctor?"

"He should call this week. He's a sensible young man."

"Why didn't they keep her in hospital?" he asked.

"To die?" Like Mother, he thought.

"Yes." Blunt to blunt.

"I don't know. Perhaps they can use the bed for somebody they can cure. Perhaps they think she'd prefer to be home. Perhaps it saves the NHS money."

"It's hard on you."

"It's been less than three weeks, Uncle Noel. I've already had one good holiday earlier this year. They don't think it will be for long. There are thousands looking after parents these days. And they get no respite. And damned little help. And that's over years." Her voice snapped. Noel laid his hand on her muscular forearm. She smiled, her eyes green.

"Are you going back today?"
"That was the idea."
"Can you stay a bit longer?"
"I suppose so. I can ring the neighbour about the cat. And let Irène know where I am."
"I think Mother would like it. She kept saying to the nurse how glad she was that you were here, that you were her favourite brother."
"Her only one." Joseph and Thomas were both gone. Tom had died younger than Noel was now. And Joe had puffed and panted on to his late seventies, outliving his childless wife. Both were successful scientists, Tom brilliant and volatile.
"She will be glad."
Imogen was in no hurry to move. The bustling, energetic woman sat still as a stone, her round face almost unlined.
"It will mean more work for you," he said.
"I won't put myself out."
They both laughed, drily, briefly, like strangers.
"Has your brother been down?" he inquired.

"When she was in hospital. Soon after the operation. She was so weak she barely knew Bill."

"Did that upset him?"

"No. He gave the impression that's what he expected of somebody on the point of death. He's a hard nut." A research engineer, he had transferred his skills early to administration.

"Why's that?"

"Billy lives in another world." A scientific civil servant. "He's never at home. Flying to this place and that. He's on loan to the United Nations."

"Does he do any scientific work now?"

"At a bench, you mean? No. He's an organiser. He came down once he thought Mother was dying, and the hospital said she had only a day or two to live, but his wife and he both gave the impression that they'd something more important to do, and that when they had to appear for the funeral that would be at the expense of, oh, God knows what international transaction."

"Your mother would be glad to see him."

"I suppose so."

The answer suggested the exact opposite, so that he looked carefully at his niece. She noticed but did not appear to resent his scrutiny. This foursquare, good-looking woman spoke from a sense of unfairness. As clever as her brothers, she had never quite had their expectations and was left now to help the mother, who in the first place had stacked the cards against her, to the grave. That was his guess.

"We all have our own concerns. It's natural. Billy's retiring this year, or next, and he and Shirley are going to settle in America."

"Why?"

"God knows. Consultancies, perhaps. Billy's not very used to explaining his motives to subordinates. He'll have had some offer. We're a competitive lot. Mother, both boys, even Ray. I'm as bad. In spite of ending up back in the same street where I was born, looking after Ma." She laughed again, coughed.

Noel Smith wished he knew his niece better. She had taken early retirement from the headship of a comprehensive school for no very sound reason, according to her mother. 'She says,' Ethel had reported two years ago when the idea was first broached, 'that she has spent quite enough of her life trying to organize the impossible.' The mother's attitude seemed ambivalent. She had worked on beyond the age of sixty-five, but tried to admire a daughter who knew her mind sufficiently well to decide to go at fifty-six, though the admiration was of the same order one granted to an honourable Roman patrician one read about falling on his sword. Noel guessed that the women had argued, and bitterly, but there was no sign of this on Imogen's smooth face. She had known her duty.

They went indoors to breakfast, but neither ate much. He gave some account of Irène's family and their affairs, and of a holiday they hoped to take later in the year in Finland.

"Won't it be cold?"

"Desperate. But dry. We'll be mostly in Helsinki or Vaasa."

"Are you lecturing?"

"Yes. Just twice. It's mostly for concerts. We're staying with friends."

He coughed. "And you? Will you be going away? When, when . . . " He had lost his boldness.

"I've promised myself a holiday after Mother has died. It's something to hang on to. But you never know. I can't guess how I shall feel. I've been expecting her death now for long enough. But when it comes it may bowl me over. One can't tell. A world which doesn't contain somewhere inside itself my mother alive and talking will be so different I don't know how I'll put up with it. Do you recommend cruises?"

"I've never been on one."

"You surprise me."

"My life seems to me a whole set of missed opportunities," Noel answered, "cruises amongst them."

Imogen rose to reach for the coffee percolator. She poured.

"You mustn't talk like that. I would have said you've been outstandingly successful. A chair, three highly regarded books, dozens of articles, time in America, offers from there which you turned down, a beautiful wife, a son. What more can you want?"

"'What then? sang Plato's ghost. What then?'"

"No doubt." She replaced the pot with a flourish. "I take it that's a quotation from somebody."

"Yeats."

"Suggesting that success is not all it's cracked up to be?" She smiled broadly, enjoying this. He realized that his niece had not held a proper conversation for weeks, had asked him to stay on for her own sake as well as her mother's.

"Yes. What about your mother? Did she, does she feel she's not achieved all she could?"

"She doesn't say so. Anyhow, she wouldn't confess to me. I guess that, like me, she feels her brothers all had an easier time than she did, all managed to go further."

"They're all scientists except Ethel and me."

"Yes. I'm amongst the boys, I'm afraid." She laughed, but without noise. He guessed her normal voice was louder, that sickroom attendance had softened it, improved it. "But you became a professor."

"Is that so much?"

They heard a groan, a gurgling sound from Ethel's bedroom. "Trouble," Imogen said. "She's awake. Well," she straightened her shoulders, "the day begins."

He cleared the breakfast dishes while she tidied her mother.

"How is she?" As he asked, Imogen shrugged, almost violently.

"Perhaps you'd sit with her a minute while I get her breakfast."

His sister lay stone still, flat to bed and pillow. Her eyes were shut, and her skin inhumanly sallow.

"Good morning, Ethel." He affected cheerfulness. His sister murmured an answer, without apparent movement. He asked how she felt, what sort of a night she had spent, said a word or two about the calm beauty of the morning, announced that he intended to stay on another day, uselessly detailing the arrangements this entailed, described his own sleeping habits and what he ate for breakfast. The sick woman made a slight sound of acknowledgement now and then, a creak of voice, inarticulate but vaguely signalling attention. She did not open her eyes or stir in any fashion in the bed. Noel paused between each sentence, waiting, listening for clues before he began to speak again.

Finally, hopelessly, he took her hand. It was emaciated, but clean beyond reason, the nails admirably cared for. He felt no answering pressure, but the flesh seemed warm. Thus they sat, he conscious most of his own discomfort and inadequacy. Searching his mind he asked about Mr Cooper in the big house, the man who had built these bungalows in his garden. He expanded his inquiry: how old was he? Retired? Active still? Not even a sound, so that he felt his sister was in some way rebuking him for inflicting his curiosity on her, torturing her weakness with his inanities. He stared at the sky through the half-drawn curtains.

He remembered being sent as a punishment to his bedroom at the age of ten, in the summer holiday before he started secondary school. His father had arrived home from work; he was chief clerk in the Beechnall Municipal Transport Offices, and had accused his son of breaking Mrs Taylor's fanlight with a ball. The neighbour had been waiting for the father's arrival — his regularity matched Kant's — with her story. Noel had been playing with a ball in the street; she had seen him earlier tiptoeing into her front garden to retrieve his ball without permission, and after the breakage she had seen him turning up the street. He could not shake her story. She was sure.

Joseph Smith was annoyed to be stopped on the way to his evening meal. He loved to step into their dark, narrow front corridor, and there remove bowler hat, hang up his umbrella, and square his attache case to the skirting board. Then he would call out a greeting, tiptoe upstairs, wash his hands, change his jacket, knowing full well that the first course would be on the table three minutes later.

This evening he disturbed his routine.

Disposing of bowler and umbrella, he called out, "Noel." He heard nothing from the dining room, then his wife's anxious, "Noel, your dad wants you." She disliked change more than her husband. The boy appeared, clean for the evening meal.

"Yes, Dad?"

"You've broken a window in Mrs Taylor's, haven't you?"

"No, Dad."

"A pane in her fanlight then?" Testily but prepared to admit initial inaccuracy.

"No, Dad."

"You were playing with your ball in the street in spite of the fact that I've told you not to do so."

"I was only bouncing it."

"You were playing with it. Moreover, you threw it over her garden wall and went looking for it without asking Mrs Taylor if you could do so. Now, don't go denying it. She saw you."

"Yes, Dad."

"And not an hour later you broke her fanlight. Again, she came out, saw you running up the street, called out to you, but you were off and round the corner into Raglan Road."

"No, Dad."

Joseph Smith had had a tiring day, trying to instruct his underlings in a new method of accountancy that would save them time and the city council money. They had been, in spite of sycophantic expressions of eagerness, reluctant to learn. This did not surprise him in that he himself saw little advantage in the proposed changes to him, them, the office, the transport system, the city's coffers. But he did as he was bid, and they must follow his example. It had been a black day, and Mrs Taylor's wordy postponement of his deserved evening meal had not improved his temper. His lips pressed hard together.

"It's no use denying it, Noel. Mrs Taylor saw you. I shall inquire about the cost of the damage and deduct it from your spending money. Right?"

"I didn't do it."

"Noel. You have been disobedient. I've told you about that ball in the street at least twice." Mr Smith rubbed his hands. "Now, don't add lying to it."

"I'm not."

"Mrs Taylor saw you."

"She didn't. She's the liar."

The boy's defiance angered Joseph Smith. He wanted the business over and done with, guilt admitted, punishment taken like a man. He also knew that the dining-room door was open, that every word was being overheard by his wife, no great matter, by Ethel about to be married in three weeks' time, by Joseph junior his eldest son, already at twenty-three doctor of philosophy in chemistry, and Thomas, a year younger, even brighter, with first-class honours in physics and halfway to his doctorate already. They would be all ears, and judgement.

"Don't use that word."

"Well, she is."

"When you've done wrong, you should admit it."

"I haven't."

Joseph Smith considered; he was fair, but knew that human beings lied, especially where money was concerned.

"You had better go up to your bedroom, young man, until you're in a better frame of mind."

"I shall miss my tea."

"That's the idea of punishment."

"It's not fair."

"You have been disobedient, if nothing else. Now, up you go."

The child turned, and walked upstairs very slowly, making his father, who came up behind him, wait. In his bedroom he left the door open, listened to Joseph's ablutions and descent. There after he heard the sounds of talk in the dining room as he sat with full throat, but could make no sense of what they said. The harshness of the world grated on him; he had not been playing in the street, but returning on an errand to the grocer's for his mother had bounced his sponge ball as he walked. It had caught the corner of a badly laid paving stone and flown, trickled rather, at an angle over Mrs Taylor's low wall. He could see it; he would tread on no plants to retrieve it; he would trouble nobody, harm nothing. Like a shot he was in and out of the front gate. The old dear must have been sitting in her front room behind the lace curtains.

From downstairs he heard a plaintive appeal from his mother. She had left the table, stood in the front passage.

"Not now, Ethel. Leave it at least until we have finished the meal."

The petition went unnoticed, and he

heard the front door open and close. In his distress he did not connect the happening with himself. A tear or two had squeezed on to his cheeks against his will. An adult had believed an adult, as always. His father had not made proper inquiries, nor had he himself advanced his defence to advantage. The accusation had been too unexpected. He rehearsed his case in his mind, over, over again.

Conversation downstairs seemed subdued. Usually the boys, cycling back from their labs, had plenty to say for themselves, and Ethel, in university vacations or as now on school holidays, would lay down the law energetically for them all. Joseph, the father, enjoyed argument with his brilliant children. He was clever, and was to be advanced to the general managership of the city transport services within the next few weeks. His application and imminent interview determined in part his present irritability. It was unusual for a chief clerk to apply for such promotion, even if like Smith he was quite capable of doing the job superlatively well: the council committee usually appointed from outside. But less than a year ago they had chosen some highly qualified high talker with a string of letters as long as your arm behind his name, only to find him both idle and incompetent. Fortunately for them, this manager, who had considered living in Beechnall as exile amongst barbarians, had applied elsewhere and supported by glowing testimonials from his dissatisfied employers had landed the post. Now a small, strong caucus had pressed Joseph Smith to put his name forward, and he fared so well in the interviews that Noel until the time he graduated from Oxford had the pleasure, or otherwise, of seeing his father's name painted on the sides of tramcars, trolley-and petrol-buses: J. T. Smith, General Manager. His wife, equally intelligent, lacked the temperament for ostentation and had gratefully retired from schoolteaching to look after husband and family. Noel's birth on the first Christmas Day of the First World War had perhaps saved her from a further spell as locum in a classroom. She took her pleasure in reading, and quietly critical, looked on her husband's constant attendance at chapel, for instance, his advancement in office there, as without great concern to her. She refused to help with the Sunday School or its gigantic annual anniversaries for which pedagogy had fitted her, politely turned down interviews from the Young Wives, the Women's Bright Hour, the Band of Hope, even the Wednesday Prayer Meeting, but attended the Sunday evening service regularly, and afterwards commented on homiletic deficiencies or theological shortcomings of ministers and grammatical howlers from local preachers. She lacked force; her voice was small, but she was not a nonentity, only made herself out to be so, occupied with the price of beef not the origin or destiny of the universe.

Noel sat upstairs, cheeks on fists. He no longer felt hungry, merely outraged at his father's misjudgement. Time and again he outlined his case, and could not forgive himself that he had not done so. He had no great fear of his father, who was a strict but gentle man. He understood that his father thought he was lying and had punished him because he wanted his boy to rate honesty as highly as he did. But justice should have been placed first. Noel hovered between anger and lassitude; he stared out of the window at the sunny shrubs, the dry lawns, and found no comfort. He picked up a book, found he could not read it. He felt thirsty, but decided against walking to the bathroom for a drink. He would be still so that they did not know whether he was there or not. They had sent him to his bedroom and they, the adult world, would have consciences troubled by the silence upstairs. He took off his shoes, took up an old Christmas annual and followed, more comfortably by the minute, the babyish, exciting pictures.

The front door was opened and Ethel's steps mastered the linoleum of the passage. The dining-room door was shut. Noel could hear the voices, though he had difficulty in differentiating between his brothers', even his father's, and could not make out a coherent word. He wondered why Ethel had left the table. Perhaps she had dropped something and had gone back to look for it: a ring, a handkerchief, a notebook. But she had not been out all afternoon; he had been helping her to make little crowns, 'chaplets' she called them, for the bridesmaids. These had not been successful at first, but they had managed something acceptable by four-thirty. Downstairs he heard the clatter of plates as the meal finished. Ethel and her brothers would wash the dishes, while Father and Mother sat on either side of the hearth, he reading the evening paper, she barely containing her eagerness to be back in the kitchen inspecting crockery or mopping the tiled floor.

Someone came up the stairs. His father opened the bedroom door.

"Noel," Joseph Smith said, clearing his throat, "I wrongly accused you of breaking Mrs Taylor's window. I am sorry. I apologize with all my heart. I should have made closer inquiries. You were apparently with Ethel at the, er," more throat noises, "crucial time. Why didn't you say so?"

"I don't know."

"Ethel went out and questioned Mrs Taylor. She established the exact time. Mrs Taylor was by no means as certain about her facts as she had been with me.

I can only repeat how sorry I am."

Now, from what little his brothers had said, he could well imagine the scene downstairs. Ethel would cross-examine her father about the time of the breakage, and if he showed any vagueness would harass him in or out of exactitude. Then Ethel rose, said she was going across the street to sort this out. Her father, guilt already in his own troubled mind, but mindful of his wife's convenience, would try to stop her. "Let us finish the meal first, and then you can go over." But Ethel was on her feet. Politely she excused herself, putting them all in their inferior moral places, and had marched out, followed by her mother who had spoken the sole sentences the boy upstairs had heard clearly. He never found out what had happened to the barely eaten potatoes, cabbage, roast pork and apple sauce; his mother would have found some means, at risk to the spoiling of her own portion, of keeping the plate and contents warm. His brothers, he guessed, would have gone on eating; they had good appetites, but would have their heads cocked in judgement. Years later, the younger, Tom, then knighted, D.Sc., FRS, had recalled the incident, had said, "Typical of our Ethel. She couldn't wait to set things right. Bull at a gate. And she hasn't changed much." "Have you told her so?" Professor Noel had asked. "Countless times, but I'm wasting my breath."

Ethel had said nothing to him about the incident.

"Your mother will give you your dinner," his father had continued. "This, this delay can perhaps be construed as a slight punishment for playing with a ball in the street against orders. I know you were only bouncing it, but it would have been better to leave it back indoors. Err, if at all, on the safe side. Still, that's ungenerous on my part. Will you forgive me?"

His father held out his hand. An adult in their circle did not usually shake hands with a child. Noel stared. His anger rekindled itself. He would have liked to refuse, but he stood up and held his hand forward. Awkwardly they sealed the pact.

The son looked at the fifty-three-year-old face, the clipped moustache, the so well-known balding head. Perhaps he realized what the apology had cost. As his father stood there at a loss, the boy stepped forward, he could not help himself, and hugged his father. The man was taken by surprise. The boy wept, and the father bent to kiss the wet cheek. Then it was handkerchief out, "Blow your nose, son. No need for that, is there?" and they linked arms. "Wash your hands and face" at the bathroom door.

Noel understood now, not then, how much that odd old stick had loved him.

Downstairs his mother fed him, even his brothers slightly fussed him, but Ethel having smiled, said a brusque hello, went about her own affairs, this duty done.

Ethel had drifted away, breathing heavily through her nose.

Time froze, in the heat. He looked at the unrecognizable features, listening to the harsh noise. This small creature on the bed could have stood up for nobody, represented nothing. It had no virtue but nearly ninety years of skin and grief, half in and half out of the world. On the street he could hear the passing of cars, the rattle of a milk float, the voices of postmen or work people. Inside, the small, ferocious intake of breath dominated the ticking of an old mantlepiece French clock and the dusty silence.

Imogen brought in the tray.

"Come along, mother, wake up." She smiled at Noel. "Wake up. The day's begun."

She lifted her mother straighter, smoothed the bedclothes, moved a strong wooden stand across the bed. Gently she motioned her uncle outside.

"Have you had a chat with Noel?" he heard the bright voice as he closed the door.

4

"DON'T be afraid to spend a bit longer over your shopping," Noel advised his niece. "Make an outing of it. You might just as well make use of my stay to advantage as not."

"Thanks. I'll think about it."

"None of this puritanical stuff, now."

Imogen laughed. "My mother has a week or so to live and you're telling me to spend my time out of her company?"

"If I thought it would do her any good, I'd keep you tied to the bed-end."

"Will you sit in with her, then? It's rather dark in there; she doesn't want the sunshine. You might find it hard to read. Come out if you wish. She'll let you know if she wants you. I'm going to take my morning pleasure, a wallow in the bath."

Noel Smith moved into his sister's room. Ethel, propped with pillows, seemed slightly more lively. Her greeting, though almost inaudible, had about it a politeness that recalled her strength. She answered his questions monosyllabically; she had slept, eaten some breakfast, felt as usual, had received a postcard from an old friend in Barmouth. He spoke of Wales, said he had never stayed in that resort. She mumbled something which he made out in the end to be a title: 'David of the White Rock'. Pleased at the communication he sang the line or two he could remember. She heaved herself round, beckoned him closer. He had difficulty with her message; her becks, breathless short repetitions, her pained expression at his misunderstanding racked her, strained him, but in the end he grasped what she wanted him to know. She had taught that song for weeks on end in a classroom, had liked it but no more, and then had heard it sung on a holiday in Llandudno, where William Wagstaffe had spent his boyhood vacations, and had been overcome with its beauty. Small beads of sweat glistened on her forehead; she had spent herself, but typically Ethel had won her way. He remembered the last lines of the first stanza and sang it to her, in a high whispering falsetto.

> "On women and children
> God's blessing remain."

Ethel nodded, seemed to smile, he could not be sure. He spoke of Elgar hearing a Welsh tune in the distance, recreating it in the Introduction and Allegro. He held his sister's hand as he spoke and waited without answer. He relinquished his hold on her hand, gently hummed the tune, whispered her name. She did not stir. Soon the nurse and then the home help would be coming in to disturb her. Her face was free of anxiety, almost smooth now, untroubled in its leanness. Noel stood; he was stiff; long sitting in one position did not suit him. He stood staring down at the hump under the bedclothes, the lifeless hair, the fallen cheeks. Quietly he stepped into the corridor.

As he took the few steps to his room, the bathroom door opened and Imogen emerged, stark naked. Though she carried clothes in her right hand, she made little attempt to cover herself. Her hair was done up in a white towel. She slipped aside into her bedroom without embarrassment, not speaking.

Noel blushed; he could not breathe. He sat on his bed, trembling slightly. At his age he could be only foolishly excited. The handsome, sunburnt head, the pale skin, heavy breasts, dark nipples, pubic tuft, the energetically working, shapely legs had robbed him temporarily of control so that he slumped weakly on his bed, a slice of his consciousness withdrawn. The bright clarity of what he had seen left him vague, dazed, dumb. The unexpectedness had proved too much; he needed these days to prepare himself for the smallest alteration of routine. Imogen had walked those few naked yards because she was not used to anyone about the house but herself. What would he say to her when they met in a few minutes' time? Would she mention it? Would he be expected to keep silent? He had begun to approve of his niece, her efficiency, her sense of judgement, of duty — and now this. He snatched a pillow from his bed and hammered it feebly at his feet, holding one corner. That seemed the gesture. An old man with a slapdash movement, done without emphasis, with a child's petulance. He groaned aloud.

When he stood his knees weakened and he stretched about with his arms to support himself. He picked up his book, *The Joke*, tiptoed out to the drawing room where he sat, novel closed, head astir. From the rest of the house he could hear not a sound. Outside the bright morning glared without movement, grey-green against unstained blue. His head dropped, the paperback fell to the ground and he dozed. At nine fifteen in the morning after a good night's sleep he dropped off.

The front door bell woke him so that he snatched up his book guiltily. Strong voices in the passage announced the arrival of the nurse. Imogen, judged vocally, seemed herself, much in command. He could now hear diminished, hurried talk from behind Ethel's closed door. He crept out into the kitchen, filled the kettle, turned it on. Imogen entered.

"Oh, good," she said. "We'll have a cup of coffee when the nurse has finished.

I'll leave you in charge. We'll be about ten minutes. No more." She pulled down instant coffee, indicated cups.

"Will your mother want one?" he asked.

"No." She shook her head sweetly. "Just three. Sugar for Mrs Jones."

Imogen, quite at ease, was not going to mention her nakedness. He set about his task, thankful for consideration, carefully squaring up the contents of the tray. When the women came in, the nurse, in uniform this morning, said she was in a desperate hurry, but she examined her chocolate digestive biscuits and talked at loud length.

"Your mother's not lost her spirit," she informed Imogen. "While I was dealing with her she wanted to know about the weather. As if it mattered. And when I told her how hot it was she said something about India. I think she'd been there?"

"Yes," said Imogen. "To Bombay and Bangalore."

"And do you know the last thing she said?" The nurse laid down her cup. "She signalled me over with her eyes. You know how they do." This to Noel Smith. "And she whispered, 'How long do you give me, Nurse?' as plain, as clear. It took me aback, I can tell you."

"What did you say?" Imogen asked.

"What could I? 'You'll last to get the Queen's telegram,' I said. And you should have seen her face. 'I hope not,' she told me. 'I hope not.' There was a lively, thinking brain at work somewhere inside that poor bag of bones."

"How long do you give her?" Noel asked.

"You can't answer that, Professor." The remembered title sharpened the rebuke. "She ought to have gone days, weeks ago. You can't say. Spirit makes all the difference." She carefully finished biscuits and coffee, cleared her plate of crumbs, said she must be on her way. "Let me know if anything happens."

Noel heard the car drive away. Imogen returned.

"A decent woman," she pronounced. "But she does talk."

"Does your mother like her?"

"It's hard to say. I often wondered if

my mother liked anyone." He thought hard about that.

"I see."

He did, and remembered how just after the war she had been appointed in her late forties from a very powerful short list to be principal of the Kay-Shuttleworth College, the largest teacher training establishment in the north-west. The local education committee had wanted to sell off part of the extensive grounds and it was rumoured, amongst the cynical or her rivals, that the chairman, a knighted retired solicitor, Jim Blagg, a dictatorial sexist character, had leaned on his fellow electors to appoint Dr Ethel Wagstaffe because a woman would be less likely to oppose his many plans. Certainly her promotion had caused surprise. She had been highly successful as head of a women's college during the war, but the KSC was an expanding mixed establishment training not only two-year teachers but preparing graduates for the Certificate of Education of Cambridge University, and their own certificate of proficiency. It needed a man, her opponents claimed, either a scholar or an administrator who knew the world, preferably a scientist. Two colonels, a fellow of an Oxford college, a headmaster who had written a highly regarded book on secondary education and a senior lecturer from Manchester had made up the short list. All had performed admirably at the interview, but the sole woman candidate had found favour. Ethel discovered her own staff, mostly newly recruited males, astonished and suspicious.

Sir James Blagg gave her little time to settle before he outlined a new scheme. It would mean some slight 'legal adjustments', he said, to the deed of trust but that would not present insuperable obstacles as long as there was no very great public opposition. The council needed the money for its many postwar developments. The idea was to build a small estate of large, architecturally first-rate houses; in those days of shortages they would be designed to the highest standard and sell for high prices, would enhance the status of the neighbourhood, would remove a mere twenty acres from her vast playing fields and would not even be seen from the administrative block, screened by an already existing copse. The college would not miss the land; the ground had been ploughed up during the war and was still let out to a local farmer; they would acquire influential neighbours, if not patrons. But they must move quickly, the developers would not wait indefinitely.

It sounded plausible enough. Certainly, a few houses for the rich round the boundary of her campus would do her and the college no harm. Ethel looked Blagg straight in the eye.

"I must think about it, Sir James. And consult my colleagues."

"Think about it, yes. But not too long. As for consultation I can tell you now what the result of that will be. For every six of your people there'll be ten opinions; the only few who will oppose it will be the reds, you have one or two bolsheviks and they'll stir up trouble for the sake of trouble. A *fait accompli* is the answer."

"And I must consult my husband about the deed of trust."

"There's no need. Our lawyers have

studied it. A King's Counsel has given an opinion. The clerk and his assistant are both legal experts; I have spent my life . . . "

"Then there will be no danger to the scheme in allowing my husband to look it over."

"It's not his business."

Blagg's face had burnt a mottled red, his jaw had set, his false teeth were clamped together.

"We shall have a further legal opinion, delivered quickly and without cost. That must appeal to you?"

"I didn't know that Will Wagstaffe specialized in . . . "

She interrupted. "You would be surprised, Sir James."

He left in a furious hurry, warning her he needed her answer inside the week. She promised it.

Ethel set out the case to her husband with almost Blaggian force, but he reacted with surprising mildness. There would be no insuperable legal objection to the selling of the land; he delivered, he said, without any great expertise. Secondly such building might be better than what could follow if they scuppered Blagg's plan. Once materials were more readily available, there'd be a spate of jerry-building and the college would at least have a line of defence, and a precedent for the status of the next burst of planning. Thirdly, she had plenty of scope to double or treble the size of the college on the remaining land. Fourthly, what did her colleagues say? Blagg had been right there, she considered; she had consulted her three deputy principals and for all the help she received she might have been asking for an opinion on Bossuet's sermons or Pascal's *Thoughts* or Montaigne's *Essays*. They had words in plenty; they were concerned with education. They held no strong views. They rushed round every side.

Disappointed she asked if Wagstaffe could voice any objections to the scheme. He grinned, drily.

"Blagg will be making something out of it."

"You mean he has a fiancial interest? Or they're bribing him."

"I can't say that. But there'll be a *quid pro quo*." Her husband held up his hand.

"It may not even be personal advantage. The builders may be putting up a school for him out of turn, or offering to extend your labs on favourable terms or earlier than expected. All to the glory of Jim Blagg, but not criminally."

"What should I do?"

"You've made your point, if it needed making. Blagg sees you're no pushover. If you like to take a moral line, you can ask him, point blank, if he has any financial interest in the scheme. Then, after his denials, you graciously agree. If you wanted to be specially awkward, you might ask him for something your college needs, and he doesn't want to give you. But I don't advise that. Not at this early stage. You've shown your teeth."

"You think I've overreacted, don't you, Will?"

Her husband waved aimless hands in vague contradiction.

"Not at all. You've shown you're capable of fighting. That's probably good in the educational world. I don't know."

Noel had heard the story from his sister, from Wagstaffe and from a junior member of staff at the time who later became professor of education at the University of Birmingham where Noel held his first chair. William Wagstaffe had been diffident with his brother-in-law, voice especially low, a hand across his mouth.

"It doesn't do to bother too much with motive in my trade. We just see whether there's any sort of chance of winning a case, and whether it's worth it in time and money. Blagg is an old rogue who does good from time to time, and it will do him no harm to have somebody stand up to him. The director of education won't, for instance. But, in my view, and you needn't broadcast it, this is Ethel, putting her father, your father back in his place again."

"Did he need it?"

"Do you?"

Noel interpreted that question as a criticism of Irène, another who disciplined her father through every male she met.

Sir James had his way; the houses were built and his elder daughter's husband bought one, became a college governor, admired and supported the principal in her successful schemes of expansion, in her initial moves to become incorporated into the polytechnic, sat with her on the Bench.

Imogen was now ready.

She looked smart, cool, smelt deliciously attractive as she set off for the bus.

"Don't hurry," he advised. "Make something of it. Take advantage of me."

"I don't need encouragement."

The niece tapped her uncle's arm. She had left instructions about the care of her mother. He felt confident. Ethel's drinks were prepared; she did not need food and he knew where to find sustenance for himself. At eleven or thereabouts the home help would arrive, and he could go out. Noel went to his sister's bedside.

"Are you awake?" he whispered. A faint murmur in reply. "Is there anything you need?" Silence.

He went back to the *Guardian*: An eloquent woman, nevertheless Ethel often had to be pushed into speech. He remembered that years ago he had established her position in the Blagg affair by dint of long-drawn-out questioning and by a confession that he needed to learn how the minds of the local notabilities worked. That wasn't the truth, she probably recognized it as mere curiosity, but it served its purpose. She seemed little inclined to boast, feeling perhaps that she had compromised or yielded too much in the affair.

"I asked him," Ethel's voice had been clipped, almost mannishly deep even when she made no attempt to speak loudly, "first of all to give me his word that he had no financial interest in the transaction. Then he began to bluster, tried to bully me, swapped tactics claiming he was the one mainly instrumental in appointing me."

"And you said?"

"That wasn't difficult. 'Sir James,' I said as innocently as I could, 'just give me your word, and that will be sufficient.' He did."

"And he was lying?" Noel had asked.

"I expect so. It's difficult to be exactly sure in these cases. Perhaps he had no *financial* stake in the project. That's why I used the word. Very deliberately. As an escape route for him. But there'd be some advantage in it somewhere for him, you can be sure of that."

"Were you acting morally?" He didn't mind putting his successful sister to the test.

"Strictly, no. I strengthened my position. And that would be to the advantage of my college and its staff. You should always give people the chance to put their best face forward."

"But don't believe them."

"Well, no. 'Be ye wise as serpents.' I think Jesus made some remarks about being as clever as the sons of darkness that used to trouble Father."

"Dad had his own troubles with councils and unions."

"I'm sure he did. And was as crafty as the next man, believe you me. But he felt in some way that religion moved in a purer, more strictly principled field, and I think he couldn't quite take it that Jesus of all men, made, for example, an unjust steward the hero of one of his parables. We argued it out one time. 'Religion needs to be able to face the realities of a twisted world,' I used to say. 'No, Ethel,' in the same lugubrious voice he'd discuss the printing of tram-tickets, 'that's where you're wrong. The twisted world, as you call it, crucified Jesus, but on the third day God reasserted Himself and raised His son from the dead.' And I answered, 'And has rested on His laurels ever since.' 'Ethel,' he said, 'you're talking without your book. There are thousands of people who will testify to the powerful intervention of God in their lives.' 'And even larger numbers who'll testify to the opposite.' I wasn't kind in those days." She clearly had not repented.

"Did it upset him that only Joe of his children was religious?"

"I guess he wrestled and prayed about it. In many ways he was a shrewd old man. He was proud, for instance, that all his four children had doctorates. We all had taken full advantage of the educational opportunities he had been denied. And I think he realized that we were prevented somehow by our training from thinking about religion in quite the way he did. But he was a meliorist. If God could turn a crucifixion to advantage, He wouldn't have much difficulty with our puny atheisms."

"But Jesus deserved the resurrection."

"He would not have liked that sentence, Noel." Ethel laughed. "But I think he tried to be godly enough himself to make up for the rest of us. Wrong-headed, but heroic."

"You admired Father?" Noel asked.

"How could one do otherwise? But I had him at the wrong end of his life. When he was young, comparatively, energetic, didn't take too eagerly to dissent. By your day, he had mellowed. And you went away to university. It made a difference."

"He insisted that I appeared at chapel with them in the vacations."

"And what did you think?"

"How many opportunities the preachers missed."

"Did you tell him so?" Ethel asked.

"Not really."

"Always diplomatic, Noel."

"Hypocritical. But I made a point of ducking useless arguments. I knew the line he'd take, that the language was less important than the message, that my attitude was like refusing to step off the sinking wreck into a lifeboat because the rescuer hadn't said 'Please'."

"There are such people."

"He wouldn't deny it. He'd just think, more fool they."

They had laughed together.

5

THE woman who came in to give Ethel her bed-bath had arrived.

"I'm sorry I'm a bit late. I can't seem to get on this hot weather. We aren't used to it." No, she knew where everything was; she would appreciate a cold drink if he would be so kind. Miss Wagstaffe often went out while she was at work and he could do the same. "I clean her up, and she feels the better for it. Then I spruce her room up for her. You would think they don't notice, but they do. Only yesterday I rearranged an old lady's family photographs on her dressing table and she thanked me. 'You've put Dad,' that was her husband, 'in the middle where he should be,' she said. 'He'd have liked that.' He seemed quite a young man in the picture, in sailor's uniform. In the war, I should think. Anyhow, he looked younger than some of his children. But she was pleased as punch. And do you know, not an hour later she was dead. It was over."

"Was her husband still alive?"

"No." The word was tunefully elongated, like an ironic cello solo. "Mornin', Mrs Wagstaffe." She pushed open the door. "Here we are again."

She carried in the bowl, the towels, the soap. "Come on, my duck. Bath time."

The term of endearment intrigued him; perhaps the home help came from his own part of the world. He said nothing, retired to the garden and the morning paper. Ten minutes into the bad news, even the hot weather brought its tally of disasters, he returned indoors to the brusquely ringing telephone: Irène calling from France just to find out if he was coping. This pleased him; his wife had her share of French thrift and would have thought twice before using the phone at an expensive period. She kept it short now; she heard about Ethel, succinctly questioned him about his health, advised him to stay on another day or two if it eased Imogen's burden and said she would herself be back for the funeral, whenever or wherever it was. She wished him brief, businesslike love and rang off. The home help was still in Ethel's room, but doing her duty in complete silence. The house seemed hot under low ceilings; curtains were drawn against the glare of the sun. It was already a place of mourning.

Noel swilled his hands under the cold tap, and trotted out to straighten the *Guardian* untidily abandoned on the garden seat. Even in the shade he felt uncomfortable, dizzy with heat. He read a paragraph on the Test Match, found he had retained nothing, turned to the arts pages, jolted, to gloom at the picture of an actor and actress he had never heard of. He blubbered his lips.

The garden dazzled about him, the lawn straw-brown, shrubs touched already with yellow. He could find no comfort, only blankness. This was all he was fit for, to occupy warm space in a suburb, with no objective; elsewhere people made themselves useful. The home help dedicated Ethel's last hours to cleanliness; Irène would be in the kitchen preparing a meal and arguing about culinary risks and exactitudes with her sisters; dozens of people from this road would be out at work, organizing life. They all did their boring duty, making it as interesting as their temperaments allowed. He alone parked himself, unable to understand a simple paragraph the gist of which he could guess, he believed, before he picked up the paper.

He dozed almost immediately and dreamed. He accompanied a former colleague, a soprano, as she sang. They seemed to be rehearsing for a concert, and as soon as he jerked awake he remembered the shape of the tune, the look of the chords which introduced the melody, quavers in E major. Enid Fisher was interested in singing, joined the ad hoc college choir, but would never have put herself forward as a soloist; she had neither the voice, verve nor nerve. The tune faded, but Enid's thin voice hung ghostly clear in his head. He had not thought about the woman for years; they had not corresponded. On the rare occasions he had called in at or accepted invitations to functions from his last college at London University Dr Fisher had not been there. He remembered untidy hair, her eager, innocent face, the sober clothes, her husband a music teacher in a comprehensive school, and how he had approved of her. She gave value for money; she taught with care; the clever students thought she did not give them enough elbow room, but she had read a great deal, and still continued to learn, to apply her mind to her teaching. In real life he had never played the piano for her. Why she had suddenly appeared in his dream he could not say.

The harder he tried to recall the dream, the quicker it dissipated itself. He could not place the room, the song, the colour of the piano, the composer. One name suggested itself: Watts. Had he been at home he would immediately have made for his old paperback Grove to see if such a musician existed, but Imogen had no such standby. He took out his notebook and carefully wrote down the name. Perhaps he had written the words? The mention, the thought of Isaac Watts in Ethel's room had provided the name. Yet this had nothing of the hymn book about it; a Victorian ballad seemed nearer the mark for this rapidly disappearing nothingness. Noel straightened his paper.

He moved back into the kitchen, provided coffee for the home help who said Mrs Wagstaffe seemed 'far gone' this morning.

"It's a shame," the woman said, "to linger on like this."

"You believe in euthanasia?" he asked, wondering if she'd understand the word.

"It does seem sensible." Gruff equality in the answer.

"There are some snags," he said.

"You name me anything that hasn't got drawbacks."

When the woman had finished her task and gone, he crept back into the half-darkness of his sister's room. His eyes became accustomed to the light. Ethel's bedclothes were almost clinically straight, her hair had been damped and combed.

"Are you awake there?"

Nothing. He looked round the tidy room and on the wall opposite the end of the bed he recognized a painting. Though it was quite large, he had not noticed it before. He cast his eyes about the other pictures in the gloom, did not recall them, and returned to the first.

It had hung in Ethel's bedroom when he was a child.

The print, framed in dark oak, was a portrait, head and upper torso, of a young woman by some minor Pre-Raphaelite. Light played over the figure, round the edges of the titian, flowing hair. Influence of Julia Margaret Cameron's photographs, the present Noel Smith advised himself. The girl had the rapt expression of Dante Gabriel Rossetti's 'Beata Beatrix', but the eyes were open and the pearly shoulders bare. It had held pride of place over the tiny mantelshelf in her room, and he remembered looking at the folds in the clothes, the naked shoulders, the great soulful eyes. This inferior print must have been the beginning of his education in the visual arts.

Not long after Ethel's marriage to William Wagstaffe the picture had been taken down and away with one or two other small pieces of furniture to her new home, and Noel could not remember seeing it since. Presumably it had adorned, he scoffed at his own cliche, the marital bedroom.

He remembered mentioning its disappearance to his mother, who had made an unexpected remark. Lily Smith had been born slightly higher in the social scale than her husband, was the daughter of a bank clerk, later manager. She was a quiet woman, rather self-contained, apparently happy in her lot of keeping the home warm, the family well fed, the husband and sons in clean shirts and collars, and the skivvies busy and contented. She was, Noel decided later, clever, would have done well academically had she been allowed to stay on at the grammar school after she had taken matric, but her father had not seen much sense in overeducating women, though he had allowed her to train as a teacher. Lilian Smith, née Pennington, said little except about matters which directly concerned her, seemed bemused by the brilliance of her children, even by her husband's apotheosis as general head of the transport service, but kept them all hard at their ambitions. She showed little overt affection for her brood, kissing them sometimes in a perfunctory way, rarely throwing arms about them, replying to their complaints with a distanced, ironical reticence that made them harsh judges of their own cause without any direct condemnation from her.

She led the family from the back. The children realized that their father was clever, quick, a man of judgement, with his loyalty to employers, his faithfulness to his church, his codes of conduct, so that his bright offspring would have mentioned him first. The mother, with her application to cooking, or ironing, household spending, arrangement of holidays seemed more formidable, once they were adults, though she in no way had threatened them. Noel remembered his father once asking her advice, and on her mild but critical answer Joseph Smith had responded with a sung quotation, common with him, from the hymn book.

'Thy kind but searching glance can
scan
The very wounds that shame would
hide.'

That was about it. Lily had raised her eyebrows a fraction of an inch at his burst of singing, not dismissing it, merely the implication that he could have put his breath to better use.

On the day that Ethel's bits and pieces were sent off to Manchester Noel had remarked to his mother about the picture, asking if it belonged to the parents not the daughter, as it was being carried out.

"No," Lily had said. "Ethel bought it."

"Was it her favourite?"

"I suppose so. Why, do you like it?"

"Yes." He'd been perhaps eleven at the time. "It's beautiful."

"Do you remember Albert Hickling?" his mother asked. Noel did; Hickling had been a fellow student at the university with Ethel, had visited the house as a suitor, a tall bony young man, very serious. "He used to be sweet on our Ethel, and he told her once that the lady in the picture was very like her."

"Like our Ethel?" Incredulity sharpened his voice.

"That's what she said he said."

Ethel was strong, firm-fleshed, physically large and handsome. The thin, yearning woman of the sorrows in the picture was the exact opposite, pale, afflicted, slim, beautiful from rejection or renunciation.

"That's what love does for you," his mother had said.

She had thereupon marched away to her jam making, overseeing furniture removers or whatever, and had never raised the matter again. Albert Hickling, Noel vaguely recalled now, had become a Methodist minister and had been a missionary in China. Must have been dead for years. Even as a boy Noel Smith had felt that Ethel had been condemned by her mother for believing what was so obviously untrue. The woman had not said as much, but he had realized that his unforthcoming mother had pointed out a weakness in the daughter who had done so well at school, at university, in her M.A. thesis on Montaigne, in her teaching at grammar school. He had wished at the time he had looked more closely at the print, remembered it more clearly.

Here it was in dimness, half-shadow,

more than sixty years later.

He walked towards it, but as he reached a suitable distance for scrutiny, he turned about, looked down over the bed, at the heavily breathing hump under the clothes. He concentrated on the picture, but the room was too dark. Ironically he questioned whether this lack of light added to its attraction. When he had last seen it more than sixty years ago, he knew little about painting: Holman Hunt on the Sunday School walls, the smudged cartoons in comics, the illustrations of Roman soldiers, Egyptian pharaohs, or Zulu warriors in the books he borrowed from the library. To the boy this had seemed fresh and direct of impact; the bare shoulders had appealed to sexual stirrings; the wide-open eyes demanded a story. At whom was she looking? But now he needed light, curtains drawn right back to appreciate the subdued radiance of that angel face. Noel touched it, glass covered, unfaded.

Screwing up his eyes he stared again, without much success. He wondered what Ethel made of it now. His sister had been in favour of the arts, visual, aural, dramatic, but had never said a word to him about pictures. The walls of the corridors of her colleges were hung with tasteful landscapes, mostly twentieth-century watercolours, and garish, big, abstract prints, but these had all been chosen by her art department. He tried to remember what other pictures he had seen when she lived in the villa down the road. He felt at a loss. There had been pictures, he was sure, but he could not remember one. It was as if no one, Wagstaffe, relatives, dependants, employees ever looked at them. What was over the mantelpiece of the great-windowed drawing room? A mirror in an ornate gilt frame, a vast glassy shining area in which the male Wagstaffes combed their hair, the girls examined lipstick and the visitors looked away ashamed. For the rest, a Mabel Lucie Attwell with attendant poem about soap in the bathroom.

Quickly he walked across to his sister's side. She opened her eyes; perhaps he had wakened her with his tread. Her eyes looked onto his.

"Anything you want?" he asked. "A drink?"

He picked up the tumbler on the lace-edged tablecloth, quarter filled it from the carafe, tried to apply it to her lips, failed, slightly spilling water on chin and sheet.

"I'll have to lift you up," he said. He returned the glass, put his arms about his sister, straightened her, shifted her towards the bedhead. Holding her in position with one hand he propped her from behind with pillows. He did this clumsily but easily; she was lighter than he expected. He kept his arm about her as he reshaped the pillows, folded, remoulded them. Now he was breathing as harshly as his sister, who had closed her eyes during his manoeuvres.

"Are you comfortable?" he asked.

She opened her eyes, stared impassively.

"Now for the drink."

He put his arm round her again as he held the tumbler to the mouth. She sipped.

"More?" She nodded, drank. "Enough?" He replaced the glass. "Do you want to sit up for a bit or lie down again?" She murmured: he did not understand and left her as she was, upright, his arm about her. "I've been looking at your picture." He pointed. "I remember it when I was a boy. It's the same one, isn't it?" Her eyes slipped from picture to brother. "I connect it somehow with Albert Hickling? Albert Hickling. He used to come with you."

"Albert," she grumbled, muttered. The forehead puckered with effort between the eyes. Her face cleared, returned to its wrinkled immobility.

"Do you know who painted it?"

Ethel made a movement, uttered a pained sound so that he understood that she felt discomfort in her present position, wished to lie down. He kissed her cheek which smelt of scented soap and eased her flat.

"Better?" he asked.

She muttered four syllables which he interpreted as 'Albert Hickling', then utterly clearly 'Mandarin Chinese' and then another sentence, buzzingly incoherent.

"Sorry," Noel said. "What did you say?"

Her eyes were closed; she did not

answer. He stood, moved his chair away from the bed, checked on her sleeping face and returned to the picture, concentrating now on shape in the dimness. For a second, a flash, he saw with Hickling's eyes; the ethereal gaze illustrated, illuminated something behind the robust, attractive, confident features that had been the young Ethel's. It had no connection with the withered creature in the bed, the whispering voice; its connection lay with the strong woman, who had ruled her roosts, her men. But for the lovelorn Hickling, master of the pu-tong-hua, she wouldn't have mentioned the language except as a sign of distinction, of having read into it . . . Noel Smith swore silently, grinned at himself, tapped the glass of the picture with a fingernail, issuing a warning to himself.

"Are you all right?" he asked.

"Perfectly," came the clear, unexpected reply.

"Anything you want?" She did not answer that. "Are you comfortable?"

"Noel."

"Yes?" He drew close.

"I'm glad you're here." That was plain. "Where is Imogen?"

"She's out shopping."

"She's a good girl. What . . . ?"

Strength petered out. He wondered how the unfinished question would have finished. Some triviality. 'What is she buying?' 'What does she want?' 'What time will she be back?' It seemed typical of Ethel's terminal hours, the drugged, damaged drift from consciousness, that she should achieve clarity only on these banalities. One expected some final jewel, nugget of wisdom from a deathbed, not the humdrum, unthought-of exchanges of the shopping queue.

Yet Ethel had managed to express her affection for him. 'I'm glad . . . '

When he had been appointed to his first chair, he recalled, she had written to him, a short letter on the headed notepaper of her college: from the Principal, E. F. Wagstaffe, M.A., Ph.D., FCP, but in her own handwriting. It had said how delighed she was that her little brother had managed to obtain a real professorship at last, unlike the rest of them. (This was unfair in that the older brothers had both occupied honorary chairs in America when they could spare the time from their industrial or civil service research. Ethel herself to her chagrin some few years before had failed to obtain the chair of education at the local university for which she was eminently, even pre-eminently qualified.) There followed a sentence or two in that distinctive, large hand about his early promise, his sharp eye, keen ear as a boy, about his youthfully revealed temperament.

It had all sounded off colour to him, as if she were drunk, an unlikely supposition. He interpreted it at the time as a clumsy attempt to express what she had never said for years or written before: her love. 'I sometimes thought,' she wrote, 'that you might be a poet. I was, for all my arts training, like Joe and Tom a scientist, but you were different, with a different sort of imagination. It used to puzzle me. Father, with the proper education, would have been a scientist, and Mother had so buried her talents I don't know what she would have made. Perhaps you inherit from her. But here you are now, head of a department, laying the law down, and I am delighted, because teachers need this creative gift. They need plenty of other endowments, I'm sure, but the two or three really outstanding pedagogues (and I use that dull word!) have been makers, poets, creators . . .'

Noel had preserved the letter, now and then taking it carefully from its yellowing envelope to read. He remembered his grum and gruff reply, thanking her, promising his best, telling her not to expect his promotion to turn the educational world upside down. Modesty and meiosis. And mockery. Ethel had tried to say something better left unsaid, that she loved and admired her brother, and he had answered her stiffly. Today, and whenever he took out the letter, he felt an embarrassment he could never conquer; he had met her generosity (which must have cost her trouble; one could see that in the awkwardness of expression) with a rebuff. And that at a time of happiness. He had been thirty-nine with a beautiful wife, a healthy, attractive year-old son, a highly praised book on critical practice not long published, and he had answered his sister's overture with a distanced coolness. He hated himself. Life was too bloody short for that sort of antic.

And yet he had only once attempted to set the matter right. Perhaps he feared Ethel, expected a curt answer from her if he showed tenderness. In the course of a conversation, not long after her retirement, he had said, "Your letter to me when I got the Birmingham chair had the best advice I ever read. You showed me the ideal."

His sister had looked gloomily at him. She had not liked the way the world of school had developed and above all hated her retirement. "I've had all the ideals knocked out of me," she answered.

"You cheered me, and I failed to thank you properly. I regret it."

"I've forgotten what I said."

She turned her bitter face away from him.

As he had rejected her, she him. He saw her distress, wanted to comfort her. He took her arm and the pair had walked round his back garden in silence, companionable on the surface, hesitant, suspicious, raw, tremulous underneath. They did not meet often, and then only shortly and in company. They occasionally called in on their way elsewhere; they had been present at the funerals of her husband, William Wagstaffe, of their brothers Joe and Tom, of her son, Raymond, but never had above ten minutes' private conversation. Perhaps he had not wanted more. He looked down on the bent figure, then back to the picture on the wall. It conveyed no message. It was thin, faint, pale, lacklustre, a third-rate daub from an unfavoured period. The brilliant light on the edges of the window blinds burnt with ardour; the picture shrank into shadows. He could see no title, could not make out the painter's name.

"Anything you want, Ethel?" he whispered. No answer. He did not know whether he had spoken loudly enough for her to hear.

He crept out of the room, and out into the heated, various dazzle of the garden seat.

6

IMOGEN returned home rather later than Noel Smith expected; she had met friends for coffee, had 'picked up' one or two things, unspecified, in the summer sales. She had bundled her multicoloured plastic carriers in from the taxi, had slipped off her shoes and had gone in stocking feet immediately into her mother's room.

"Has she been comfortable?" she asked, re-emerging.

He made his report as he poured China tea.

"Have you had anything to eat?" she asked.

He detailed his snack. She seemed uninterested; her questions were not to be answered. "We'll eat earlier," she said. "There's plenty going. Let me just recover."

Imogen now occupied a settee, had arranged cushions at her back, seemed more relaxed than he had seen her before. Perhaps the morning with friends or in and out of boutiques had done her good. She complained about the hot weather, but said that her mother had refused to countenance an electric fan in her room.

"Why was that? Is she cold, do you think? Or is it noisy?"

Imogen complimented him on his tea-making.

"My mother never grew out of that thick black Indian brew of her childhood."

"Sergeant-major's," he said.

"Is that what you call it? Tea is a delicate taste." After a time with a second cup and two digestive biscuits, she returned to the subject of the fan. "I think she still feels she ought to suffer. She can't resist injections, but a fan represents luxury or undeserved relief. The beggar was not allowed to bring a drop of cold water over to Dives in hell. The nonconformist conscience has much to answer for." She crossed her silk-clad legs.

"She's too weak now to object," he said.

"Probably. But she said 'no' and I

. . . oh, let her stew in her own juice." She smiled to herself. "That's a crude expression of love for one's own mother." She spoke without force.

"Do you think your mother's had a happy life?"

"I don't suppose so."

"She's been very successful."

"Not in her eyes. She's a perfectionist and fighter. She stood no truck with opponents or rivals. She did extraordinarily well for a woman of her age and background. But I think she resented not becoming a professor."

"That's little enough."

She wagged a finger at him. "You can't talk. You've achieved it. What did you want next? A knighthood?"

"I didn't get it. That's for vice chancellors. Or some of them. Those with influential friends."

Imogen regally handed him her cup, said she wanted no more, and arranged her dress over her shapely legs.

"Whether it was temperament or upbringing or on-going experience I don't know, but I guess that every time she achieved something she felt that an extra obstacle was banged across her road. Take me for example."

"With pleasure," he drawled, not understanding.

"She had the boys and went back into teaching. It was unusual, because women at that time did not usually work once they were married. She would have none of it, and was forceful enough to win her way, choose places where it was possible. She'd been appointed headmistress of Grafton Girls' School and was making a marvellous job of it when she becomes pregnant with me. As it happens it didn't altogether ruin her career, in that Grafton was a private school, and wanted to keep her. So they gave her leave; very far-sighted for the Thirties. And she was well able to afford a nanny and servants to look after me. But . . ."

"You don't think you were properly cared for?"

"I don't know. I had the same sort of parental neglect as many of the well-to-do. I saw more of my mother than a royal princess would, and wasn't sent away to boarding school . . ."

"Don't you wish you had been?"

"Don't be ridiculous. But my mother felt I had been an obstacle. She could have done better without me."

"But you weren't to blame for your birth."

"No. But rationality doesn't always rule. I'm not telling you that she treated me badly on this account. By her own lights, she was a just woman. But she could not help feeling that she would have been better off without me."

"Did she show this? How did you find out?"

"Things she said later. Half in jest."

"If you didn't feel it as a child, then it didn't matter."

"You may not have noticed," Imogen said tartly, "but there's a tendency in this family to put two and two together. I've looked back, since she mentioned my unwelcome arrival, and decided I could have been better treated." She smiled at him. "I know it's not sensible, but there it is. I don't brood on it. But the conclusion's there."

"But you've taken your mother in." They sat silently.

"At long last. She was a disillusioned woman when she retired. She stayed on an extra year, though she was suffering. The Swinging Sixties were in full spate. Not only were the students promiscuous and unbiddable, they were also ignorant; they hadn't learnt anything. They didn't know a full-stop from a comma, surds from indices, or acid from alkaline. These were the days of self-expression in schools, and sit-ins, teach-ins at universities."

"I don't imagine Kay-Shuttleworth College was a hotbed of sedition and fornication."

"I suppose not. But it was bad enough to make Mother's life a misery. She believed that you got out of life what you put in, that no subject could be mastered without long hours of study. The opinions of students were valueless unless they were based on careful research. Mother believed in discipline, self-discipline, learning, effort to improve."

"Don't we all?"

Imogen ignored him.

"She employed staff who were, she

APS8

hoped, scholarly, who would pass their knowledge on. She found lecturers who encouraged students in their free and easy ways. She felt embattled and with no one to support her."

"Why didn't she resign? She was sixty-seven before she left."

"You don't know Mother. And she must have had some success in promoting the old educational virtues for the governing body to ask her to stay. I think that's true. She kept standards up at KS; the majority left the place knowing a great deal more than they did when they arrived, but it took it out of her. She lost weight, couldn't sleep, developed nasty physical symptoms."

"Were you at home?" he asked.

"No. I was teaching in Farnborough. My father used to write."

"Not your mother?"

"No. She kept her troubles to herself. My father wanted her to resign, but she wouldn't."

"He was still working?"

"Oh, yes. But he kept her going. You know the old saying that behind every great man is a good woman; well with them it was the opposite. He was quiet, didn't throw his weight about, but he supported her."

"I always thought he was very intelligent," Noel said.

"Yes, in a common-sense sort of way. While I was still at university my mother was sitting on the Conran Commission on Secondary Education, and she used to discuss their meetings with Father. He had a field day with her, asking questions, putting objections. She used to be quite wild sometimes with him. 'Will,' she said, 'you're too concerned with fiddling details. Try to have the wider view.' But she paid a lot of attention to him."

"And he encouraged her to retire?"

"Yes. Always. He saw it was making her ill."

"And why didn't she?"

"She didn't like to be beaten. She was obstinate. And I don't think, at first at least, that she believed that her students could be as stupid or bolshy as they made out."

"She'd outlived her usefulness, in your view?" he asked.

Imogen examined her silken legs, delicately caressing them with fingertips.

"I'm not saying that. She played a very large part in the introduction of the B.Ed. degree. She chased the university people, many of whom she condemned as arrogant and uninterested. But she went for them, stood none of their supercilious nonsense. Of course she had allies. Professor Alexander she always praised, but he was near the end of his time."

"He's still writing."

"Is he? He supervised me a bit at Cambridge when I was there." She raised her eyebrows. "I didn't like him. He left to go to Canada, I think. Still, my mother thought the longer she hung on, the more chance for her ideas to be adopted. She was wrong. They appointed a man not fit to black her boots, and . . . " Imogen slapped her thighs heartily. "And now we hear the secretary of state, no less, demanding just the things that she wanted."

"That's called educational advance."

"Noel," she warned, "you're an old cynic, and it's a good job my mother's incapable of understanding what you're saying out here."

They both laughed, and then like comedians straightened their faces, woodenly serious. Imogen put her feet to the ground, resumed her shoes, and knees neatly together, faced him.

"I wonder," the woman spoke slowly, word on word, "if any of these things pass through her mind as she lies there."

"Her disappointments, you mean?"

"Yes. Because on the whole, at least by the time she was on the way to her eighties, she felt a failure. One can put up with setbacks as long as one has plenty of other things to do. Don't you find that?"

"To an extent."

"You're a right old diplomat, Noel. You're just the sort of professor she would have hated."

"Too bland by half. I know." He smiled, not believing his lie. "But Ethel's so drugged that she won't be able to think straight about anything. And so weak."

"I hope so. If you knew you could give her an extra tablet or two and bring her life to an end without anyone finding out, would you do it?"

"In principle, yes. In practice, no."

"Why not?" Imogen spoke strongly, her voice lively.

"I'm a suspicious character. I'd not ever be certain that I'd not make some mistake and be found out. I also think I might be snuffing out some valuable piece of human wisdom."

"That doesn't apply to Ethel, surely." He'd never before heard her call her mother by her Christian name.

"No. But ending a human life seems deeply serious. Perhaps because I never had to do it."

"Even in the war?"

"It would be at a distance, and as part of a predictor- or gun-crew, not one to one."

They talked for half an hour; he learned, he thought, a great deal about his niece. Before, on the infrequent occasions they had met, she seemed an attractive, self-contained woman, aware of her place, relative importance, planning her life. She had none of the usual headmistressy drawbacks; she did not lay down the law, demand subservience, appeal to inferiors for confirmation of ideas. More formidable than that, she seemed ordinary, with a lively mind ready to question, but not to draw attention to herself. More than once he wondered what she made of her mother.

"Do you admire people like Ethel?" he asked now.

"She achieved something."

"But was it worth it? You said she was disillusioned by the end of her time."

"Let's suppose everything she fought for has disappeared now, and that's by no means so, the struggle would not have been wasted because it allowed her to display or develop her temperament."

"You might say the same of Hitler or Stalin."

"Easily. And even if you don't approve of what they've done, you have to admit that somehow they made a considerable mark on the world. They're dismissed now as evil or mad, my mother as old-fashioned. The virtues she paraded — what about that for a verb? — aren't altogether admired. Perhaps our world is better because some of her pupils rebelled against her."

"Do you believe that?"

"No. But I'm sure my mother, because she was what she was, made a considerable impact on her small world, let's say the educational systems of the north-western side of England. And how many of us could claim that?"

Imogen stood, a new woman, restored, stalked in to see her mother, called her uncle after her. She wiped her mother's face with a flannel, dampened her hands forced her to drink iced lemonade.

"Now, sit up, Mother, for a few minutes. Here's Noel come to see you. You talk to him while I start on the dinner. He goes back tomorrow, so make the most of it."

Ethel's face, unbespectacled, was as expressionless as that of a tortoise. She opened her eyes fractionally.

"She's a good girl," Noel began, meaning Imogen.

His sister nodded, spoke.

"Like her father."

"William?" Who else? "Is she? And are . . . were the boys more like you?"

"Billy was. Not Raymond. He was like himself."

Ethel spoke so that he could understand. Her voice lacked power, slurred consonants and modified vowels, but showed that she knew what he asked. Ethel's speech had never been incisive; she had a warmth, a contralto depth that was attractive to men. It was perhaps what one expected from her large frame, but it did not boom, rather it convinced listeners of her humanity, her wish to consider, if no more, their point of view.

"Clever," she moaned. "The boys."

William, Billy, the elder still served with distinction on the board of the Atomic Energy Authority, was a world authority on the building of power stations. Raymond, a mathematician, had worked in some kind of biological research establishment until he committed suicide at the age of forty, for love, it was said. Very like his mother in looks, he had driven his car full-tilt into a brick wall, having just written short notes not of explanation but of apology. 'Make no attempt to bring me round if I am not killed outright. I have no wish to live in full health, let alone as a cripple.'

That had happened twenty years ago.

Ethel spoke again, mumbling brokenly. He asked her to repeat whatever she had said, as he bent close.

"Love to see him doing his mathematics. Line after line. Pen never stopped."

She smiled slightly. He was sure he had correctly interpreted her message. Raymond's speed or neatness or skill pleased, calmed her now. She did not mention the suicide. She perhaps thought that her son was somewhere about the house, sitting at a table, surging on through these jungles of equations.

"Never properly understood way minds work."

Each word came separately after a slight break. Presumably she was still thinking about mathematicians. He salvaged a few stories about scientists, and switching, said their brothers must have been fair mathematicians to achieve their eminence.

Ethel had left him. Her eyes were open, and she looked over in the direction of the Pre-Raphaelite picture.

"Are you all right?" he asked.

"Lie down," she whispered.

He moved the pillows, eased her flat. Though she had hardly any flesh on her, her bones were large. He tucked the one flannelette sheet round her limbs and up to her chin. Her skin chilled.

"Is that better?"

She nodded.

"Noel."

"Yes." Again he bent his ear down to her mouth, but she had floated away. Imogen looked briefly in.

"Leave her now for a bit," she ordered. Outside the door, "Did she say anything?"

"Raymond."

"Oh. Was she upset?"

"No, she seemed to be remembering how fluent he was with his mathematical equations or whatever. It pleased her, I think."

"It's salad again. Do you mind? It's too hot for slaving over the oven."

"Great."

She parked him in an armchair with the evening paper.

7

NOEL insisted on washing the dishes after the meal. The nurse came earlier, still in uniform, complaining about the enervating heat. She and Imogen spent ten minutes in the sickroom, talking in rapid, fierce whispers.

"Do you see any difference?" Noel asked Mrs Jones when she emerged for refreshment.

"No. Not from this morning. No." She put on her look of professional wisdom. "It's not likely. She's very low, very weak, but not in pain. Has she spoken to you today? Sensibly, I mean? Putting two or three words together?"

"Once or twice."

"That's good. It's done her good to have you here. Are you going back tomorrow?"

"I thought of it. Is she likely to die," he forced the word out, "in the very near future?"

"We couldn't say to a few days. Soon, yes. No doubt. When she goes, to tell you the truth, I expect it to be sudden. No change for hours on end, and then, gone in a flash. The heart couldn't take the strain any longer. It could be tomorrow. It could be tonight."

"Is there any advantage in my staying?"

"Only to Miss Wagstaffe here. And fleeting pleasure to her mother."

"I'm a bit of a nuisance, rather than otherwise. Like all men."

The nurse smirked. Imogen said nothing.

Later Noel and his niece sat out in the garden in what she ironically called 'the cool of the evening'.

"What did my mother say about Raymond?"

"Very little. Except how good he was at mathematics."

"Nothing about his suicide?" Imogen had no fear of bluntness.

"No. And the memory seemed pleasant. I thought she smiled."

"Yes."

Silence fell between them; Imogen sat taut.

"How long is it since he died?" Noel

asked to ease the situation.

"Twenty years. He was forty. He fell in love with another man's wife. He was a bachelor, hadn't seemed particularly interested in women before. I mean, I don't know. He was always very self-contained. A loner." She laughed nervously. "And then he took up with this married woman. I think she worked as part-time secretary for him. She had three children. Her marriage was pretty well over; her husband would have been quite relieved to divorce her. And then Ray must suddenly have realized what he was doing, making himself responsible for a family, all still at school."

"How did your mother take this?"

"It was her worst time. She'd retired a year or two before, and hadn't properly come to terms with that."

"Your father was still at work?"

"Yes. Part-time. But he took her on a cruise to Greece and Palestine. He was very good. They often had holidays in Italy. She loved Rome and Florence, and seriously started to learn Italian again, to read Dante. But she was unsettled, felt herself a failure."

"And what about Raymond's . . . affair?"

"She spoke to me about it. Before he died. When it was just starting, I imagine."

"How did she find out?"

"I suppose Ray must have told her. I don't know. Perhaps he asked Dad about the legal side. Anyway, she knew. And took a relaxed, distanced view of it. What we call laid-back. Her line was that he was old enough to know his own mind. Dad was much more worried. He thought Ray didn't quite measure up to what was going on."

"And did he?"

"Ray was very clever at school, and a talented pianist. He did outstandingly well at university, but Mother used to say for all the good it did him outside his degree he might just as well have been taking a correspondence course. He didn't attend many concerts there, and certainly didn't take any part in them. Just did his everlasting mathematics. And then he landed a job which didn't involve much direct contact with other people. It suited him. He never had to teach anybody anything. Just come to some conclusion, and then explain it to some other dry-as-dust civil servant. I may be exaggerating, but I think all three jobs he had were of that sort. Communicating with computers."

"He wasn't homosexual?"

"Not as far as I was aware. There was Denise."

"And when he killed himself, how did your mother react?"

"That did shock her. She had this puritanical view that you should soldier on however badly things went against you. And it hit her where she didn't expect it. She thought it a bit of a joke, one of life's ironies, that Raymond, her cold fish, should take a tumble for a not very attractive girl lumbered with three children. But that he should kill himself she could not come to terms with."

"What happened? To the girl?"

"Denise? I don't really know. I never kept in touch with her, and I'm sure my mother never did. I hope Raymond left her what money he had."

"Was he well provided for?"

"I don't suppose so. Though he wouldn't waste his money."

"Did she and her husband divorce?"

"I don't even know that. I expect so. Now I come to think of it she had probably got her divorce before Raymond died. I met her only once. She was nondescript. And terrified of the family, especially Mother. We weren't very kind to her."

"And did that weigh on your mother's conscience after Raymond had gone?"

"I shouldn't think so. Not for one minute."

Imogen sat straight on the patio in the heat, exhausted. She rose, making up her mind.

"I'll go to see the patient," she said, clinically efficient.

After a few minutes she returned to the garden carrying glasses of iced lemonade. "Have a drink," she invited. "Mother's well away. I couldn't rouse her. Mrs Jones came earlier than usual. I hope this doesn't mean Mother's due for a restless night."

Noel raised his glass in a mock toast. She did nothing to acknowledge the gesture.

They sat unspeaking, but Noel felt

eminently comfortable. He had learnt something about his own family. Ethel had left home to be married when he was eleven, and they had never since that time, sixty-four years ago, spent a whole week together. They had corresponded sporadically, but rarely at length. Perhaps six times a year they might talk on the telephone. He had always admired his sister; she was forceful, had ideas, could argue, sometimes made small headlines in the quality newspapers. But at bottom he knew little about her.

When Raymond had committed suicide, he had attended the funeral, setting aside other important commitments, but had not managed any intimacy with his sister. She had been upright, unemotional, putting on a good public face. He respected, approved her stoic demeanour, but he had not touched her grief.

Imogen replaced her glass on the tray, looking at him with satisfaction, as if weighing up a favourite pupil, confirming the estimate of worthiness.

"My mother had trouble with love," she began, small-voiced.

That was enigmatic enough. Her own

love, other people's? He assumed an almost comical expression of interest.

"She went overboard for some man at her college."

He waited. He would not force his niece into untoward admissions. He could not help wondering if Imogen herself had been troubled by love, and the form her own desperations had taken. He gripped the seat of his cane chair.

"I suppose nothing of it ever reached you?" She dropped each word softly, separately. "It was all very hush-hush." She giggled into her fingers. "She was discreet about anything likely to affect her career."

"No," he answered. "Who was he?"

Imogen bit her lip.

"And when was all this?" he continued. "And how did you find out?"

"His name was Leslie French. He taught literature at Kay-Shuttleworth. How long ago? Oh, thirty-odd years. She would have been well up in her fifties."

"And French? How old was he at the time?"

"Thirty perhaps. Certainly no more.

There was a big difference."

"Did you ever meet him?"

"Yes, I did. He was a big drama man. He wrote some sort of pageant when they opened the new science block. Yes, I met him several times up at the college."

"And he was impressive?"

"Yes and no. Tall and good-looking. He reminded me of publicity photographs of film stars. Excellent head of waved, greased hair. Dreamy look. Rather effeminate. But yes. He was handsome, and knew it. And as I say did a great deal for the dramatic side of the college. Took the Theatre Royal over for a week every year. Edinburgh fringe and into the newspaper reports. And marvellous debates and classes for those who weren't so gifted. Made confident speakers. Yes, he earned his money."

"And how did he react to Ethel's, um . . . infatuation?"

"He wouldn't know."

"How did you learn about it? Was there talk?"

"No." Imogen paused. "My father told me."

"How did he find out?"

"My mother confessed to him. That shows it must have been very serious, though by that I don't mean to imply that there was any physical relationship between them. In Kay-Shuttleworth I guess he was seen as a favourite of the principal, that she made a great fuss of him, but in view of all he did, that wasn't surprising. There'd be jealousy, I don't doubt. I remember one middle-aged woman saying that Mr French had only to hint, to suggest anything to Dr Wagstaffe and it was as good as done. But I don't think they regarded him as anything but teacher's pet. Nothing sexual about it." Again Imogen stared ahead, patted her damp palms with a small square of ironed, lace-edged handkerchief. She slightly moved one of the glasses on the tray as if attempting some more aesthetically satisfactory placing. "Those were innocent days."

"So they say."

She darted a quick glance at her uncle.

"But, and this is the surprising thing, she confessed to my father."

"Why surprising?"

"She could easily have kept it to herself. In some ways Mother was secretive rather than otherwise, but she either thought this was so serious that something public might come of it, or was so obsessed with the man that she had to talk about him to somebody."

"Was Deirdre Commons working with her then?"

"I can't remember. I guess so. Why?"

"She didn't tell her about French?"

"I've no idea."

"She didn't," Noel pressed, "confess to your father out of justice to him?"

"That's just possible." Imogen spoke quite firmly, with her far-back voice, but thoughtfully, without confidence, as if some newer idea would break in to wreck the theory. "She admired my father. In some ways he was stronger than she was, though it didn't seem like that. He kept within his limits, whereas she was . . ." She hesitated.

"'For ever roaming with a hungry heart,'" he ventured, smiling.

"That's right. She was never satisfied with what she'd done. It was partly personal ambition; she had that all right, but she really did want to make colleges of teacher-training a kind of, oh, what they call now 'centres of excellence'. Was that a quotation?"

"Tennyson. 'Ulysses'. Didn't you read it at school?" She shook her head.

"I was another scientist. Translating scientific papers from German now and again was as near as we got to the arts."

"Why did your father tell you?"

"Again that's baffling. He'd talk to us. To Billy, and Raymond, and me. Quite freely about all sorts of subjects. But this came as a bit of a shock. I was home on holiday from my second job, Erith Grammar School. And we were out taking the dog for a walk. Ethel was away at some meeting. Even in the holidays she drummed work up, and her sort of activity always involved other people. I don't think she enjoyed sitting at a desk by herself."

"And?"

"Oh, yes." Imogen laughed at herself. "My father suddenly stopped, and tapped the toecaps of his shoes with the ferrule of his walking stick, and said, 'Y'know, Immy, I oughtn't to tell you this, but your mother's fallen in love with another man.' I was shaken; it seemed so unlikely. Ethel was no great beauty, and she'd always seemed elderly and extremely sensible if not strait-laced to me. Love was for young people, or so I thought." Imogen meditated on that at length. Noel decided she would not continue.

"And didn't he comment further?"

"Yes. I'd recovered my wits by this time, and wanted to poke my curious nose in, so I asked questions. He told me Leslie French's name, and how much younger he was than Ethel. And then he said, 'This is to go no further. Don't mention it to your mother. Or your brothers.' And then he straightened up and said, 'I wanted to tell you, Immy.' He never called me that when Mother was about; she hated it. 'I don't know what will come of it. Nothing, probably.' And that was all."

"She recovered, presumably?"

"I don't know. How can we know? I raised it once or twice with my father, and though he always answered, he didn't seem much concerned. He shrugged it off as if I had somehow misjudged the situation, that it had never been all that serious."

"You think it was?"

"Yes. She told Father and he confided in me."

"There was no scandal? In the college?"

"No. Well, not as far as I know. And this was the period of her biggest success. Kay-Shuttleworth prospered; she sat on national committees, appeared on radio programmes and the television, produced her book *The Bounds of Education* which was really highly thought of at the time. I don't know if the two things were connected, love and success at work. You see I don't know how long it lasted or what happened between them."

"There was no talk of divorce?"

"Oh, no. But this was also the time when this stupid university here ought to have given her a chair of education, and didn't. She also applied to the Institute at London University."

"That would have meant living away from your father."

"Yes. She would have done that."

Certainty rang in Imogen's pronouncement. Here she spoke with her mother's rich voice, a sumptuous sound.

The pair sat in silence.

"A curious story," Noel said, at length.

"You may say so now, but I guess at the time it turned their world upside down. For good or bad. It might have shaken both out of a rut." Imogen smiled grimly. "Even if the rut was valuable."

"And where's French now? What happened to him?"

"I don't know."

"Is he still alive?"

"I've not heard to the contrary. He'll be about sixty. He went to a job in the Department of Education at Cambridge, and then he went out to Africa. Or the other way about."

"Where in Africa?"

"Again I don't know. I never talked to my mother about him.

But she once mentioned she'd had a letter from him. As she would with some of her other notables."

"How long did Deirdre Commons live with her?"

"Oh, she came to them when she retired. She visited them a great deal before that. She'd retire at sixty. When she moved in, they were hanging on to this great big house, and my father was just beginning to be ill."

"I see."

"She died, oh, eight years ago. She'd always been healthy, and so it was unexpected. My mother had been ill three or four years then. With cancer."

"I never knew that."

"Nor I. For a long time. She did not want to mention it."

"Isn't that unlike her?" Noel asked. "Wouldn't she want to speak plainly about it?"

"You'd have thought so. But no. People are odd about illness. She'd hardly been sick in the whole of her life. I'm not saying that she'd argue that disease was moral weakness, but I guess that's how she thought of it. Or sometimes. And since she started she had operations, and some quite horrible treatment, I believe, but she did not broadcast it. Not to me, even, or Billy."

"Deirdre knew?"

"Must have. But Mother — well up into her seventies, into her eighties

— didn't broadcast what was wrong with her. They removed a breast."

"When I saw her she'd always give me the same story. Bronchitis, arthritis, old age, creaks and bones."

"I know. She was a brave woman. When I found out she swore me not to tell Billy or you. But that was well after Deirdre died. She lived on her own in that barn. She had help, but it must have been a struggle. I had the biggest battle with her about buying this place when I decided to retire two years ago. Why couldn't I go and live with her? If we took a bungalow we'd be in each other's way. She didn't like these modern places with low ceilings and jerry-built walls. But she was pretty well finished by then. She's lasted here a lot longer than I, or she, expected. She must have a robust constitution."

"Will you stay here?"

"After she's gone, you mean? I doubt it. But I haven't had time to think it over. I've still kept my house in London. I've rented it out. Nor is my mother's house sold."

"I thought . . . "

"Yes. That's what she wanted you to think. But she couldn't make the break. She knew damned well she'd never go back, but she didn't like to admit it to herself. That's the curious thing. Ethel, the plain speaker, the advocate of let's-look-facts-in-the-face, was utterly secretive about her own illness."

"She was getting on."

"And lonely. She had Deirdre after Father died, but when she went, Mother still said nothing. She stuck it out on her own. And I was busy. In fact she lied. When I asked her outright if it was cancer, she looked me straight in the face and said, 'There are hundreds of other inconveniences and illnesses besides cancer.' Absolutely brazened it out."

"Does your brother keep in touch?"

"Yes. Occasionally. He came last week. And they phone sometimes on Sundays. He's very busy. Shirley his wife has offered to come and stay."

"How old is Billy now?"

"Sixty-one."

"He's not thinking of retirement yet?"

"He hasn't said so. He enjoys his work." William was a structural engineer, into atomic energy, and travelled the world a good deal.

Imogen gathered the glasses, but allowed him to carry the tray indoors.

"We'll go to see Mother," she said.

They tiptoed in, almost farcically.

"Are you awake?" Imogen called.

"Yes."

"I'll put the light on, then. Close your eyes." The curtains were still drawn. "Are you warm enough?"

"Yes. Thank you."

The room seemed stiflingly hot. Imogen plucked efficiently at the bedclothes and Noel moved forward.

"Is that Noel?" Ethel asked, mumbling.

"Who else?" he asked.

A smile lit his sister's face, wrinkling it more deeply, but giving it humanity, making her seem more like the Ethel he remembered.

"Give me my glasses, Imogen, please."

The words were softly clear. Imogen complied. Noel took the invalid's hand. Again a smile lit the features.

"It's lovely to see you," Ethel said.

"Noel's going back tomorrow," Imogen intervened.

"I expect he's busy. Are you?" A ghostly chuckle from cracked lips.

"I still find a bit to do now and again. I'm trying to write an article on Robert Southey, to say whether he's worth reading or not."

"Is he?" Imogen.

"I can't make up my mind. I don't think so, but it may be my sort of prejudice."

"Had you read much of him before?"

"No. Not really."

"Have you, Mother? Robert Southey? What do you know about him?"

Ethel opened her eyes wide, struggled about.

"'I charm thy life / From the weapons of strife,'" she repeated with an effort, but clearly enough for them to follow.

"Is that Robert Southey?" Imogen asked.

"Learnt it at school." Ethel's face was momentarily ajig with mischief, as though she knew she had put one over on them. "The 'Curse of Kehama'. We had to recite it."

"Do you know it, Noel?"

"It's in the anthologies." He shrugged.

Ethel had closed her eyes, allowed her face to sag into this image of disease and death. She was no longer herself but a shallowly breathing corpse. Noel, as surprised at her foray into sense as at the speed of her exit, held on to her hand.

"Don't you feel like sleep?" Imogen asked.

"Yes." Nodding of head.

"Have a sip of lemon first. Your lips look parched." The operation completed, and the bedclothes straightened, Imogen signalled her uncle from the sickroom.

8

TWO hours later Imogen and Noel idled with glasses of whisky. Three or four times she had been in to her mother, grumbling that this looked like the beginning of a disturbed night.

Marginally cooler, put at ease by alcohol, Noel Smith felt comfortable for the first time that day. His niece was in no hurry to go to bed; she was a poor sleeper, she claimed, and if her mother was going to play up she might as well be ready. Besides she enjoyed having someone to talk to. It didn't happen too often.

"I came here last November, and moved my mother in. She was ill, but herself, if you know what I mean. Then she became worse. She's had three spells in hospital this year, came out three weeks ago, and wasn't expected to last."

"Does she know she's dying?" He had

asked her this twice before, but found her answers unsatisfactory.

"Difficult to say. She's so weak and drugged. Besides, I guess that she won't know either when she's finally going. Her heart will just stop functioning. Or if she does realise it, she won't mind. It will be a relief."

"But she seemed lucid?" He questioned her answer. "Just now."

"When you were in, you mean? When she quoted that Southey? I don't understand the way her brain functions. She remembers her childhood. But time's disappeared. She asked me what her father was doing out in the garden when I went in last time."

"But she knows me and she was fourteen or thereabouts when I arrived."

"It's all beyond comprehension. When my time comes, I just want to snuff myself out, with no trouble to anybody."

"We're all too well built," Noel said. "You and I and your mother have the Smith constitution."

They had looked up the Southey 'Curse', and read it again.

'From sickness I charm thee,
And Time shall not harm thee
But Earth which is mine
Its fruits shall deny thee . . . '

"They taught children some odd stuff," Imogen said, offended.

"They did indeed. There's always been, I guess, not that I've had much connection with schools, a minority of eccentrics who stuffed down the throats of their charges all sorts of ill-gotten bits and pieces that ran temporarily riot in their crackbrains."

"Is that good?" Imogen asked, primly a headmistress.

"I wouldn't stop it. I imagine you had a great many very intelligent people in the teaching profession in Ethel's day. That was the limit of ambition for many clever, poor children."

"And it's not so now?" Sarcastic question.

"What do you think? You worked with them."

"I see what you mean." She drew in her polemical horns.

"The large majority were conformists.

Of course they were. They did as they were told. They were rising a social class or two and so acted circumspectly. And the eccentrics often had no great background on which to base their oddities. So they were reduced to hymns or pub songs, horrible puns, wild scientific theorizing based on the popular newspapers and magazines. Why, my science teacher in the grammar school, first-class honours degree and all, told us flatly that it would never be possible to launch a rocket from the earth to reach the moon. He was convinced, and convinced us; and yet he was a superb teacher."

"That's not eccentricity."

"No. But I quote it to show how teachers are influenced by what they read."

"What was his reasoning?" Imogen asked.

"I can't really remember. I think, I can't be sure, it was that the rocket would need to be fired off at such a speed to counteract gravity that it would be burnt up in the earth's atmosphere before it barely made a start. I may be wrong. Does that sound logical?"

Imogen hummed.

"Do you think Ethel encouraged eccentricity in her student teachers?" he asked.

"I doubt it. She was determined to educate them. She instituted qualifying units or modules with exams, and made sure people knew something. All her students, for instance, did a science course each year they were with her. I guess at the end it was just a case of mugging up Dr Somebody-or-other's notes or an elementary textbook, but at least they had heard some of the terms and glanced at some of the problems. She was serious. People coming out after three years at her place had learnt something and been tested on it. She chased the university when they were preparing for their B.Ed. course, argued that they set the standards too low. But as to eccentricity, I doubt it. She'd think there was no time for it in real teaching. Teaching wasn't entertainment. An unusual approach she might approve provided it didn't go too far. I remember a man I taught with who did his post-graduate certificate there. Apparently one day he was delivering a short lecture to his fellow students when Ethel walked in. She stood and listened, and at the end the tutor asked my mother what she thought of the talk. Sycophantically, I expect. She made a complimentary remark or two, and then said, 'You need anchoring to your table. I can't see the necessity for all the strolling about you did.' Now this man was, he said, a cheeky young devil and he answered her, 'Aristotle used to walk along the Lyceum to do his teaching.' And she said, 'Hasn't it crossed your mind that Aristotle is remembered because he had something important or interesting to say and not for his walking?' That was Ethel. You were there to learn."

"And did you take that line?"

"To some extent. That was the grammar school ethos, at least when I was young."

"Were you eccentric?" He began again.

"Not really. Science teaching is more open. The lab assistants hover around.

And one learns to be careful with valuable or dangerous equipment about. So circumstances were against it. Not that I haven't come across some lunatics."

Imogen chattered on, freely, scattering anecdotes.

"How did you like it when you became a head?"

"I was lonely at first."

"Unexpectedly?"

"My first school was a small, well-organized grammar school, so that there were whole long periods when nothing happened. Then there'd be short spells of intense activity and decision, and then back to the vacuum. I was energetic and found myself work in the end."

"You could have been idle?"

"Easily. When I moved to a bigger place, it was different. And besides there is more and more paperwork these days."

"Useful?"

"Some of it. But the schools would function just as well without it. At the end I had four deputy heads to help me make work. Still, as you can see, I'm a very conventional person. I did as the education office thought right."

"Do you ever regret spending your life in teaching?"

"I tell you this, if that's what you're getting at, I wouldn't have been any use as a research scientist. Not like my uncles. I was Mother's daughter."

"You haven't answered my question."

"Do I regret . . . ?" Imogen rubbed her chin, almost apologetically. "Often. There are many more options these days."

"You might have been a lawyer or a stockbroker?"

"Yes, or worked abroad. The diplomatic service. What I don't know is whether such a career would have been intrinsically more interesting than teaching. I doubt it. All work has its longueurs. The trouble these days with teaching is that it is neither highly regarded by society nor adequately rewarded. And I guess this is so too in the universities."

"I'd agree."

"Of course," Imogen continued in her mother's rich, winy voice, "when it's all over and done with, one must feel regrets. One sees mistakes and lost opportunities. And the more successful one has been, the greater the disappointment."

"Were you successful?" he asked.

"Yes. People said so. Good examination results. Oxbridge if the bright ones wanted it. Some line careers. Mediocre students looked after. Outside interests. Well-publicized community work. I was lucky. I chose or was chosen by the right schools. Yes."

They sat in easy silence again. Imogen wagged the whisky bottle towards him. When he shook his head, she helped herself.

"I suppose," she opened slowly, "you mean on a personal level, do you? I never married, have had no children. My mother managed both a career and a family. My father's money helped. And from what she has said lately — well, since Deirdre died — there were enormous snags."

"You mean she neglected you or failed in her work somehow."

"That's what she felt."

"But you've no complaint from your side?" he asked. "You didn't feel your mother treated you badly?"

"Not really. But she demanded high standards of herself." Imogen smiled broadly. "You're wondering, aren't you, why I never married. I hadn't quite my mother's force. If I'd have married I think I wouldn't have minded taking ten years or so off from my career to bring up a family. I shouldn't have been bursting keen to get back in a hurry as Ethel was."

"Did you ever think of it?" Noel asked.

Imogen stroked her chin, smiled broadly, not put out.

"Yes. Three times. Seriously." She waited for a further question which he was too polite to pose. "But just as I would have been in no hurry to rush out of housewifery, I was a bit loth to break off from a successful career. I'm postwar, Noel. Marriage didn't seem quite so necessary to complete life." She laughed as she looked at him. "You understand what I mean?"

"I think so. Did your mother?"

"That I don't know. She never spoke to me about it. She backed away when I raised the matter, though she was always most polite when I brought young men home. I guess she believed that she would have achieved more if she hadn't been hampered by husband and family."

"Such as?"

"The professorship for one thing. I don't think she had political ambitions. She limited herself." Imogen pointed a finger. "Like you and me." Silence stalked. "She taught children, trained teachers, talked publicly about both, but she never came to grips with, well," a pause, almost laughingly broken, "philosophy or, let's say, the problems of evil." Imogen thinned her voice so that a modest scepticism denied undue pretension. "She taught teachers to deal with snags, intellectual or emotional or moral, that our sort of society, that of a moderately large nation on a small island off north-west Europe, would be likely to pose. God, predestination, suffering, were outside her remit."

"Good Lord." She had surprised him into the ejaculation.

"There you go. Another modest violet. Isn't that what's wrong with this country? We'll clean our little hole and corner up, and forget the rest of the world. I'm as bad as you are. If you're as bad as I think. And when somebody moves out of his little field, somebody like C. S. Lewis, I just read a book about him, and starts to ask questions about the soul and innate evil and eternity and God, then the rest of the scholars say he should have stuck to his *Allegory of Love* or *History of Sixteeth-Century Literature*. Why the hell should he?"

"I could think of several reasons."

"Such as?"

"He's convincing, or puts up a good case, in literature, but not elsewhere."

"You might just be jealous of his fame or his money."

"Possibly."

"Do you never," her voice had her mother's beautiful insistent power, "consider what George Steiner said: that people who think highly of art can still be thoroughly wicked."

"That the commandant of a death camp can sit down at night to enjoy a Mozart quartet?" Now Noel rubbed his chin, then pointed his finger. "Yes," he continued. "And I'd even be bound to admit that the highest art could have no moral effect on many people. Or even have a deleterious effect on some. But, and let me say this, if I thought literature, and I speak only of my own subject, was no more than entertainment, a way of passing leisure time pleasantly, I'd still do what I have done, and that is teach people to read carefully, and bear all kinds of important considerations in mind while they do so. I took my pleasures seriously." He looked down. "Here was a great land of plenty, which had fed me often enough, and my work was to indicate to my pupils what they might find there. It would be better, doubtless, if they did it for themselves, but many wouldn't, and so guides like me performed usefully."

"You sound quite unlike yourself."

"Not such a dry stick?" he coughed. "Now I've given it up for nearly ten years I see what I ought to have been doing."

"And didn't?" Imogen laughed.

"The detail, the side issues, the administration, the bits and pieces got in the way. By the time I retired I was going through the motions, moderately efficiently, I hope, and not hindering the one or two young people, teachers and students, who were doing the job properly." Again a bout of coughing scraped his chest as if he'd spoken too frankly and now wanted to blanket his confessions under raw physical noise. He recovered, growled out, "Weren't you the same?"

"Yes and no. But I was too much of my father's daughter. I could stand back and look at myself in a way that my mother, and perhaps you, couldn't. Ethel was in the middle of it all, flailing about. She'd plenty of critical sense for detail, but she had to be into anything right up to the neck. My father wasn't like that."

"How do you come to know about C. S. Lewis or Steiner?" he asked.

"You think a chemist shouldn't? No, I had a very good woman teaching on my staff who used to recommend all sorts of reading to me. She still sends me the odd book."

"Young?"

"No. Late forties. Unmarried. An educationist. Or is it — alist?

She thought even headmistresses could

learn. I liked that. She was not forceful; she'd sidle up and say, 'I think you'd enjoy this' or 'You know what you were telling the sixth in assembly, well this man is most interesting about . . . '"

Imogen laughed, stood. "I'll go in to Mother."

When she re-emerged, she answered his "Comfortable?" with a reassuring nod, and "Creep in and see her." He did so, clumsily, stood by the bed in a room lit only from the crack of a nearly closed door. His sister did not move, and he, uncertain whether to touch her, shuffled on the spot. The counterpane and sheets needed no straightening; glasses and bottles stood neatly on a side table. He was useless in a way his father would not have been. J. T. Smith would have prayed, perhaps not aloud but with intensity inside his head, for God's blessing on his suffering daughter, for a quiet night, a holy rest, peace at last. The petitions would range from pulpit clichés to Newman's luminous, late-evening phrases, but the old man at least would have known where to turn, how to put all into God's hands. His son could do nothing, had no equivalents. Noel closed his eyes, said "God bless her and keep her", and then quickly, guiltily opened them again. What right had he to such words? Almost blasphemously he felt better for the sentence, and raked round for the rest. It was biblical, Old Testament. He'd heard it often enough, both as a child and at the official services he'd had to attend: university, civic, memorial. 'God bless thee and keep thee; The Lord,' yes, that was right, the Lord, not God, 'make his face to shine upon thee, and be gracious unto thee.' His excellent memory stumbled, righted itself. 'The Lord lift up his countenance upon thee, and give thee peace.' He straightened himself, comforted. Ethel lay there still; he did not bend to her, but turned. The portrait on the wall could be made out as an oblong of darkness barely different from the dark wall behind it. He slipped out into the brightness of the corridor, leaving the door slightly ajar.

Imogen waited outside.

"How is she?"

"Fast asleep."

"Good. I'll get myself to bed."

He pondered whether to tell his niece about his prayer. To confess would erase some of his shame. He stood, hesitating, not moving.

"Is there something?" she asked. Her smile was rare, broad, open; he saw the attraction and strength of the woman.

"Not really."

She continued to question him with her expression. He kept silent.

"Let's get to bed, then."

"It was in there." As soon as he spoke she turned easily, companionably towards him. "I said a prayer."

"Yes?"

"I feel now I've no right, I had no right to do it."

"Why not?"

"I'm a nonbeliever. God doesn't exist. And yet I prayed to Him."

Imogen approached, stood shoulder to shoulder, not touching.

"May I ask what?" she inquired.

"That Ethel had an easy end. That's what I wanted. Of course it was. And I could do nothing about it myself. So I asked God, in Whom I don't believe, to do something about it." Now he explained himself, in simple words, his competence returned. "That doesn't seem right."

"I'm not surprised. In these last few weeks I've often been at my wits' end, and would have loved to turn to somebody or something. But, unlike you, I hadn't been trained to it. When you were a child you were taught to say your prayers, so it's not unexpected that you drop into the old habit. We're not prepared to face the reality of death, as perhaps nurses or doctors are. We see it intermittently and then only when it affects our nearest and dearest." She sniggered at her phrase, dissenting at any great protestation of affection for her mother. "So you slip your wish into the form of a prayer. Almost without thinking. Now, let me guess again. You made some quotation. How's that? From the prayer book or the Bible?"

"In the end, yes, I did. Once I'd made my wish."

"There are the old habits," she pontificated, "reasserting themselves. It's superstition now. Pulling the turkey's wish bone."

"You know, Imogen," he spoke firmly, "we should have seen more of each other."

"I doubt it. I've enjoyed your company, certainly, even in these circumstances. But that's no reason for further misjudgements." The short sentences dashed him.

"That sounds grudging. But will you come and stay with us, once this is all over? Irène would enjoy it. She loves entertaining visitors, and she'll trail you round the shops and theatres."

"I'll think about it."

"You'll come?"

"Yes, sir. Very good, sir." She shoulder-charged him lightly, giggled and made for the door. "You're very like Ethel."

"I lack her big gestures."

"Not a bad fault."

They left the room, pleased with each other.

9

NOEL left before lunch next day. Ethel, who seemed unchanged, recognized him, called him faintly by name, but said nothing more. When he spoke to her she nodded like a preoccupied child, perfectly willing to act properly, but with mind engaged elsewhere. When he kissed her for the last time she opened her eyes; he held her hand but the pressure was not returned. Imogen drove him to the station, as a neighbour came in to keep watch.

"It's a bit amiss," he said awkwardly, "leaving you like this."

"No. I can manage. You've seen the help I get is good. It's just that I'm tied to the spot. After fifty-six years of pleasing myself a week or two more in confinement won't harm me."

She kissed him on his lips, her breath slightly sour, and left him to find his own way. On Manchester Piccadilly Station he felt, guiltily, enormous relief, enjoyed searching the departures board, buying a paper, watching the railwaymen, the screens, the trains. A middle-aged man greeted him by name and title, claimed to have attended his lectures in London, though he had been a modern languages student.

"I came to hear you talk about the Romantic poets. Our prof., Leyland, insisted on it. We were ignorant, he used to say."

"Your name is?"

"Alan Faulkner." He explained that he had just paid a professional visit to an engineering concern which made small components for car and aircraft manufacturers.

"Was it interesting?" Noel Smith asked, daily uninvolved.

"Bloody hair-raising."

Faulkner, apparently the principal of a firm of accountants, began to explain how the firm he had seen, excellent, up-to-date, wasting nothing, with modern technology, barely survived.

"And you're called in to bring comfort?"

"No fear. They don't want soft soap.

They want accurate summaries, and sound advice."

"Can't they do that for themselves?"

Faulkner explained, shortly, drily, why it was worth the money employing him. In the ordinary way he would have sent a subordinate, but here he was a friend of the managing director and so had come up himself.

"I like to go out in the field from time to time. Figures aren't everything, though you'll be surprised to hear an accountant say so."

Noel Smith listened now with a subdued pleasure to this middle-aged man in his good suit, with smooth silver-grey hair and clipped moustache. Faulkner's exposition was clarity itself, and short. He took his listener's interest for granted, because nobody was bored by plain money-talk, but he spoke without exaggeration. He rarely used his languages now except on holiday. Yes, they had plenty of work; he'd taken on two newly qualified women last year, he spoke proudly of that, and they would have to extend their premises in the next months.

"Do you ever read French or German literature?" Noel asked.

"Poetry, you mean? Or plays? Novels? That sort of thing. No. I glance at continental newspapers. Useful to be able to do that, I suppose. I don't get a lot of spare time. Often don't leave the office until seven."

"And does your wife approve?"

The one-twenty-five express powerfully appeared. Faulkner jumped up, grabbed his silver-bound box briefcase and made for the first-class carriages at the front of the train.

"She's fucking left me."

The ferocity of voice frightened Smith, so that he sat timidly in his non-smoking second-class area, trembling. That beautifully dressed striding figure, making a handsome way in the world, a paradigm of all that was admirable in the country, had flung a bitter sentence back at his old teacher. Ethel's dying had left Smith vulnerable; he saw himself almost as incapable these days. Thankful that he had no longer to talk to Faulkner, he hated the shudder in his shoulders. His newspaper lay unopened on the table; the woman opposite with her magazine and wicker basket sat unobserved.

The Pennines lacked beauty under the summer sun; the moors spread dry, the grass yellow, the trees already fading, the rivers shallow. The hills interested him vaguely, large and shapely, but surfaces had been burnt dim by unusual months of heat. Even the simple houses seemed exposed, stripped of green background, desiccated, dry-stone as the walls. Noel made himself look and record; for all he knew he would be back on this way to Ethel's funeral in a day or two, but from this time the grandeur would remind him of Faulkner's unconcealed discontent.

They swiftly took the length and darkness of a tunnel, made for Sheffield, in and out over the same tracks and so into the dullness of the flying Midlands, and Beechnall. There his taxi driver, a formidable figure a yard wide, sounded off his anger.

"Did you see that man? Wouldn't tell me where he wanted to go. 'Just drive off,' he said, 'and I'll give you the directions as we're on the way.' 'Which way do I turn out of the station?' 'I'll tell you once we've started.' 'You won't, y'know. Out.'" The man changed gear with violence of movement. "I reckon he wanted me to take him to Leicester."

"Why?" Noel asked.

"I don't know bleddy why, but I wasn't takin' him, that's for certain."

He went on with further tales of chicanery; four young women had halted the taxi after a long journey and jumped out, but he had chased one, threatened to beat her so that she had coughed up the £20 fare. "I don't want to threaten women at one o'clock in th' morning, but it's the only way."

"Would you have hit her?" Noel dared.

"I'd have left her black and blue. It's the only language they understand."

At home Noel Smith sorted his post: junk mail, bills, appeals, nothing of interest. August was a blank month. His friends holidayed abroad. He walked half a mile to the shops to buy a loaf, and felt guiltily free. Imogen was caged up there in Manchester in the heat. He could turn aside as he liked.

For an hour he lounged, drinking tea, unoccupied even with the newspaper on his lap. He walked the length of his land, and spoke to his neighbour. From three doors up he heard the shrill shouts of children playing in water. The neighbour, an affluent wine merchant who spent all day in his garden with his bedding plants and horticultural machinery, had not realized he had been away. Noel turned on the six o'clock television news and fell asleep.

He woke feeling drugged, in time for the weather forecast; more heat and drought. The broadcaster smiled; this is what the holiday-makers needed, Mediterranean sunshine on your own doorstep. Noel would have to water this evening; he ran the hose half way up the garden in preparation. He ought to have asked Lawrence if the council had banned their use. Sluggishly he rang Imogen in Manchester.

Her mother was much the same. She had asked, surprising her daughter, if Noel had gone back home. "She was pleased you came; in all her confusion she knew you." Niece and uncle comforted each other, without foundation. The nurse would be in within an hour or so. Imogen had arranged to go out shopping next day. He said he must irrigate the garden. The pair did not speak easily, had lost their recent intimacy. He said he would phone again; she advised him not to work too hard. Back in his armchair he felt low, without energy, but he forced himself to his feet, played out his hose fully, thanking God he'd invested in winding gear, and set it trickling at the top of the garden. The soil was free of weeds, he noticed. He was busy trimming the edge of his brown lawn when he heard the telephone. In no hurry he made his way indoors. The phone rang on. He gave his number rather breathlessly.

A male voice asked if it would be possible to speak to Professor Noel Smith. Smith named himself.

"You won't know me. French. Leslie French. We have never met, but I'm a close friend of an old colleague of yours. Tom Luke. I've recently returned from Japan and I'm ringing from the Lukes' home. In the course of conversation I mentioned my old mentor Ethel Wagstaffe, and asked if she was still alive. He did not know, but said he had not read any obituary. In any case, Tom said, I could ring you, her brother. I did not realize there was a relationship. I knew your books on Keats and Spenser and Shakespeare, but had not connected you with Dr Wagstaffe."

Coincidence.

French did not pause, bubbled on with his apologies, giving Noel no time to intervene.

"I hope I am not interrupting at some inconvenient time. I realize that you must be very busy, even though you have retired." There followed a long paragraph on the many calls on emeritus academics' time. "But I had, have every reason to be grateful to Ethel Wagstaffe, who was most kind to me in my first post at a teacher-training establishment. We did keep up our acquaintance by letter when I first went out to Africa, and we met once or twice at conferences when I came back to Cambridge, but then I was offered a post in literature and drama in Tokyo and our correspondence lapsed." Without hesitation he described his life in the East, his marriage to a Japanese wife, her sudden death, his return to

England, his indecision over whether to retire or to fly out for a further three years at his university. "I have the energy. I love the country and the work. My children are still out there." Noel thought the man would never stop. Perhaps he missed his attentive classes. More likely he was nervous, and this spilled over into a rush of confession. Apart from confirmatory murmurs or an infrequent 'Oh, yes' while the other drew breath Noel had played no part in this conversation. Tom Luke's phone bill would rocket if this performance was typical. Now he was only half listening. "But Professor Smith, you won't want to hear all this, and so I wonder if I could trouble you for news of Dr Wagstaffe." The request was repeated in four ways, with much complimentary reference to Ethel, to Noel himself who wondered if this oriental volubility was the result of a long stay in Japan.

At last, French came to a stop.

Briefly Noel gave an account of his sister's illness. At once French broke out into a torrent of regret.

"You must remember," Noel interrupted,

strongly, "she's eighty-eight, eighty-nine, and has lived a very full life."

An explosion of questions followed. They were answered.

"Would it be possible to call round on you?" This was the shortest unit French had so far managed. Impudence had reduced loquacity. Noel, unimpressed, did not much want to see the man, but invited him for coffee, stressing that if he had to return to Manchester then the invitation would be cancelled at short notice. French expressed gratitude, said he understood, launched himself again into encomia of Ethel and brother so that it was Noel Smith who rang off on the pretext that he could hear someone at the door. He put down the phone as French was still speaking.

His left ear rang, drilled through. French was obviously used to making himself heard on the back row of the gallery. Noel sat down, trembling. When he had recovered he discovered that he was pleased he'd invited the man, gasbag or not. There had been mention of old photographs of the Kay-Shuttleworth days which he'd bring along. Noel would enjoy them. If French was as bad as he seemed hc could bc dismissed after an hour.

Next day when he rang Imogen he described the phone call.

"What a coincidence. And he didn't make a very favourable impression on you?" she said.

"We'll see when he turns up tomorrow. Suppose he wants to visit your mother?"

"I can see no sense in that. She wouldn't recognize him. It would be a journey wasted."

"What if he asks for your address or phone number?"

"Give it to him. No harm there. Just make it clear that we don't want him up here."

Imogen knew her mind. She had arranged to spend a day in London. Two nurses would come in over forty-eight hours.

"I don't know if I'm doing right. She's no different. Having another person in might stimulate her. At least I tell myself. I feel guilty. Her last few days and here I am playing truant, but I promised Yvonne Young that I'd go down to her exhibition. She was the art mistress at my school. Very hard working and talented. And like me she never married. I bought several of her pictures; there was a seascape on the corridor outside my mother's bedroom. I don't know if you noticed it. I don't suppose I shall be able to afford anything now at London exhibition prices. But I'm glad she's doing well."

"Is she still teaching?"

"Not now. She retired early, just before I did. She's in her fifties, a bit younger than I am."

"Enjoy yourself, then."

"Thanks, Noel. I like talking to you. I wish we'd had more to do with each other. How's Irène?"

"I'm just about to phone her. They'll have finished the evening meal. I have to gird my loins because she more often than not puts me on to her mother. The old dear is said to appreciate it, though I don't understand what she's saying, and she doesn't follow me. We're both a bit deaf so we bawl at each other."

"Give Irène my love."

The evening before Leslie French's visit

Beechnall was drenched by a spectacular thunderstorm. Rain washed an inch-and-a-half deep round the blocked drains in the streets and Noel feared for his garden border in the violence of the downpour. The air smelt immediately sweeter; damage to plants was not too extensive, and next morning the sky stretched cloudless blue as ever.

French appeared two minutes before time.

"I hope I'm not too early. I found it without any trouble."

"Didn't Tom Luke bring you then?"

"No, I walked. Exercise is essential at my time of life."

Noel looked his visitor over; the word he would have chosen for him was 'faded'. The thinning hair brushed back from the forehead seemed dusty. In the warm weather French wore no jacket, but a multilinear tie in the collar of his pale blue shirt. His slacks were light grey, sharply creased, the brown shoes not quite clean.

The hair, the skin seemed lifeless; the face too thin for comfort. One could imagine how handsome he had been

APS

thirty-five years ago, with luxuriant wavy dark hair, long-lashed blue eyes, broad shoulders, athletic carriage. Now the strength, the blood had gone; French had not run to fat but had melted to thin awkwardness. In the sitting room he crossed his legs as he sat with a huge swoop of movement to expose a length of grey, hairy shinbone.

As soon as they had settled to coffee French began.

"It's most kind to invite me here. I'm sure you have plenty of interesting matters to pursue rather than to entertain every casual stranger who takes it into his head to telephone you."

Noel listened to the banal flow, the balanced sentences, the trite observations. To be objective, he admitted that the visitor had a beautiful speaking voice. What had been strident, metallic over the phone, was now a pleasant, varied, attractive instrument, matched exactly in volume to the size of the room. French smiled, modestly, stared one straight in the eye, but imagined he had to talk his way into his host's good graces.

This was the man, Noel thought as

words tumbled, with whom Ethel had been in love.

True, Ethel had been no expert. Then again he did not know that. He had never thought of her in that way. At the age of eleven he had attended his sister's wedding to William Wagstaffe, and that had been, as far as he was concerned, the end of her love life. He realized how mistaken he had been. Ethel had kept that poor Pre-Raphaelite print because somebody had said, foolishly wrong, it resembled her. Ambition, work, family had not filled in every minute of her life. She had looked with favour on this chatterer. It was not surprising once one thought it over; she had power and influence, was flattered, had the capability of reorganizing the careers of other people, and it was now only too obvious that she misconstrued the attention of a young, handsome, gifted man who had set himself out to please. A masculine boss would not be harshly judged if he made a pass at a younger colleague; it would demonstrate his virility. Tom Luke, dry-as-dust mathematician, French's friend, had once injudiciously bedded his secretary, a young married woman. And Ethel, saying nothing to the beloved, afraid to make an open declaration, had suffered the pangs of 'dispriz'd, despis'd' love, undervalued not by the man but by herself and had said nothing, except, creating the worst of all worlds, to her husband. That seemed heroic to Noel now, to feel the power of love with no chance of reciprocity.

French described life at the Kay-Shuttleworth College thirty years ago. There had been minor trouble, demonstrations, marches, one sit-in, a rise in the pregnancy rate, but Ethel's staff chose their pupils carefully, worked them hard, so that the disturbance was kept to a minimum. Ethel had dismissed two leaders of unrest. "They hadn't the sense to make a decent showing in college examinations, and so were warned, then expelled. Ethel stood no nonsense. Some of the students grumbled, but it came to nothing. Your sister was a powerful figure. She received threatening letters, unwanted tons of coal, unordered books, taxis, tree surgeons, but she did not waver. It must have taken its toll, but she held to her views."

"Would it have been better if she had shown more pliability?" Noel asked.

"I doubt it. You know what it was like."

"Were the staff on her side?"

"By and large. There were some radicals." French laughed at his word. "But most were apathetic outside their own sphere. They didn't care for politicking."

"How did you stand?"

"Slightly liberal and doing nothing either way. I got on with my drama and my career. Rightly or wrongly I thought our students a pretty eventempered lot, and that the leaders of the revolution, such as it was, acted as they did out of personal inadequacies or crises. The climate of the time gave them half a chance to work off, or out, their neuroses. I realize, of course, I talk like one of the gerontocracy of modern China."

"You were a young man then."

"Yes. And I could see right on both sides."

Noel saw himself condemned by the sentence. At this period he had been a new professor, having exchanged a provincial chair for a more distinguished post, and he felt sympathy for the ideals of some of his students who had urged that their courses should be more relevant to life. He had contended, reasonably he hoped though he feared they had found him patronizing, that the great texts of literature were as relevant to their needs and aspirations as the psychology and socio-political ideas they bandied about. He had soon realized that half his students had not understood the drift of his argument; they felt a vague resentment against authority as represented by him. He, or his like, laid down areas of study, without the students' permission. They could only choose between the authors or periods he had put into the syllabus. Their suggestions seemed to him ill-thought-out; they were ignorant and scraped the bottom of an unfilled barrel. As he complained to a colleague, 'I don't doubt that the *Dandy* or *Beano* have sociological significance, but they do not repay careful study as *Hamlet* does, or *The Epistle to Arbuthnot* or *Copperfield* or *Middlemarch*.' But he had felt guilty as if he betrayed his own ideals, for he remembered the time when he had regarded his mentors as old-fashioned specialists in their own ivory towers with their insistence on philology and ablaut or *Beowulf* or *Brennu Njáls Saga*. One of his own professors had once, primly off the cuff, said he found more of interest in the *Battle of Maldon* than in any Shakespeare play. Noel had been shaken.

French launched himself into an account of his dramatic productions during his six years at Kay-Shuttleworth. In his second year he had chosen to stage *King Lear*. Now he laughed at himself. "Lear with twenty-year-olds. But it wasn't without merit." Shakespeare, Sheridan, Goldsmith, Eliot, Christopher Fry, Arden, early Pinter, Joyce's *Exiles*. Some were full-scale productions; others publicly delivered but without meticulous preparation. Ethel had produced money; the college had taken Osborne's *Luther* to full-scale performances in a city church, not without opposition and scandal.

As Noel listened his attitude changed. French boasted, in a civilized way, but he recalled to Noel Smith's mind what it was like to be a young teacher, in an institution one admired, where one was proud to work, where one could choose to do what one did best and where the effort expended was appreciated. Noel warmed to the man, and yet could not help wondering whether he would have thought very highly of his productions. Ethel had never invited him. But Shakespearean poetry rang in young heads,

> 'Oh, you should not rest
> Between the elements of air and earth
> But you should pity me.'

Noel Smith poured out more coffee. French refused a second chocolate biscuit, keeping his figure trim. He patted a waistline bulge, saying when he came back from his three years in Africa he weighed ten stone.

"That was my finest hour," he claimed, his voice only half ironical, "at Kay-Shuttleworth. I enjoyed Africa, though I felt off colour a lot of the time. Cambridge gave me time to think, and then Japan. I met and married my wife when she was a student in Cambridge and she encouraged me to take a post I was offered out there. We had a child and I think she wanted her son to be Japanese. Her parents pulled strings. But I never again seemed to fulfil myself as I did at KS. I was both young and experienced. I was twenty-six-seven when I started, after a good grammar school and a public school. I didn't do national service. I knew what I wanted. The students were young enough and bright enough to make it all rewarding. And Ethel provided tremendous backing. She wanted KS to excel, and wasn't afraid to take risks. Theatre's an expensive subject, or can be, but she saw to it the money came my way."

"As opposed to sports?"

"It seemed so. Both the schools I had been in had strong musical and athletic traditions, and drama seemed less important. They were single-sex boys' establishments with high academic standards. Drama wasn't discouraged, especially in the classroom, but if one put on a play in public it seemed against the nature of the beast." French laughed, sat upright, pulling at his shirt-collar. "With Ethel Wagstaffe it all changed. I began to believe in Santa Claus."

"What was she like personally?"

"To young people, students, and my end of the staff, and remember I was only six or seven years older than the students, she could be formidable."

"Distant, you mean?"

"No. Not at all. She'd be on you like a ton of bricks if you transgressed."

"Got across her?" Noel glossed, mischievously.

"Yes. That certainly came into it. I remember a chap there, a few years older than I was but by no means decrepit, who gave a lecture on Dewey, the American educationalist. The event was semi-public, I don't exactly recall the circumstances, and Ethel attended. At the end she sent for Tim Rainworth the lecturer and asked him what the hell he thought he was about. He argued a bit, but she soon had it out of him that he'd read nothing of Dewey's, he'd taken it all from some crib-book, and, my word, she didn't half lace into him. Not in public. He told me all this. I suppose he thought

I'd a sympathetic face. 'Mr Rainworth,' she said, and walked round and round the chair he was sitting on, 'you ought to be ashamed of putting up such a pitiful performance. I wouldn't mind so much if you were without ability, but you are not. You are clever and talented, but you choose to be lazy. How do you expect your students to excel if they see you — and they are not fools, see you they will — idling your way through your classes, through your marking, through your lack of any manifestation of interest in college affairs.'

"Apparently she dressed him down like this, and he tried to argue, and lost his temper. She never strayed from politeness with that plummy voice of hers but in the end she pinned him back because she had read Dewey and he hadn't. He tried to wriggle out of it; claimed Dewey had no relevance to the give-and-take of classroom teaching, but she wouldn't have that. He'd no right to make the criticism until he'd read the man. 'What about Marx?' he asked. Wasn't he dismissed unread? Had he read Marx then, Ethel demanded. That was a good tricky question because the Cold War was on, and he'd find favour with nobody, or at least not with anybody on the governing body, if he confessed he'd studied Marx, while if he hadn't he ruined his case." Leslie French laughed again, a dry, asthmatic sound unsuitable to his easy personality. "It all seems a storm in a teacup now. Nobody, but nobody has read Dewey these days."

"But the principle holds, doesn't it?"

"Read before you criticize? Oh, yes. That's so."

"And what difference did it make to the man? Rainworth?"

Leslie French looked up, slightly afraid.

"You looked rather like your sister when you said that. Well, momentarily."

Noel waited for his answer. French moved his haunches. "I don't know. He knew she didn't love him, that she'd watch him, that he wouldn't be promoted."

"Did he leave?"

"I think he did in the end. But it was after I'd gone. I think I heard he went into business with a relative. Probably made a fortune."

"Did Ethel show favour to the handsome young men like you rather than the women?"

"Not as far as I noticed. There were a fair number of women on the staff, because the place was a women's college before Ethel went. In my day it was about half and half. No, I don't think so. Ethel knew what was going on, kept her beady eye on us."

"Had she friends at the college?"

"Personally, you mean?" French considered, stroking his face. "No. Or did you mean favourites? Again, I don't think so. If she noticed somebody making a first-rate job of something she approved of she saw to it that backing came his or her way. And she'd praise, show warmth. She was good at that. She lived in Manchester, some miles away, and her husband was one of the Mancunian aristocracy."

"Were you ever invited to her home?"

"Once or twice. For semi-formal functions. And once I took a group of mummers there for some charity or other. It was a large house. But you'd know that."

"She's living on the same street now."

Noel Smith gave a brief account of the bungalow Imogen had bought.

"I met the daughter. She had just left Cambridge and was teaching somewhere in the south of England. A stocky, attractive girl. Did she marry?"

"No. Headmistress of St Mark's Day School for Girls when she retired."

"I see. There was some young man, some beau, hanging round her if I remember rightly. How old is she now? Middle fifties?"

"Thereabouts."

"Is she like her mother?"

"In some ways. I hardly know her. I went once with my wife to present the prizes at her school, and she seemed very much in charge."

They sat in the first silence of their meeting. French roused himself. "I always had the impression that the husband, William Wagstaffe, was a powerful character," he began.

"He was very quiet."

"I've got it wrong, then?"

"I don't know. He was a shrewd lawyer, looked after some large affairs, wasn't ever short of money."

"He'd be a source of strength to Ethel?" French mused.

"It's possible. It's an advantage to know the law. But I guess Ethel would have made her way on her own. She was a considerable personage in her own right."

French agreed, recalled Ethel at staff conferences, as a public speaker, as a supporter of good causes, as a sensitive counsellor, as a generous spender of time and money. As his voice rolled on through well-prepared paragraphs, Noel remembered that frail body under the bedclothes, cold in the hot weather, mere bones, flitting consciousness, a helpless barely alive carcase with humanity all but extinguished. He listened without conviction, was glad when French said he must go.

"Tom Luke and I are going swimming this afternoon. You wouldn't care to join us?"

Noel refused, walked the length of his front garden path with his visitor. Mrs Luke was already waiting there in her car. Noel greeted her, but she did not get out of her Golf, merely bent forward to talk. French said he would be in touch.

As he strolled back, Noel found himself hating the heat.

10

NOEL SMITH worked the next few days on an article on the art of biography for the *Guardian*. He enjoyed himself trying to find out what he thought. Was it possible to convey to a modern reader any sort of truth about Alexander the Great, King Alfred, Alfred Lord Tennyson, Bernard Shaw, James Joyce, Sylvia Plath? And what of business tycoons, newspaper owners, international financiers, politicians? He became more puzzled. The greater the skill of the biographer, the more specious the whole enterprise seemed to be. One had a string of interesting facts, anecdotes, coloured with some social history. 'Interesting' was the key word; those writers skilfully caught attention, but how near were they to the truth? He did not know. Each biographer forced his own interpretation on 'fact' and so darkened the path of reality.

Noel became both feverish and frustrated.

He'd come to no conclusion; it must be better so, but that would please nobody, not even himself. A correspondence would begin; he'd be assailed from all quarters, and he'd be invited to reply with a judicial calm he would not feel as he pointed out minor scholarly errors. He doubted whether there'd be any clearer understanding of the art, or the limitations, of biography.

That would have to do.

He'd only been invited because an ex-pupil was at present in charge of the literary pages. As he stood this morning in the already sun-splashed garden, putting off the moment when he sat down at his typewriter, he continued, though he tried to empty his mind, to puzzle himself.

The telephone rang. He turned indoors.

Imogen? Ethel finally gone? Irène? Home this weekend?

A male voice demanded to speak to Professor Noel Smith.

"Speaking."

"Alan Faulkner here." The man on Manchester station. "I hope I'm not disturbing you. I found your address in *Who's Who*. You remember we had a word or two at Manchester Piccadilly about a week ago. I said my wife had left me."

Smith murmured agreement.

"Well, she hasn't."

The voice hit hard.

"I'm pleased," Noel whispered pacifically.

"Yes. I was wrong. But that's as may be. Well, now. Here's the point, because I don't want to waste your time. We're talking things out. Helen and I. If that's the way of putting it. I told her about my meeting with you. How I'd confessed. Now she's coming to Beechnall today and expressed a wish to see you."

"Why was that?"

"There you have me. No, that's wrong. We still haven't come to proper conclusions. She's in Beechnall on business this morning, and would like to visit you after lunch. She may want to confide; she may not."

"You didn't suggest it to her?"

"I bloody well didn't. Things are still unsettled between us. No. It was her own idea. But if you agree, I'll ring her now and tell her."

"Where are you phoning from?"

"My office. Christ, man, I start work here before eight. None of your cosy provincial hours. Is that all right with you? Helen's visit?"

"Yes." It was not. "As long as you give me a phone number. I may be called away." He explained about his sister.

"I'm sorry. If I'd have known I wouldn't have inflicted this on you. But she said she'd like to see you. I knew you lived in Beechnall. I'd already looked it up. I must have said something about you that caught her attention. Quite suddenly she said she wanted to see you. About our marriage. It didn't seem sensible to me, but I didn't want to start an argument at that particular moment. I said as pacifically as I could that I didn't know whether Professor Smith made a habit of giving advice on marriage guidance to strangers. Do you?"

"No. I'm an old man. I lead a very private life."

"But you don't mind, in this case?"

"I don't know that my views will have

any value. I'm old-fashioned. I dither."

"I expect you underrate yourself." Alan Faulkner spoke briskly, as to an underling who needed correction. "But in any case, she suggested it herself. For some reason she thought it might sort us out if she could say her piece to a stranger." Faulkner stopped. "One she thought wise."

"For whatever reason."

"Exactly. You would do me a favour if you'd fall in with her plans."

"I take it you'd like the marriage to continue?"

"Yes. You can take that as read."

"Is there anything you would like to tell me? That I should know?"

"I don't think so. I don't want her to get the impression that I've already been putting ideas into your head. Let her come and do her thing. I can't demand any more from you. The whole notion baffles me, but I try to appear flexible, compliant. Will two o'clock do? Good. I'll tell her. And many thanks."

The phone was replaced.

Noel Smith tidied the room where he'd entertain Mrs Faulkner and made sure the biscuit tin was replenished.

His visitor did not arrive on time, and this annoyed him. Outside the sun blazed. At two-eighteen he heard a car draw up.

Helen Faulkner smiled solemnly at him, and apologized. A tall, beautiful woman in her late forties with black hair and blue eyes who wore a severe dress of darkish green. She spoke with a pleasant modesty, sat down carefully, opted for an iced drink, complained mellifluously cool about the heat. Once the social chatter was over, she asked, "Were you surprised when Alan asked if I could see you?"

"Yes."

She waited for further explanation but received none. "I saw you once before at Kay-Shuttleworth College. You made a speech, and your wife presented the prizes. I still have my set of Jane Austen." She smiled courteously. "Though I finished my course there, I never taught."

"Oh?"

"I had met Alan, and I trained in his firm as an accountant. The year wasn't altogether wasted. I sometimes take a class in accountancy at the local poly." She seemed not altogether easy. "Weren't you a brother of Dr Wagstaffe?"

"Yes. Your husband told you about her, did he?"

"Told me? No. Nothing."

"She's very ill, dying. We don't expect her to last beyond a few days."

Helen Faulkner took the news easily, with a sad note, a serious face.

"I'm sorry," she said. "She'll be quite old."

"Eighty-eight."

"As much as that? Yes. She was a great lady. A personage. I hadn't much to do with her. I did the PGCE, and was only there for a year."

"Did you know a man called French? Ran the drama?"

"Not really. I remember the name. I went to one play with Alan. I'd just met him. Alan not French. It was very good."

"What was it?"

"That's the odd thing. I just can't remember. We met and had a meal. I can see the foyer quite clearly, where I introduced the new boy to some of my college friends, but as to the play, it's just disappeared."

"You said it was good?"

Helen laughed. At herself. "I can remember Alan saying what a high standard they set. I could take you to the exact place where he said it, but the play . . . no, it's gone."

"More interested in the new young man." Noel spoke drily.

"I suppose that was it."

"But it's not so now?"

He had called the meeting to attention. She nodded, her mouth pouting fetchingly, her eyes away from his, as if he had come to the core of affairs before she was ready.

"We can't expect that now, can we? After all it's twenty-six years ago." A voice without harmonics.

"You've celebrated your silver wedding?"

"Yes. Alan didn't want to hang about. Typically. We were married in the summer. I began to train with his firm after the honeymoon. He arranged all that."

"Was he working for himself?"

"No. Price Waterhouse."

"You qualified with them?"
"Yes."
"You work in his firm now?"
"I do."
"Are you a partner?"
"No."

They sat silently in the room after this exchange, both uncertain how to proceed. Helen Faulkner apparently unembarrassed held her back straight, while Noel leaned forward, fingers locked, elbows on thighs, as if he wrestled with an intractable problem. When Helen finally spoke he felt a surge of relief.

"I don't honestly know why I've come." Again the cagey delay.

"Did your husband advise you to see me?"

"No. Several times he mentioned meeting you, and that you lived in, had retired to, Beechnall. One thing led to another. As it does sometimes."

"I don't understand you," Noel said gently.

"He said he'd told you I'd left him, and then that he'd wished he'd talked to you about it."

"He made no attempt to contact me

during the journey."

"Weren't you sitting together?"

"No. I travel second class."

"I think he hoped to see you in London. Your college was there, wasn't it? In fact he hung about the platform, but you had left the train elsewhere." She smiled at him. "He looked you up in *Who's Who*. We talked, and I said, rather foolishly perhaps, because I didn't know anything about you, that it might do me good to see you. It was then that he pressed me. He can be forceful, and I suppose it had its effect. Perhaps there was something you could manage for us, he said."

"Such as?" Noel.

"I don't know now. But he'd rushed off and fixed it up." Again the engaging smile, elegant but unpatronizing. "Perhaps you could suggest what you could do."

"I can't. I'm no counsellor. I've no experience of this sort of work."

"But you have common sense? Or a knowledge of literature?"

Noel shrugged.

"If this is going to be sorted out," he said, "it will be through you, not me." A paradox? "Perhaps it's already done. You take the trouble to come here. You think, to a greater or lesser degree, what you want to say. We drink lemonade. You look at the furniture or the pictures on the walls, and you go over the trouble between you and your husband. But you do it in a different place, in comparative peace, and though I can't promise anything it may work the oracle. It depends how deep the rift is. Had you really left him, as he claimed?"

"I'd written saying so."

"But you changed your mind?"

"Yes. I did. On the cowardly grounds that it would hurt me more than him. So I went back home." The words sounded unserious.

"On your own account. Unpersuaded by anybody else?"

"I stayed two nights with a friend," Helen admitted, "and I poured out my troubles to her. Or at least I thought I did. We had no long-faced sitting-down confessionals, but I talked."

"A female, you say?"

"Yes. And a doctor. An anaesthetist.

Divorced. Sensible. Busy. My age. Children like mine off her hands. She listened; she even said a thing or two about her own marital troubles, but she gave me jobs to do about the house."

"Did you not go to work?"

"It was the weekend. I rang her Friday, returned home on Monday night. I knew Alan would be away in the north of England."

"I see."

Again they waited. Helen Faulkner seemed in no obvious trouble. Certainly she gave little away and that could be a sign of danger, but she spoke to him as to a client discussing some hiccup in trade or change in taxation laws that needed attention. She grinned at him now companionably.

"How are we doing?" she asked.

Noel stood, pointed at her glass, asked if he might refill it.

"Please," she answered. "It's delicious. And home-made."

He went out to the scullery. On his return he said, "I'm not helpless. I can look after myself. My wife spends a good deal of the summer with her family or at our house in France. Separation is good. In moderation. Now, to answer your question." He shook a bony forefinger at her like a jovial schoolmaster. "Let's see. I'm enjoying the visit. The interlude. The conversation. You are making no great demands on me. Or not so far. You appear much at your ease. But we are not seriously discussing your problems. We could have had just as pleasant a conversation if you had come to discuss with me a thesis you were writing on the poetry of Philip Larkin or the sermons of Lancelot Andrewes. You might find my advice more helpful there. I'd refer you to a few books." He laughed drily, fell to coughing. "But whether we are getting anywhere this afternoon is, let's say, open to doubt."

"Why?"

"We hardly know each other. I have no qualifications to encourage you to trust me with your confidences."

"So we're wasting our time?" she asked.

"I'm led to believe that people suffering from psychiatric disorders are statistically just as likely to recover while waiting for treatment as by actually undergoing official therapy, so on those flimsy grounds there's hope here for us."

"If I were screaming or kicking my heels in the air there'd be more chance would there?"

Noel considered that, making nothing of it. "These marital differences must be painful, and must, by their very nature, exacerbate the hurts."

"Sounds good," Helen smiled at him.

"You're making fun of me. But I don't mind."

"All I'm doing then," Helen said, "is going through the motions? Is that about it?"

"Possibly. I don't know."

"You think you can help, don't you?" Acerbity there.

"No. I'm very uncertain about that," he answered.

She lifted her glass, and with a second ironical tilt to his health wetted her lips. "What impressed me was that Alan mentioned you, so frequently, as if he thought you had some sort of key to our difficulties. Perhaps he saw you as wise because he remembered you from the time he was a student."

"It upset me," Noel answered. "He'd been talking in a very interesting way about his job, about this firm in Manchester he'd been to see. He was very clear-headed, a first-rate teacher. Knew the sort of question I'd want answering. And then just as we were getting on the train he swore violently, when I mentioned you, really blew up and rushed off. It was as if another man had appeared who spoke with a different voice. I was, well, disturbed."

"But what did you conclude?"

"Nothing at the time. How could I? I was physically shaken as if he'd punched me. I was left quite breathless. I suppose that afterwards, next day, when I'd come back and had time to settle I decided that he was deeply affected by the trouble."

"I'm sorry," Helen murmured.

"I'm old, and unused to violence these days, even verbal violence. Perhaps my mention of a wife triggered his anger. But he was furious. Or gave that impression."

Helen Faulkner touched her nose, and, reassured, began to speak.

"We hadn't done too well with each

other these last two or three years, once the children had gone, and both left us at eighteen. Or to all intents and purposes. They didn't come back from the university very much in the holidays."

"What do they do now?"

"Mike's a trainee stockbroker. Liz is just finishing at college."

"Married?"

"Neither."

"I'm sorry. I edged you off the track."

"You did. Where was I?" She knew well enough. "Alan and I hadn't much interest in each other. We'd a pleasant home, well-paid work, not a great deal of time for leisure . . . "

"How did you use it?"

"I, on the house and garden. Alan, I don't know."

"Not women?"

"I couldn't even guess. There'd be plenty available. If he wanted them. I don't expect he was altogether chaste; he's not the ascetic type. But I didn't inquire too closely. As long as he acted sensibly. With circumspection." Helen smirked at her word. "As for me, now. I have a long-term lover."

"Does your husband know?"

"He knows the man, and that we are friends. No more than that. I don't want to say too much in case you identify him."

"Is he so well known?"

"Not at all. But Alan is, I guess, very likely to ask you and your wife to stay with us, and if you do I don't want you to recognize my friend. Alan's specially likely to press you to visit us once he knows I've been up here to see you."

"He doesn't know that? I thought he'd arranged it all."

"No. That's nothing like it. He knows I'm here in Beechnall, of course, but he has no idea whether I'd take up his suggestion of calling in on you. It does him no harm to be kept in ignorance. Or uncertainty. I expect you don't approve of any of that, do you?"

"You don't intend to make the clean break, to live with your lover?"

"No. He has a wife. And children still at school. Besides I don't think he'd be any better than Alan as a long-term prospect. Sometimes we go for longish periods, say a month without meeting, or meeting to make love. It's becoming conventional."

"Don't you feel guilty?"

"Not particularly. We've fallen into this arrangement almost by chance. It's comfortable now, it makes me feel wanted; there's an element of risk, or naughtiness, about it. We're both old-fashioned in some ways. But there we are. I'm sometimes quite surprised that it's happened this way."

"Why did your husband think you'd left him?"

"I've told you. I wrote him a note."

"But why did you do it?" Noel pressed.

"Rush of blood to the head." She smiled at her own wry phraseology. "I'd made a hash of a task I'd set myself at work, and that so annoyed me that . . . " Helen flung her hands about, dismissing words, the irrational world. "Actually, it didn't matter in the least, as I've since found out. It might even be an advantage. But it annoyed me at the time. I went home, flared up, wrote my letter and cleared off to Caroline's."

"And when did you realize," Noel said

slowly, "that you weren't serious about running away?"

"Realize? Running away?" Amusement spiced her repetitions. "Serious? You like that word, don't you? It was more like a realization that I'd be ditching much of my comfort for no great advantage."

"Comfort is important?" he asked.

"At my age, yes. It is. Though I'm still young enough to do without it for a good cause."

"Did you make this clear to your husband when you went back home?"

"I didn't make much clear at all. I felt, oh, sheepish." She trilled a laugh. "I said I'd come back. I had changed my mind."

"And he?"

"He asked questions. He always does. But he accepted my explanation that I was annoyed with myself over my misjudgement at work. He even said one or two sensible things about that. In fact I thought he was rather more interested in that than in my desertion. But that's unfair. We did talk a bit and he said he was glad I'd come back. It was all pretty painless. And then he told me about this meeting with you."

"He didn't lose his temper?"

"No. Not at all."

"He was relieved, if anything?"

"Yes, you could say that."

"Why?" Sharp, almost brutal, but she seemed undisturbed.

"He has a great deal to do, even in this holiday month, and he doesn't want his boat to be rocked. Or not unduly."

"Are you going away for a holiday?"

"Not together. No. He's going to South Africa at the end of the month. That's only half business."

Noel now considered what she had told him. When he began to talk, it was quietly, as if to himself.

"I'm not sure that I see your problem," he said, "or even if a problem exists. You and your husband have grown apart, but find it convenient to live together. I can understand that. I can see it might be unsatisfactory. But why was he so angry?"

"If he was, then it might have been like my aberration," she glanced up at him on that word, "the result of something else. Something connected with the investigation he'd just finished. I don't know."

"He's not a violent man?"

"I'd say he was capable of violence, but he gets rid of it making money."

Helen Faulkner suddenly changed her mode of sitting. Before she had been relaxed, her legs slightly extended, ankles crossed, hands lightly in lap. Now the back was straight, the feet together, the hands slightly clenched outside the thighs. She lifted an arm to examine her wristwatch.

"I shall have to go," she said. "I've wasted too much of your time as it is. And I have another call to make this afternoon during working hours. Thank you very much for hearing me out so patiently. It all seems trivial to you, I guess, but I'm not so sure. We've managed to put into words what were mere vague feelings, and that must be helpful. You've made me see straighter."

"Putting plain words round vague feelings is not always sensible. Changes are made."

"I won't argue."

She stood; he did likewise. She thanked

him, not effusively, before she moved towards the door. "I hope you don't think you've wasted your time on me."

"Not at all."

"Will you perhaps come to see us? When your wife comes back to England?"

"I'll put it to her. We're governed in the next week or two by what happens to my sister. She may die at any time."

They were now outside in the neatness of the front garden; he had used the spray on his lawn; its green shone almost chemically vivid. As they had stepped through the front door the ferocity of heat struck them. The place dazzled with violent sunlight.

Helen thanked him again as he accompanied her to the gate. She unlocked the nearside door, wound down the window, slammed the door shut.

"It will be like a furnace," she said. "These black seats are too hot to sit on." She repeated the opening, the winding on the other side, but stood on the road. "These matrimonial troubles aren't very important, are they?" She sounded wistful. "Compared with the wars and famines and political changes."

"I don't know about that," he said. She waited for further explanation which was not forthcoming. She bent, tested the temperature of the seat with her hand, slipped inside, pulling the door after her in one movement, straightened the dress on her thighs, buckled the belt round her, waved briefly, regally, and drove away.

Noel returned to his house disappointed, picked up the lemonade glasses, placed them on the kitchen draining board and stared down to the orchard at the bottom of his long garden. The man at the window. It's all he did these days, stand behind glass and look out without commitment or even understanding at the shapes outside. He picked up one of the tumblers, filled it at the tap and drank the water thirstily. As he returned it to the sink he was convinced that he had used Helen's glass. He swayed. It seemed unimportant, that. They had shared a source of comfort. Again he lifted the glass, held it precariously between thumb and middle finger, restored it to safety. Dizziness attacked him; he clung to the sink; its steel provided no coolness, but he did not care.

Two human beings had wasted an hour together.

Helen did not need him, he concluded; she had come out of curiosity, made her presence felt and that was that. A beautiful woman had appeared, and it mattered to him. She had not found any advantage. He remembered the natural grace of her posture, the quiet rationality of her speech. And yet she had been here, had sat by him, had appealed for his advice, whatever the pretext. He felt pride.

That she was beautiful had made a difference.

He walked out into the tropical heat of the garden. The world puzzled him, wearied him. This afternoon he knew its blankness. Through his thin hair he felt the ferocity of the sunlight, and disliked it. He did not want to go back into the empty house, nor stay out here to be burnt. He returned indoors, reached for a book from his shelves: the works of Charles Stuart Calverley. He opened it near the end. At random. XLIV Christmas.

'Lanigeros, acclinis humo,
pastoria pubes
Custodiebat dum greges;
Splendescente polo longe lateque Jehovae
Descendit ales nuntius.'

Noel made no sense of the words. Wool-bearing? Pastoral young people? His eyes caught the introduction . . . 'translations made for *Hymns Ancient and Modern* . . . 1867'

'While shepherds watched their flocks
by night
All seated on the ground.'

Of course. The bird, the winged messenger, the angel of the Lord. It seemed unsuitable for broiling summer. He lazily, against his will, stumbled through the rest. *Colit*, inhabits; *Virisque pax arrideat*, and let peace smile on men. Ah, well.

He replaced the book, straightened it, marginally preferring the boredom of the window, his own company.

11

THE news of Ethel did not change over the next few days.

Imogen, cheerful almost, said her mother grew weaker, vaguer, but was not uncomfortable. Irène rang from France to announce she would take another week if he did not mind; she and a sister would visit an aunt in or near Bordeaux. Why they had not gone before he did not understand, but the Dalsaux suffered from sudden decisions, rushes of blood to the head. He preferred weeks of careful planning and irreversible decisions. It was, in any case, time Irène came home; he wondered whether now in her late fifties she preferred France to England, the baggy lack of routine in Périgueux to the calculated, restricted regimen in Beechnall.

He walked out into the garden already too warm.

His neighbour, on some perch, looked down on him over his high fence. The two men exchanged red-faced commentaries on the heat wave. Alec Swarbrick, in his sixties, owned and ran four shops, men's outfitters. He had announced his retirement but spent most of five days a week behind one or other of the counters. This morning in white shirt and flannels he said he was fixing a climbing rose which had broken loose from the fence.

"Aren't you at work, then?" Noel asked.

"No. Annie insists we're out today, so it's early lunch. Twelve noon sharp."

"Going anywhere interesting?"

"To Newark. To look round the antique shops. Boring. Tiring. Hard on your feet. But Annie loves it."

"Does she spend all your money?"

"No. She's a reasonable woman. I think she likes to have something to talk about. To her friends."

They chatted thus for a few minutes before Swarbrick bent forward, tapped Smith's side of the fence with his hammer. Now some advice or demand would follow. The neighbour's face was still, head cocked, eyes half-closed, mouth pouting with words not yet emerging.

"Do you know that foreigner, lives at the bungalow at the end? Thickset fellow?"

"What's his name?"

"Smollett, now. Must have changed it. They tell me you're entitled to call yourself anything you like."

"I believe that's so."

Swarbrick tapped the fence again with the hammer, tentatively.

"You know the man I mean? Lithuanian, Estonian or something of that sort?"

"Yes. Elderly. About my age."

Swarbrick set down his hammer, and grasped the top of the fence with both hands.

"They say he's a war criminal."

"Who says?"

"They were talking about it up at the golf club. Arthur Warden's nephew has something to do with this group that hunts them down, and seeing the name of the road asked his uncle what he knew about him."

"Oughtn't Arthur Warden to have kept his mouth shut?" Noel asked, censoriously.

"Why? It isn't a secret now."

"Might he not escape?"

"Escape where? He's been living here getting on for forty years. Where would he escape to?"

Swarbrick had puffed out cheeks and lips in exasperation at the stupidity of the question without expectation of irony.

"What's he accused of?"

"The usual, I should think. On duty at one of these death camps for Jews or ethnic minorities."

"What work did he do here? In England?"

"He was a foreman or supervisor at the iron works for years. Saved all his money. Invested it in that bungalow. Very nice place. Worth a bit."

"Is he married?"

"So I believe. His wife's a small stout woman. They both look foreign. It's very strange, isn't it, that a harmless-looking man like that could have been such a bastard? Or a murderer? He doesn't look any different from dozens of other Poles and Ukrainians who live here. I wonder if it preys on his mind?"

"What would he be? Late sixties? Seventy at the outside. Forty-odd years ago he would have been in his twenties, and that means he would have been fairly low in rank."

"You and I know," said Swarbrick, "plenty of sergeants who were bastards."

"A few."

"Well, a few then. Still . . . "

"Would it make a difference," Noel asked, "if these minor officials had treated their victims courteously on the way to the gas chamber? It would have been a temptation to use or misuse what bit of power they had, but you were an NCO for a time as I was, and I expect you flashed your chevrons as I did."

"But putting people to death by the hundreds?" Swarbrick put on a puzzled look.

"You get used to anything. There are decent, quiet grandparents about in England and America who bombed Dresden until the streets ran fire. I agree they didn't actually see what they were doing to people and buildings, and they stood the chance of being killed themselves, but still."

"You wouldn't prosecute these people,

then?" Swarbrick asked, leaning ludicrously back.

"No, I don't think I would. It's too long ago."

"But they'll think they've got away with it?"

"Yes, but in wars all sorts of behaviour that would be utterly unacceptable in peacetime will go on. This man may have acted like a swine. Did they say so? At the golf club?"

"No, they didn't know any details."

"Does the man Smollett know what's being said?"

"Oh, yes. He's been interviewed several times."

Swarbrick examined the rambler rose, invisible to Noel Smith, with his head held comically to one side.

"It doesn't seem right that a quiet suburban street like this should be connected with world-shattering events, does it?"

"It's only the form of words you use."

"Eh?" Affronted, Swarbrick tapped the fence again.

"There must be hundreds of people

around who were present in some capacity or other at important happenings, the invasion of Europe or the Coronation, let's say, and they will live, on the whole, on humdrum streets. They did not play large parts, but they can claim they were there, in minor rôles or as spectators. Call these 'world-shattering events' and we can expect many ordinary people to have had some connection."

Swarbrick's face fell.

Noel pulled a wry mouth, feeling himself pompous, a pedagogue, making a useless point that needed mathematical straightening out. He was interested that Smollett had been an official in a death camp, but he had to put Alec Swarbrick, with his golf club chatter, into place. That was ungenerous.

Swarbrick had returned to his hammering.

Later the same day when Smith went out to post a letter, he saw Smollett and his wife walking down the street, the first time for weeks. Just before they passed, he called out "Good afternoon." The man, startled, raised his trilby hat from a bald head, round as a football, the grey hair on the fringes cut mercilessly short to a stubble. Mrs Smollett creased her fat cheeks into a smile. Noel Smith had never spoken to them before, but felt the better for it now, though he did not know why. Smollett's polite gesture in lifting the hat from his head, his wife's piggy smile, the fact that both had responded seemed cheering.

"Very warm again," Noel said.

"Yaas." A deep voice but diffident growl. The two did not pause, waddled past. The man's feet in brown shoes looked small; his wife's ankles bulged. Smollett was big; he had run to fat now, but one could imagine him as a young man, husky, broadly powerful, a bully, worse.

Noel Smith turned to watch their slow progress along the street. They neither spoke nor touched nor looked back at him.

Faulkner telephoned early in the evening to thank him for receiving his wife. Noel replied with moderate truth, that it had been a pleasure. Faulkner several times seemed on the edge of confession, but finally shied away, as Noel offered no encouragement. He and his wife must spend a little time on a visit if ever they came down to London. Noel gravely thanked him, saying he would have to wait until Irène returned from France and he learned what her plans were.

"She wears the trousers?" asked Faulkner, heartily.

Noel made no attempt to prolong the conversation.

Helen Faulkner telephoned at ten o'clock, as he settled to the ITN news.

"Am I interrupting anything?" she asked. He reassured her. "I wanted to thank you for your kindness the day before yesterday."

"Your husband has already done so."

"Today?"

"Yes. About six forty-five."

"It must have been from the office. I haven't seen him at all since breakfast. He's attending some function, a committee meeting, I think."

"You don't know?"

"I could look it up on the calendar, if I were interested. We're both quite meticulous in keeping that up to date. I think it's some charitable committee.

I remember because it seemed off to arrange it right in the middlc of the holiday season. But these people are a law unto themselves. They'd find a spare night and make arrangements." She sounded grudging. "But I had to thank you."

"I enjoyed your visit."

"Are you lonely?" she asked. "With your wife away?"

"I'm beginning to think it's about time she came back. Let's put it no more strongly than that. On the whole I can occupy myself. Are you well?"

"Yes. Very busy. A whole lot of tasks before September when we fly down to St Tropez."

"I see. Are you looking forward to that?"

"Yes and no. We both ought to rest, swim lazily and go to bed early, but we think that it's only a week and so we ought to cram the nightlife in. It's silly, but we'll never learn. We come back with bags as big as portmanteaux under our eyes, and fit for nothing." She laughed. He would remember her as one whose small talk was interjected into conversation to keep it unserious or acceptable. "Do you not go to France with your wife?"

"Yes. Quite often. But she spends a good part of the summer there, and Christmas. It seems fair. As one grows old, one edges towards one's childhood, I find. When I look back now I see myself standing by one of those old-fashioned hydrants at the side of a wide but traffic-free road; I'd be six or seven years of age. That's nearly seventy years ago. And it must have happened once, though why I remember it I don't recall. I went to look at the place recently, and the hydrant is still there. They pulled down some cottages and built a cinema and the road was quite wide, but nothing like as broad as I remember it."

"You're an interesting man, Professor Smith."

"Is that so?" He felt foolish once he'd posed the facetious, flirtatious question.

"That's not the sort of thing I'd expect you to concentrate on. Especially as it seems you didn't do anything, just stood about. I should have thought you'd have remembered your academic highlights, or the publication of your books, or your wedding, or your son's birth, or something of that nature. How old is your son?"

Noel reckoned up.

"John, now? Thirty-eight."

After more of this chatter, Helen Faulkner thanked him again, and suddenly hung up. She had not said whether her visit had any effect, good or bad. An odd woman. He returned, disgruntled, to the news, terrorist outrages, a road accident, another test-match disaster. Sitting after rising to switch off the television, he wondered what Imogen was doing, but decided against ringing her. He thought about Smollett, the prison-camp official, and his stout wife. Were they asleep yet? He reached for the directory, looked up their telephone number, but did nothing further about it. Out in the garden it was pleasantly warm, and the sky luminous. He had wasted another day, had read hardly anything outside the newspaper and that not thoroughly. If he forced himself to buckle down to a task, reading a new novel, pursuing a chapter of some critical work, a biography, he could have mastered the contents and marshalled his opinions almost as easily as forty years back. He had not done so.

That morning he had enjoyed an hour's walk; all old men should tramp the streets, but the exercise had been taken in lieu of serious reading, and he despised himself for the specious excuse. It was too hot for a stroll later in the day, but then he had not set himself down to his books in the blaze of the afternoon, and he had known this would happen. As he paraded the streets he made himself look out for significant events, changes; he'd replace literature with life, a vain hope.

His perambulations had led him to an industrial estate, where the late-Victorian factories in dark brick were gradually being torn down and replaced by smaller units, service industries with wide car parks and newly planted trees. An old, three-storey pub which crouched in his boyhood under the towering factories and giant warehouses now stood tall and alone. A man walking in front of him suddenly turned off into a space, carefully marked with white lines on tarmacadam for half a dozen vehicles, and there carefully walked round his car, examining it, bending, peering. As he stood, slightly breathless, his eye caught that of Noel Smith who had now drawn level.

"Some bogger pushed a broken bottle under my back wheel last time I parked here. Cost me a bomb."

Noel making sympathetic noises passed on.

Farther down the hill he reached a newly erected tall flat fence round the ground where a great warehouse had been flattened. This street had been for years cramped, invariably shadowed, even on the brightest days, under the purple brick of high factories, with black barred windows, the roads damp and the narrow pavements occupied with long, iron grates or oblongs of thick opaque glass, metal bound, above basements. Now one could see in the distance lopped rows of houses, trees, a clear urban landscape, the wide stretch of sky. Noel paused by the fence, which unpainted showed the grain of the plywood sheets from which it was made. Its plainness offered a raw promise.

Near the middle some vandal had concocted, one needed such a description, a huge graffito. In darkish blues and yellows it consisted of four words, in chunky, intertwined, blackly outlined letters of such extravagance that Noel found himself reduced to being able to read only one in every two or three. It was, he thought, rather like making out a banner inscription in Cyrillic characters from a smudgy newspaper photograph, or a Russian magazine, hoping for a name he knew. Here he found an equal trouble; this was presumably the name of a pop group, and God knows they were often outrageous or unintelligible enough. He did not like to be beaten in his own language. The letters were backed in a chalky, dappled, rippling flag, itself outlined by wavy thick black brushstrokes like those round the letters. The whole was spattered by delicately long explosions; a burst, a thin, straight rod, an elongated line, a blob of white paint which danced lurid interruptions irregularly across the darker inscription. It constituted, he decided, a kind of art; a human had taken trouble; it had cost money and time.

He stepped back to the other side of the road to try again.

Four words, three short, one longer.

The penultimate from this distance was most easily deciphered: 'of'. The first word, an intricate, overlapping Laocoon of a scrawl, ended in a flourish, with an arrowhead like that on the devil's tail for a serif. 'The', of course 'the'. The final short word on three levels ended in a 't'; the first letter writhed too wildly for understanding but the second could be, must be an 'r'. 'Art.' The blank of art. Now for the longer word. The opening letter was perhaps the plainest of the lot, an 'm' even though its final stroke overlapped crazily, disfigured the second, presumably a vowel. The word seemed to end in a 't' and the letter before that an 's' or an 'r'. The most of art? Not long enough. The mostest — the hostess with the mostest — unlikely. The answer presented itself. 'Mozart.' He should be able to recognize 'z'; it was just possible, though the letter was so entangled, bloated, disfigured by those pressing in, on, above, below from either side that he could not be sure. If the word was Mozart then its last three letters should match the last word 'art'. They occupied approximately the same length; but their slopes were different, while the final 't' of 'art' had a largeness, a pomposity of its own. Perhaps like the semitic languages some letters had final forms, perhaps even forms indicating the end of writing, a celebratory flourish.

Noel was convinced.

'The Mozart of art.'

That did not sound even to his ignorant ears like the name of a pop group. One never knew. He recrossed the road, stood under the design, which stretched twelve or fourteen metres long. 'The Mozart of art.'

There was, a few hundred yards away, he remembered, an art college, the annex to an establishment for further education. He imagined some deranged student rushing out with his sprays and brushes and signing his paranoia on to the fence. Was it in the daytime, when one or two of his fellows might have watched or encouraged him or helped him carry the tools? But surely passers-by must have noticed the painter at his convoluted work. Or was it done at night by the distorted glow of street lamps? "'The Mozart of art', but not the man's name. Man? He felt sure the painter was male; no woman would have flung her elaborate, highly wrought answer to inadequacy on a fence that would stand for a few months at the most.

The graffito exercised his mind, his emotions, and that was the function of a work of art, ephemeral or not.

He walked a few steps along the street. 'Beechnall Mods, Mods, Mods' in plain, six-inch, not ill-formed capitals, and then in smaller, cruder script, staggering into four lines; 'WARNING. Writing on this fence can seriously damage your pride.' He smiled grimly. Who had answered, mocked the Mozart with this pseudo government health warning? This was a working-class district and had been so for the past hundred years or more. Were the children of the remaining terrace houses profiting from their education, and plastering the walls with their new skills, colourwork and cold satire? Or were newish ethnic minorities involved? The 'Mozart' had a Caribbean extravagance of gesture. He felt immediately ashamed of his prejudice; blame anybody but ourselves. He took a last look at the design, reduced now in his narrow, oblique field of vision to a coloured lump, a dumpling of non-meaning. He raised his right hand in salute to the painter, clicked his heels. He was convinced and pleased by his interpretation; the human race grew fractionally more valuable on account of this illegal act, this piece of vandalism. He turned his back, walked on down the hill. The sprawl of houses in the valley lay indiscriminate, roads winding as intricately as 'Mozart's' letters. The elaborate, perpendicular tower of a church seemed at a distance as square, as utilitarianly spare as a shoe box. Still descending he passed a Salvation Army barracks, largish now, once a dwarf amongst the warehouses. Its wayside pulpit proclaimed: 'This is part of Christ's Universal CHCH! Something is missing!!' Verbal jiggery-pokery was the order of the day in these streets. He stepped down the steepness of the hill. 'Permanent Shop-Lifting Exhibition' he read on a fascia board, and jerked himself to attention. 'Permanent Shop-Fitting Exhibition.' He stood in a triangle of shadow nodding to himself. A woman toiling uphill with a shopping basket eyed him curiously. He wished her good morning; she shied, and said nothing. On the corner, half way down the hill stood an early nineteenth-century house, the date worked in bricks on the west wall, AD 1823. It was now attached to a factory, and acted as a storage place. On the north side shop windows blotted by modern blinds occupied most of the wall of the bottom storey, but from the south the building retained its rustic, provincial solidity. It must have stood here on bare hills, looking down to the distant church tower, the river, the cluster of houses in the hamlet, the home of a sheep farmer, high and isolated, monarch of all it surveyed, one amongst the few farm buildings in the local stone, until the railway pushed forty years later into the valley and the first factories were built to prosper into vast, stern palaces of industry of the 1890s that the modern age now began to find redundant.

It had been interesting, but a waste of time. 'I wasted time, and now doth time waste me.'

The 'Mozart' man must be young, with elbow room, years to develop his talents. Now Smith knew his time was limited, not to be thrown away. That presupposed that he had something still to say, and this he doubted. What he offered to criticism now had all the usefulness of his sister's groans as her nurses moved her. He had finished; the graffito artist wrote his sorrows and inadequacies large with a ridiculous claim, but the hope shone, if not to be the Mozart, not even perhaps the Spohr or Max Bruch, but a decent craftsman, giving pleasure, earning money, maintaining self-respect.

He washed the dishes on the draining board, tidied his kitchen, the floor round the chair where he had been reading, locked the doors. He saw no signs of his cat; he'd be outside in the warm darkness, hunting.

Deciding against a bath, he made for bed and the upstairs radio.

12

FIRST thing next morning Imogen telephoned.

No, there had been no change. The doctor would call in tomorrow.

"There's one thing I want to ask you," she said. "Did you give Leslie French our telephone number?"

"Not to the best of my recollection, no. Why?"

"He's telephoned twice."

"He knows where you live. It would be easy enough to get the number from directory inquiries."

"He called to see you, didn't he? What was he like?"

"Forthcoming. Not unpleasant. Rather handsome."

"He wants to pay us a visit."

"I did explain to him," Noel said, "that Ethel was unlikely to recognize him, or get anything but discomfort from his appearance."

"Yes. He said as much, but he still

wants to come."

"Did he say why?"

"Oh, he pitched some tale about how much he owed to my mother, and that he felt he must pay her the honour or the duty of a call. Something like that. His language was odd. I thought perhaps it was the result of his long periods abroad. I did my best to put him off."

"Do you remember him at all?"

"Yes, I do. I'd left home, had started teaching by the time he arrived at Kay-Shuttleworth. He must be four or five years older than I am. But I used to go up there to see some of their dramatic productions. My mother pressed me; she didn't want me to be just an ignorant scientist. And I must say that they did some remarkable things. I can remember a quite striking *Enemy of the People*. I always thought of that as too earnest, but not the way they did it. And the actors were all very young. And there was this handsome bachelor to hand."

"And so you . . . ?"

"No, you don't." Imogen cackled with laughter. "I was at a susceptible age, I suppose, though I didn't think so. But

I didn't see enough of him. We were briefly introduced. When I went home for long periods in the holidays, he wasn't there."

"And you didn't notice any signs of your mother's infatuation?"

"None at all until my father made his suggestion."

"Mightn't he have been wrong?" Noel now pressed her.

"No. He didn't mean they were having an affair. Or even that she had said anything to French. Only that she had felt strongly enough to confess to her husband, and for him to take it seriously enough, or to be surprised enough, to tell me. He was shrewd."

"Because he told you?"

"No. I guess it put it into perspective, and thus made it bearable."

"You greatly admired your father?"

"Yes. He was quieter than my mother, less in the public eye, though I suppose he had a very successful career as a solicitor. But he held her steady." Again Imogen laughed, this time more lightly. "I'm making all this up. I don't know if it's true."

APS

Noel enjoyed these conversations with his niece. She seemed in control of herself; ready to argue a point, think it out, see his side of the question, while only a few yards away her mother was dying with all the consequent distress or disturbance to a daughter.

He had not taken six steps from the telephone when it rang again and Leslie French asked if he could call. The arrangement made, he arrived that same afternoon, cool and suavely clothed in the uncomfortable heat. He made much of Noel Smith's kindness in receiving him.

"I won't beat about the bush."

He rolled the ice-cubes in his glass of fresh lemonade. Noel did not reply. He lounged sleepily, though mildly pleased he had a visitor to keep him awake. French was now straightening an already immaculately tied silk neckerchief.

"I have rung Dr Wagstaffe's home once or twice."

"I know."

"And have offered to pay a visit."

Noel looked suitably judicious.

"You may wonder why this is so. Especially as you made it clear to me that there would be no advantage to anyone, not to Dr Wagstaffe, to her daughter, to me in such a call." He waited for Noel's comment, and receiving none, clasped his hands, brightened his expression. "It is," he continued, "almost a matter of superstition. Or at least that is how you will see it." Noel disliked people who instructed him about the direction of his thought. "I think I made it clear to you that my time at Kay Shuttleworth now appears to me to have been the high point in my life. I've held interesting posts; I occupy one still. When my wife died eighteen months ago I was shattered. She had been seriously ill for three months, so that I had time to prepare my mind, but the death left me," he paused, reached with his fingers into the air, "desolated. I continued with my work, but when the opportunity for a sabbatical half-year came up I took it. I have two boys aged sixteen and fourteen. I intended to bring them with me. They both speak English, study it at school."

"Have they been to England?"

"Yes. Twice. On holiday. My wife's

family was, is, very generous to us, helped us with fares. But this time they were against my children's coming. They perhaps suspected I would settle here, sever my ties with Japan, make Europeans of my sons." French read the question in Noel Smith's face. "No, nothing was further from my mind. My parents-in-law, who are fairly well-to-do, I'll put it no more strongly than that, offered to look after the boys. They are, in fact, not much older than I am, and have the room, the leisure, and can afford the necessary domestic help. I was not keen. I argued it would do the boys good at their age to live for a few months in Europe. They said, not without reason, that it would be a shame to interrupt their formal education in school at this particular stage. I could bring them over for a short holiday, but then I should be inclined to return with them to my own detriment. That would have been the truth, I think. Instead, they argued that I should spend the whole of my sabbatical in Europe; I deserved it. I had worked hard. My wife's early death, she was forty-two, had taken its toll. They would see that the boys did not suffer."

"And are you convinced?" Noel.

French looked up with a jolt of surprise.

"I am not," he began with a mischievous leer, "one of these people who knows his mind easily. Except in a few small areas. I tend to shy away from decision. Not when I am producing a play, or commenting on a text, perhaps, but in the common ways of life. I was forty-three before I married." His face modestly expressed the hopelessness of his case. "I don't know whether I did right here. I like people to show me a plain path, to give me directions. That's why I made so much progress under Dr Wagstaffe. I wasn't even sure I wanted to come back to England."

"But you did."

"My parents-in-law thought it sensible. For a thorough change. My father-in-law cunningly reasoned that it would give me a chance to catch up with modern trends. In language, literature, the stage."

"Have you?"

"I've tried. I've only been over for a month." He sounded pathetic. "I've read. August is not a great month for serious theatre, but I have made a start. The trouble now is that I am not sure that I want to return to Japan."

"Not to see your sons?"

"Yes. But it will not be too long before they leave home to start their adult lives."

"How long will your job last?"

"I can sign a contract for another three years at least."

"And could you settle for good in Japan if you so wished?"

"Yes. That's not impossible."

"You speak the language, I take it?"

"Pretty fluently now. I have been there nearly twenty years. That was really my intention, in so far as I thought about it, until the time of my wife's death." Noel noticed that French did not call his wife by name, but that was perhaps out of deference to his English auditor.

"That changed your mind?"

"It unsettled me. My boys are Japanese, not English, in spite of dual nationality, and for anything I may think otherwise. I have come to accept that. It is a problem that expatriates have to face."

"You write to them?" Noel asked.

"At length. And in English. And they reply. They also say they miss me. As I miss them. But just this last week or two, I have felt myself English again. The first time for years. Oh, there are many things about the country which I dislike, changes which I abhor, but, but . . ." He waved a despairing hand. "The strength of the feeling has surprised me, shocked me. 'Patriotism is the last refuge of a scoundrel' is something I agree with. But here I am with this deep feeling that this is my place."

"You may grow out of it." Noel tried cynicism. "You have another few months left. Could you afford to retire here?"

"As easily as in Japan."

"Tell me," Noel spoke pacifically, "how does this tie up with the visit to my sister?"

"I thought it might make me see straight again, that Dr Wagstaffe would put my longings into perspective. I know now from you that she can't. Then I could visit Kay-Shuttleworth again and see it for what it is, a provincial college for training teachers, of no very great distinction. And that it would sort me out."

"You'll have to go back to Japan to see your sons."

"Do you think I don't know that? Your wife, I understand, is French."

"And she spends a month or two at least with her family or on holiday there. We seriously considered retiring to France, but decided against it. We own a small place in Normandy. I think it was my wife who made up my mind for me to stay in England. We sold our London house, and I came up here. I was born in Beechnall."

"Was the move successful?"

"I'm still alive to tell the tale. The London house was far too big. It's not altogether sensible to leave an area where one has friends and connections, but it has not been disastrous."

"Do you spend any time in France?"

"Yes. At least a few weeks. Mainly in our house in early summer. It's let out the rest of the year. It's at the seaside. And visiting Irène's relatives from time to time. She spends longer there than I do. That's sensible."

They talked on until both discovered it was almost five when French leapt guiltily to his feet, apologizing for wasting time.

"Go and have a look at Kay-Shuttleworth," Noel found himself advising his visitor. "I expect it will be closed, unless they let it out for conferences. In any case you'll come across caretakers and the like. You can walk the grounds, and the streets round about."

"What will be the point?"

"If your difficulties are connected with nostalgia, then it won't do you any harm to see clearly what it is you're nostalgic about."

"But I mustn't visit Dr Wagstaffe?"

"No. My sister is likely to die at any moment. She seems small, a little heap of bedclothes as she lies there. Once she was a commanding figure. She's unconscious, drugged probably most of the time, incapable of speech, not even recognizing her daughter."

"I'll keep away."

"You can ring Imogen if you wish. It might do her good to hear new voices. Did you ever meet her?"

"Yes. Once or twice. I remember her quite well. A good-looking woman."

"She still is. And sensible. A recently retired headmistress. Something of her mother about her. She is coping admirably with this, this illness. She rarely goes out of the house for more than an hour, and that must come amiss to somebody who's pleased herself all her life. She never married."

"You surprise me."

"Offer to take her out to lunch. It might give her a break. Say I told you to."

French held his head proudly quizzical like a film star in one of the black and white shiny photographs which decorated the advertisement cases outside the cinemas of Noel Smith's youth.

"Thank you."

13

LESLIE FRENCH sat with Imogen in her car outside the wrought iron gates of the former Kay-Shuttleworth College, now part of the Northwestern Polytechnic.

He had rung Miss Wagstaffe from his Manchester hotel, explained his presence, followed Smith's suggestion and invited her to lunch. She had replied that this would need careful arrangements which themselves might have to be cancelled at the last minute, but she would see what could be done.

Later the same evening she had telephoned saying that she would pick him up at his hotel next day at noon, would drive him out towards the college; with his agreement they would have a pub lunch at the Wheat Sheaves en route, and then continue to Kay-Shuttleworth only ten minutes away by car. She suggested that he contacted the college to see if it would be convenient to make the visit.

They would arrive at two, two-fifteen. She gave him a number. They would be back at his hotel between five and six. It was all very efficient.

Dressed to the nines in a lightweight summer suit he had waited for her in the car park, according to orders.

Imogen arrived exactly on time. She was shorter than he remembered, had dressed rather soberly, seemed formidable, unsmiling, making no effort to charm as she invited him into the car.

He described his efforts to get in touch with the college as she drove easily through and out of the city's noon traffic. The girl who answered the telephone had not heard of him, he had not expected her to, but seemed equally ignorant of the name of Dr Ethel Wagstaffe. The building would be open, yes; there would be someone in the office at two o'clock, and workmen and caretakers or groundsmen about the place in the afternoon. To the best of her knowledge no members of the teaching or administrative staff would be in, but she felt sure that there would be no objection to Mr French's looking round the main rooms or the surrounds provided he made his presence known at the office. She would leave a note, as she would not be on duty.

Imogen parked near two other cars, by the main door of the college, and from a vantage point on the steps they looked out down the wide drive.

"Has it changed much?" she asked.

"More buildings." He pointed right and left.

"Were those big trees there by the gates?"

"They must have been, but, do you know, I can't remember. You've been since I have. Were they here on your last visit?"

"Yes."

She seemed cold, unwilling to be too friendly. Over lunch she had been guarded, polite but preoccupied.

Now they stood in the foyer, with its glass dome and parquet floor.

"This hasn't changed," he said.

"Does it smell the same?"

"I can't really say." French felt he was failing some crucial examination. The faded baize notice boards had been cleared of last year's litter. On one only, headed Theatre Studies and Dram. Soc., a small notice was lopsidedly pinned advertising an M.A. course in 'Playwriting Studies' at a Midlands university.

"That makes me look twice," said French.

"What?"

"'Playwriting.' The spelling. A course for playwrights. I suppose that's the idea. Attracts attention."

"Does it?"

Imogen did not seem impressed.

He rang a bell at the inquiries guichet. A middle-aged woman presented herself, a sheet of paper still in her left hand.

French explained his presence, introduced Imogen.

"Oh, yes. Linda left me a note. What was it you wanted to see?"

The woman listened carefully, nodding, flapping her paper. Yes, the hall would be open; they would be able to go up on to the stage. The lecture rooms on the second floor were no longer in regular use; they were now demonstration rooms or storage spaces. No, the library was a conference area, though there were some books there still. The main library was in one of the new blocks, N 11. She pointed. By 'new', she bit her lip, she meant ten years old. They were to walk round as it pleased them provided they reported back before they left the building. "We don't want you locked in overnight," the woman said. "It has happened." The office closed at four. If they were in any difficulty she'd be glad to help.

"Is that the principal's room there?" French pointed.

"No. That's the head of the education department, Professor Schofield."

"Would it be possible just to look in?"

The woman started back affronted, but stepped away to find and jingle keys before accompanying them across the foyer. She unlocked the door, ushered them forward. Pine cupboards lined one wall. There was one short shelf of books. On an otherwise empty light-oak desk, with swivel chair, stood a silver coffee percolator, with four cups and saucers on a metal tray. A table, two armchairs, a settee occupied spaces in the width of the room; there were no carpets. An academic gown hung on the antlers of a coat stand. A notice board, standard baize, carried half-a-dozen drawing pins. No pictures decorated the wall.

"Utilitarian," French said to Imogen. He stepped across to the large window.

"Professor Schofield's computer has gone for servicing," the woman informed them.

"What's that?" French politely asked about a large, windowless building in light brick.

"That's part of the physical education department.

"A gymnasium?"

"Three. We lay stress on physical education and development."

French's face lacked animation. "Is there a drama department?"

"Yes. Beyond the new library. It has its own stage.

"You don't put on performances in the main hall?"

"Not usually. We might on special occasions."

"Who is in charge of drama?"

"Mrs Sefton-Brown. Dorothy Sefton-Brown. She's well known."

Not to French, nor to me, Imogen decided. They shuffled out of Schofield's room, but their guide insisted that they inspect the large committee room. This, they were told, adjoined the vice-principal's office, and was often used for important meetings between the polytechnic director and his chief advisers. "The Hauptkommando," French facetiously interjected. "They will often come out here so they are not disturbed as they might be in town or on the other sites." Godlike figures walked these corridors, sat on these black leather chairs, drank coffee from this polished table and took world-shaking decisions. Large photographs hung on the wall, all in modest sepia and white. French stepped across to stand in front of a handsome portrait of Ethel Wagstaffe. In doctor's gown and hood Ethel faced the camera with a clear conscience, eyeglasses sparkling, right hand holding on to a book. On the dark oak frame he could see the mark of the name tag, now missing, a paler oblong with two empty screw-holes.

"That's how I remember your mother,"

he said to Imogen, who now stood beside him. Their guide sidled across.

"Who is it?" she asked. The visitors turned to and on her.

"Principal Wagstaffe," French answered.

"When was she here?" Not put out, willing to learn.

"She retired more than twenty years ago," Imogen answered.

"That's before my time." Then appeasing them, "I have heard the name." She had regained in her own mind her position as the knowledgeable one. "They looked well in their robes, didn't they? They had . . ." She paused.

"Gravitas," Imogen said sarcastically. The woman opened wide eyes.

"They don't wear academicals now?" French asked. "Gowns and hoods?"

"Not here, no. At the degree ceremonies, yes. But they're never held here."

Imogen had walked out into the corridor. The other two followed, not altogether at ease.

"We'll just look round if we may," French spoke pacifically.

"The drama department is the other side of the library, did you say?"

"Yes. It will be locked, though. I can't go over with you, really. I'm the only one on duty. Not that we'd see anything except bare rooms. The costumes and the equipment are all stowed away, double locked. We have to be so careful these days. But take a look at what you like. There might be somebody in the library — I'm not sure. And I'd be grateful if you let me know when you're leaving. I go at four."

French thanked her. Imogen gravely lowered her head. The woman locked the door of the committee room, bade them good afternoon, clacked away over the parquet floor to her office.

The visitors stared at the dome, at the sloping lights in the high ceiling, at a loss.

"At least it's cooler in here," French said, subdued.

"What next?"

"The main hall." French led the way.

The place with its wall-high windows to one side and its aisle to the other looked smart, and smelt of furniture polish. Chairs in brown leather were neatly stacked in one corner. The stage curtains were velvet and gold. Those on the windows were partially drawn.

"New since your time?" Imogen asked.

"Yes. They were blue in my day." They had walked on to the stage; French thrust out his left arm to lean against the proscenium arch, at home.

"What was the best thing you ever put on here?" Imogen asked him.

"It's hard to answer that now. The one I remember with most pleasure was *The Devil's Disciple*, but that's because the cast was so talented."

"I didn't see it. Did any of your students take to the stage professionally?"

"Yes. John Chetwynd's perhaps the best known. But several others did. I'm out of touch."

"Did my mother approve?"

"Oh, there you have me again. On the one hand she'd want to produce trained, well-educated teachers. But I suppose it did the reputation of the college no harm."

"She quite enjoyed the theatre. She and Diddy Commons used to make trips into Manchester, and now and again to London, on theatre outings."

French, neck cricked, examined the high barenesses of the dismantled stage. No lights, no flats, mere spaces for work.

"Has it changed much?" Imogen wanted to know, staring down the hall, great, irregular patterns of sunlight brightly oblique along the floor.

"No. Not at all." He stood by her.

"Is that sad?"

"Well, yes, I suppose so. But it's something we have to come to terms with." He signalled her down from the stage, and they crossed the hall. "You won't be able to tell your mother anything about this?"

"No. She's unconscious most of the time now." They marched towards the old library. "It doesn't seem right, does it, that she's barely alive and we are looking round the place where she was so powerful, influential."

The old library was locked, as was the new when they found their way out by a small door. A man in overalls mopped a corridor in the physical education complex, but took out his keys to lead them to an immense gymnasium, coolly severe, utilitarian, almost beautiful, lit by small windows under the edges of the high ceiling.

"It's quiet," the cleaner said. "No shouts. No balls thumping."

"You don't like the noise?" French.

"Some of them girls. Worse than the men," he shook his head, "by a very long chalk. They squeal like banshees. And the shorts they wear. Talk about modesty."

Imogen cut him off by curtly thanking him. She had handled garrulous caretakers before. The man retired, disgruntled, to his bucket. The visitors walked round the unrevealing, empty corridors, past interminable locked doors, and out again into the bright acres of playing field. They tried the new library block at the far end, but it was closed. They failed again further on at the theatre building.

"We're not doing well," Imogen said cheerfully.

"No. But it's not this new part of the college I came to see. Though they were beginning to expand in my day, most of the activity went on in the old building. As you know."

Imogen walked towards the original edifice, 1920s Georgian, her face set.

"And does it mean anything to you now?" Grim.

"No, not really."

They had halted, shoulder to shoulder.

"Buildings are only buildings," she said. He sucked in his breath loudly and they set off again. While French went inside to speak to the woman in the office, Imogen sat on a low, hot wall outside. When he emerged and walked smartly down the main steps, a youthful figure still, flaunting his silk neckerchief, she rose. He pointed in his descent at two reddish trees on the grass bank by the steps.

"What are they?" he called, gruffly.

"Rhus," she answered. "Smoke trees." He stopped two steps from the bottom, and swayed.

As he came up to her she saw his face was wet with tears. His hands clenched and unclenched. Very gently she laid fingers on his sleeve, held them briefly there before she turned away and with her back to him made for the car.

When he caught up with her, he had

a handkerchief in his hand, had wiped his cheeks though his eyes brimmed.

"I'm a sentimental idiot," he muttered. "Getting old."

"Are you all right?"

"Yes, thank you." French's voice was now quite steady. "You must think I'm mad." They sat together in the roasting car. He looked away from the college. "For just a moment I felt overcome, dreadful. As I stepped out into the light. I remembered doing exactly that on the day I was appointed."

"Where did they interview you?"

"In the old library." French brandished, then shook his handkerchief. "I spent five years here and I did the finest work of my life. I reached my peak."

"How old were you?"

"Nearly twenty-eight when I was appointed. I don't think I've wasted my life, as I was explaining to your uncle; I've given value for money, but by the time I left for Dar es Salaam at thirty-three my best was over."

"Why did you leave?"

"Ambition. It seemed sensible to widen experience. Your mother encouraged me to do so. Though it's quite possible that even if I'd stayed on here, those first five years would have been my best. And as I stepped through those doors the realization hit me. My wife is dead, and she had never seen this place. My sons are in Japan; they're cut off by upbringing and culture from understanding what this college was and what I managed here. I know you're thinking I'm exaggerating, that nostalgia is misleading me, and you may well be right, but as I came through that door and out into the sunlight I was shaken by a pang that took all the strength out of my mind, left me desolated."

"But you asked me what those smoke trees were?"

"Did I?" He groaned. "That must have been the actor in me." He paused and she did not move. "I felt that the whole of the world meant nothing, could never mean anything again, came together as a series of chances, and that if we made sense of any part of it, it was because we did so of our own volition, not from inherent purpose or providence in the world."

"But you with your volitions must be equally the result of chance?" she said.

"That is so, and that surely makes it worse, unbearable. We, a random mixture of molecules, appear to be able to conjure up sense, to trace patterns. But this universal desolation that flattened me there was only a secondary effect, the emotional impact of my acknowledgement to myself that I had done my little best by the age of thirty-three and in this place."

"It may not be the truth," she said firmly. "You have had a wife, two sons, dozens of other pupils, some of whom may have achieved a great deal on account of your encouragement. You're asking too much of yourself."

"That's probably so. I'm an emotional man. I have always been so. And perhaps I am not properly over my wife's death. And in my narcissistic way I interpreted my momentary qualm and changed it into a godless universe. Your mother would not have approved."

"My mother would have understood the need for such exaggeration from time to time. It wouldn't have done for everyday behaviour, but rarely, once a year, in a gifted individual it would have offered her a valuable insight."

"Of such pessimism?"

"Pessimism has its function," she answered. "Believe you me."

He straightened his back, then in a light, pleasant baritone he began to sing, "'This shall be my shining hour.'"

"What's all that in aid of?" she asked, the demotic phrase exactly matching the cut-glass voice.

"It's a song from an old film. I've forgotten the title. Or who was in it. I don't know why I remember that one feeble line. So much for human endeavour."

"Yes," Imogen answered, the headmistress, grimly sensible.

"But thanks for bringing me out here."

"I suppose it was quite an impressive building in its time." Imogen looked over the white windows, the shrubs, the lime trees. "Anything else you'd like to see, or do, before I deliver you back?"

"I must apologize." French, abashed. He now seemed less spry, withered rather than slim, mocked by his own smart clothes. "Your uncle suggested that I bring you out to lunch. And all you get is a look round a provincial college you must have seen dozens of times before, and an emotional outburst from an aged adolescent. Not good."

"Mr French," Imogen spoke without fervour but with a clarity as if she'd prepared every word, "you took me out of my house, which is why Noel Smith suggested it. I'd as soon see this college as I feel now as anything else. Life's still going on. My mother is a small, shrunken heap under the bedclothes. There's no hope. The sooner she dies the better for all concerned, and it's no use saying or believing otherwise. But coming out here has made me realize that in her time, for good or bad, she had an influence on a great many people, you included. It doesn't matter a damn whether or not the universe is a chance concatenation of atoms or events, we're most of us given our seventy or eighty years, at least in western civilizations, and Ethel Wagstaffe made the best of hers." French made ready to speak, but Imogen checked him with a gesture. "It's even possible that all that was predetermined. It seems to me to be very likely; it's just that it doesn't feel like it to us. But I am slightly more cheerful than, let's say, I would be if we'd have traipsed round an art gallery looking at products of genius. Why that should be so I can't say, but it will give me something to think about."

"You're a remarkable woman."

"Bullshit." She laughed out loud. "That's what my brothers used to call it when they were doing their national service. Haven't used or heard the word for years. Now, shall we go back?"

She drove without haste; he seemed to recognize none of the landmarks she pointed out. She dropped him without ceremony at his hotel, merely instructing him to give her regards to her uncle back in Beechnall, and slid into the afternoon crawl of traffic.

As she finally parked in her drive Imogen wondered what he would have said if she had told him that Ethel Wagstaffe had once been in love with him.

Indoors the nurse reported no change in her mother's condition; she had hardly moved during the day. Imogen carried a small drink into the sickroom, jostled her mother up into a position to sip. The wrinkled eyes tried to open wider as the glass was pressed to inert lips.

"How are you now, Mother?" No answer to that was given, or expected. "Do you know where I've been today?" Nothing. "To the Kay-Shuttleworth College." Not a flicker, as the dying woman attempted to drink. "I went with Leslie French. Do you remember him? Leslie French, he was one of your staff at one time." The faded, almost colourless eyes looked, saw and revealed nothing. "We went into what used to be your room." The nurse came in, urgently, dressed in her outdoor clothes.

"I'll be off now, Miss Wagstaffe."

"Very good. Many thanks. You saw . . . took . . . the envelope?"

"Yes, thank you. 'Bye Ethel. 'Bye, my darling." The mother hung, a limp scarecrow. "'Bye Miss Wagstaffe. Ta-ra."

She left. The front door banged.

Imogen sighed, settled her mother back, quietly straightening the sheets. She wept.

14

AT the weekend Irène Dalsaux Smith returned to Beechnall.

"How are you?" she asked Noel, hugging him outrageously.

"Can't grumble."

His wife inspected the house, congratulated him on its tidiness, affirming that it fared better than when she was in charge.

"How's Ethel?" Irène was now in the kitchen, watching him pour lemonade. Outside the sun burned. He explained his sister's condition. "And her daughter? Is she coping?"

"Very well. As far as I can tell from phone calls."

Irène led him out into the garden. She seemed, as always after these visits to France, incapable of sitting, determined to restore herself at breakneck speed to English life. Soon she'd be mocking her relatives, detailing their marriages, law suits, wills, house hunts, holiday jaunts, funerals. By her account her family consisted of eccentrics if not lunatics. Noel knew they were middle-class lawyers, teachers, civil servants, small landowners. He used to think that Irène reinstated herself as an Englishwoman with these exaggerated sagas of domestic bedlam *in partibus infidelium*; now he believed that she spoke somewhere near the truth and any embellishments she provided were entirely for his entertainment.

While she was abroad, and she spent two months of the summer in France, she did not write to him, but telephoned regularly. He kept a small journal of local happenings, with never more than half-a-dozen lines to a day. She had named this 'The Dullsville Diary', and treated it to an oral commentary as fantastic as her own account of life in France. Again he never quite came to terms with this, taking exception to the name Dullsville which she'd picked up from some magazine or American novel. She knew quite well of his distaste, but made no attempt to change. She had established a little realm, *royaume*, of authority for herself here, as in so many other areas, and refused to cede these harmless powers.

For the rest she'd soon be back to shopping, stocking the freezer for winter, driving out with the doctor's wife, signing up for classes in randomly chosen subjects, Greek Art and Geology for Beginners last year. At fifty-eight she was energetic. She spent Sunday afternoon writing to her son, typically in French, and complained to her husband because John replied to one in three or four, and never at length, in clichés and in English. This winter, January or February, she had convinced her husband, they should visit their son in Sydney.

"Does he want to see us?" he had inquired.

"I want to see him."

"And Australia?"

"Of course." They had been out twice before. "You're a stick-in-the-mud."

Now sauntering along the hot flagstones of the garden path he was delighted to have his wife back, even though he was unwilling to say as much. She had returned indoors leaving him to walk about in a new sense of irresponsibility. He could see her through the kitchen window, reading a letter or a newspaper or even the advertisement on a packet; her curiosity was unbounded but never shallow.

She'd thoroughly inspect the house and decide on changes. Tomorrow morning she would take the car, having issued instructions to him about lunch, and tour the district. She would call in on no one, though she might make a random purchase or two. In a suburb, she'd sit for ten minutes in her Nissan, or stroll round, then set off for some lane or out of the way road where there'd be another short pause. Noel used to pull her leg about this 'getting used to England again', but not now; he was convinced that this was sensible behaviour.

In the afternoon Irène would be herself again, making lists or phone calls, questioning him on any of his plans, bringing her diary up to date. She always appeared sad, or pensive and not to be cheered or joshed. 'You will never make an Englishwoman of me,' she used to say years ago, but by the morrow she'd be herself again, a lively housewife with her hands full. Since John had left them and Noel had retired she spent longer periods in France and this made her returns easier rather than otherwise. Family life in her native country was judged by her to be too frantic or inconsistent for her acquired northern temperate taste.

She returned from her jaunt in the car to announce that they should go to Manchester. Noel hid his surprise.

"It's not to see Ethel; it's to give Imogen a break."

"How shall we go?"

"Car or train as you like."

"Have you rung Imogen?" he asked.

"No. I had to consult you first." He judged her answer to be ironical.

"Mrs Peters left a message for you. Would you ring her as soon as you're back? It's absolutely urgent." Her friend, the doctor's wife.

"It can wait."

He liked her in this imperious mood. Thy judgement is a right judgement.

They drove by easy stages to Manchester, starting early in the morning, breaking for coffee, for lunch, for leg-stretching.

"Imogen will want to feed us?" she asked.

"Depends what's happening with Ethel."

"She said there was no change when I phoned."

The pair walked by a dry stone wall outside a Pennine village. This was the sort of place he should have retired to, up in the hills, where even on a day of exceptional summer's heat like this, the air moved, knew freshness.

"Did you like Ethel?" he asked.

"We didn't meet often, or long enough. Your family's not mine. Did I like her? No. Her French accent was appalling. She knew a good deal about some parts of French literature. I suppose in her day it only mattered that grammar was correct and you'd read the important books."

"Did she know French well?"

"In an old-fashioned way. I guess she reads it still, but she gave up teaching the language quite early in her career."

"They had holidays in France, I think."

"I'm sure they did. But that's nothing to do with my like or dislike. I found her formidable. She knew her mind, I mean, she was old enough to be my mother, nearly my grandmother. I think she quite took to me, and enjoyed hearing me talk French. But she had made her mind up about the important matters in her life."

"Such as what?"

"A woman's opportunities. Upbringing of children. Religion. Science."

"And that's not good?"

Irène gently stroked the sun-heated stones at the top of the wall where they stood.

"I think I agreed with the general thrust of her ideas, especially about opportunities for women, but it seemed," Irène stopped, drawing magic ovals and circles on her capping stone, "I may be wrong, but I had the impression that the way she had done it was, in her estimation, not only the right way but the only one."

"That's not surprising when you consider the struggle she had to rise in a man's world. There were no token female appointments in her day. Heads of women's training colleges were women, but Ethel took on a mixed college, and one filled with ex-servicemen."

"I'm sure."

"And moreover she had three brothers."

"Of whom you . . . ?" Irène screwed her eyes at him.

"I was the youngest and quietest. The other two were scientists. They knew their way around in their fields. Tom was really successful, here and in America. He was barely forty when they made him an FRS. Joe was different; he was a simple soul, a great grafter. They were both good mathematicians."

"Wasn't Ethel?"

"Oh, yes. But in her day in her sort of girls' school there wasn't much of a science side, if any, and all the bright scholars did modern languages or history. Oddly, not classics. I think she regretted that she hadn't done Greek at school."

"Not English?"

"Not many." He looked down the white road to where they had parked the car on a grass verge. "Ethel was organized. She loved getting it right, making it work. Just like Father, except she'd continued her formal education to a post-graduate level."

"Was he clever?"

"Father? Oh, yes. And hard-working. A good organizer. Loved puzzling anything out. If it could be solved. Not religion, though. What he'd learnt as a child was good enough for his maturity. He never had doubts."

"Why was that?" Irène loved these slightly bristling sessions with her husband.

"Don't know." He laughed, a sudden burst. "I guess he worked so hard six days of the week that he thought he deserved a rest on Sundays. And the places of worship he patronized dealt in certainties. They preached a Providence that God had established. The purpose of creation and its final end were known, existed in the mind of God in spite of apparent flaws and setbacks. That's what he believed in."

"But evil? And earthquakes? And wars?"

"He'd argue, that's if he argued at all, that he was capable of organizing a public transport system which worked as it said it would, and the awkward facts of some drivers not turning up to work, or of delays on account of floods or trolley-poles coming off, or people being killed by buses, or mechanical or electrical failures, didn't cause the whole arrangement to break down. It was there. It worked as he'd promised it would. And if he, a mere mortal, could manage such a system, then an omniscient, all-powerful God would have no trouble."

"He made God in his own image?"

"Not at all. He was a modest man. He was clever, but recognized his limitations. He strictly bounded his imagination. I guess he'd been told about God in his childhood, and it seemed absolutely satisfactory to him."

"But so were you. So was Ethel. You had this strict religious upbringing, and neither of you are either believers or churchgoers."

"That's so. We broke away, on account of our education. But this assurance in Ethel's behaviour derives from her upbringing. Once you've laid your hands on the truth you don't let it go easily. I see this in some politicians who've lost religious certainties only to replace them by social or economic orthodoxies. It's interesting. It's like James Joyce who was always some sort of Catholic though he'd jettisoned his beliefs in God."

Irène herself was a lasped Roman.

"I went to church a time or two with the family," she confessed.

"Good, good."

"Why do you say that?"

"I approve when you think seriously about where we are and what we're doing."

"It seems the opposite," his wife answered. "It's emotional. It prevents real thinking. It's like attending a pageant."

"Thinking and feeling are often very close. In literature, at least. One has to be careful, that's all."

"Shakespeare's not always careful," Irène answered, daring him.

"I see what you mean." He rubbed his chin. "Shakespeare was very gifted in a period when the language was expanding. What he can get away with you and I can't."

The moors stretched sun-brown; the

leaves on the few trees were sallow, already autumnal. Noel Smith found the landscape benign; even the mountains seemed gentle, suitable for amateur watercolourists, for a flat wash of yellowy green, with faint purple tinges of shadows. This could be grim country in the winter, with cold rain cutting, or the road blocked thick with snow, ice locking the land, bleak, uncompromising, unfriendly. Today it lay tame as a suburban garden.

"Sunshine doesn't suit this landscape," Irène said. She often appeared to read his thoughts. "It's at its best when the weather's wild. We must come up then."

"We'd be struggling," he said.

"Poor old man." She stroked his right arm, which he then put round her waist. Her arm encircled him and they stood in the heat like lovers, still and content, untouched by lust.

"I'm seventy-five."

"This," she waved with her free right hand at the hills beyond the valley into which they looked, "will be here, constant in outline and changing, changing, changing from minute to minute when Ethel has died."

"I don't mind that. Geological stability's proper. It's the other bits and bobs."

"Bits? Bobs?" Her intonation was suddenly French.

"Graffiti. Human detritus. I saw a scrawl the other day. In thick felt-tip. 'Don't think I'll pack Jo in just for you.' There it stands in a gents' urinal. And the writer has probably left Jo, or she him, months ago. And when Ethel dies or I go, it'll still be there, fading but legible, for somebody else to read."

"A cry from the heart?" she asked.

"I expect it was. Some schoolboy Romeo, giving hundreds a text for transience."

"But it's not the actual message, is it," she asked, "that tells?"

"No, it would have been the same if the lad had written, 'Liverpool FC' or 'The Who!'"

They unwound arms and walked slowly and apart downhill towards the car.

"There wouldn't be hundreds," Irène objected, arm in arm now, "musing on ephemerality. Not dozens. Only one or two."

"Daft old men."

"You are right."

"Dead right," he joked.

Quite suddenly they could hear music so that they stopped, exactly together again, in the road to listen.

"What is it?" Irène asked. They could not make it out properly, and walked on.

"I know," he whispered in excitement. "Handel. One of the concerti grossi, Opus 6."

Below the road in a gully she could see a cloth-capped man working at a stone wall. He had perched a long radio by his side on a flat rock outcrop. The music came and went slightly uncertainly whether on account of some fault in the set or obstacles in air and landscape they did not know, though they could now recognize Handel's eloquent variations. Noel hummed.

"What number?" she asked. He loved quizzes, opportunities to air out-of-the-way knowledge.

"Give me a minute." She did so. "The B minor concerto. Largo."

Satisfied, they looked down at the

workman who laboured on, bent back towards them. Irène clutched her husband's arm more tightly; the lightness of sky, the broad swathes of sunshine on the yellowish ground and the short, ordered beauty of Handel's entertainment touched them, edged them towards happiness.

"The music in my heart I bore
Long after it was heard no more,"
he quoted.

"I ought to know that. Who is it?"

"Wordsworth. 'The Highland Lass'. That must be Radio Three."

"Or a cassette tape."

"I'd forgotten."

They reached the car; she took the wheel. Strapped in they could not hear the music. The whole landscape stood massive; no cloud, no breeze moved, existed to disturb.

"Ready?" she asked.

"Manchester, here we come."

Imogen walked out into the front garden of her bungalow the moment they arrived. She had clearly been waiting at the window for them. The two women fell into immediate rapport as Irène dawdled through the Pennine journey once more. They quenched their thirst before straightening their faces to process into Ethel's room. They had been warned to expect no recognition. Though Imogen tried to rouse her mother, Ethel merely stirred, eyelids momentarily flickering. The visitors stood, watching, then shuffled out discomfited.

When the luggage had been carted through, Noel and his wife, washed and combed, reported to the kitchen where Imogen was completing her preparations for the evening meal. No, they could not help; she'd almost finished. Noel suggested that he should sit by his sister's bedside to allow Imogen and Irène the opportunity to walk out, or chat in the garden.

"There's no need for you to be in with Mother. She won't know you."

"I think I'd like to." Modestly.

"Yes. Do. Please yourself."

"He's a puritan," Irène pronounced.

"Take something in to read," Imogen comforted.

Noel sat in the wicker-bottomed chair

by Ethel's bed. His sister barely moved. The curtains were drawn against the evening sun, though he found that he could see after a minute in the room. On the other side of the bed, a fan whirred; it appeared to be placed too high for absolute efficiency, but perhaps the medical authorities did not want the draught to be directed at the patient's head. Nowadays, he reflected, they cooled feverish patients with fans in hospitals; his childhood had instilled the opposite notion of treatment into him. If one had a high temperature one swaddled oneself with blankets. 'Sweat it out.' Not so now. The hum sounded slightly metallic, not unpleasant; one did not hear it as anything but a machine, without human or insect connection. Outside he could vaguely make out the voices of the womenfolk, but subdued, with gaps of silence. Once a door banged. His sister did not stir.

There had been no changes in the room. He noted the tray with glasses, bottles, though she must now be beyond the help of casual medicaments. The picture of the Pre-Raphaelite beauty who resembled Ethel in some youth-stirred imagination, the imitation Blessed Beatrix hung by the door. He stood unsteadily, stepped forward, positioned himself in front of it. This half-light suited the subject and her dim ecstasies. He saw no likeness of Ethel there, either at the time of her young womanhood or her powerful maturity. This girl looked upward and outward, to God or romance, caught up in something beyond her understanding, whereas Ethel, in memory or photograph, concentrated in quite a different way, bringing the force of her intellect to bear, making head or tail of what could be solved and dismissing the rest, not as beneath notice for Ethel knew how limited her own mental horizons could be, her brothers saw to that, but as pabulum for spare moments, leisure, not for the serious consideration that her everyday exigencies demanded.

And yet Ethel had been flattered by the suggestion that she was not unlike this young woman.

And Ethel in her fifties, at the height of her powers, a national and admired figure in the educational world, had fallen in love, whatever that meant, with the younger Leslie French.

Pouting he cursorily examined the bare shoulders of the model. More light and the illusion of flesh would disappear. Or? He remembered how this daub had troubled him sexually in early adolescence. He wondered what his father had made of this, if the old man had ever entered Ethel's bedroom and stood poking his moustache at the length of neck, the soul-drenched eyes. Had he remonstrated with his daughter for her temerity in bringing this temptation, this incitement to lust, to immodesty, prurience, lubricity, lechery? Noel pushed the words about his head. Did his father know them?

He stroked his own upper lip. He hardly knew his father.

Joseph Smith had died during the Second World War while Noel was away in the forces, and during the twenty-nine years they had known each other the father had never spoken a single word about sexual matters to his son. It seemed incredible. True, in those days fathers from the provincial middle classes offered nothing to their children by way of sexual advice, not even obscurely or obliquely. No pamphlet, however misguided, had been left for his perusal; the large volumes of the home medical encyclopaedia, adjudged to show in small prose or pink illustrations the differences between the sexes or gynaecological mysteries, were kept locked away from young hands at the top of the tallest bookcase. The father left the education of his son to the schoolyard wiseacres or forward girls.

Noel could not now guess whether his father's sexual drives had been strong or easily subdued. The old man had been twenty-seven when he had married and Ethel had been born a year later; his parents in their innocence had wasted no time. He himself had been conceived fifteen years after his sister, thirteen and twelve years behind his brothers. Had the long gap betokened the use of contraceptive devices or methods, or had his parents in their thirties practised chastity? He did not know. He wondered how far Ethel could have enlightened him, had she so wished. His brothers, Tom and Joe, both dead now, had been equally reticent. Tom might have said something, if pressed. His sister had probably acquired her picture at the age of twenty, say, while she was at college. Had she smuggled it into her bedroom, once it had been framed, in conspiracy with her mother? Lily, he could imagine his mother combining sternness with mischief, looked the picture up and down to pronounce, 'You'd better not let your dad see that.'

Ethel would have argued for openness, her mother for common sense and convenience, but not for long. Again Noel looked at the uplifted face which had lost all attraction for him. This conversation between mother and daughter was his fiction; he ran an exploratory finger down the slightly chilling glass and then returned to his seat, resumed his superior perusal, from a distance. Outside, presumably from the kitchen came a shriek of shared uninhibited laughter. He smiled with satisfaction. When he was a child a woman who lived over their back-garden wall had screamed thus with wild joy and at length on summer nights when doors and windows were open, and then his father would say to him,

'Mrs Henshaw's swallowed a feather again.'

He leaned towards his sister, stroked her face with his fingertips. He found no response. When he spoke, and the sound of his own whispering voice startled him, he received no reply. Ethel's skin was not unpleasantly warm; arms and hands lay under the coverlet, so that only the wrinkled inches of face, the thin tipple of hair over pale and half-naked scalp could be seen. Air slouched hot, a mixture of small, unpleasant stinks, not foetid, at worst humanly disagreeable. Noel dismissed his fastidiousness.

As he sat in the dark room his head drooped and he dozed.

He woke guiltily, with no idea how long he had slept. Ethel lay as before. 'What, could ye not watch with me one hour?' He sat dizzily, then helped himself up by fingertips on the bed to lean over his sister.

"Ethel." Nothing. He repeated the name, once, twice. On the third time she breathed heavily, a sigh as if she broke into a half consciousness. He waited. She did not move. No reward. Noel tidied the edge of the sheets, already straight. Her hair was thin, already dead. Barely touching her, he stroked the grey strands, then the forehead. In the end, unrewarded, he felt backwards for his seat.

From the next room he could hear the women's voices in cheerful conversation. He listened carefully to make out what they were saying, but failed. Confused, he sat, hands clasped between knees. They were talking as he wished. Irène was doubtless describing her family eccentricities or encounters with French butchers and bakers, and Imogen would realize that the world went on outside this prison of a house and manage to laugh. Then he was pleased. Once Irène embarked on her aunts, she'd raise a smile from the Blessed Beatrix.

Imogen opened the door, peered in.

"All well? The meal's ready." She tiptoed forward, looked down at her mother, ushered him out.

As they began to eat, they did not talk much. Noel asked a question or two about Ethel, and this perhaps deadened their spirits. He enjoyed the food: home-made lentil soup, a complicated salad with dry ham, Stilton cheese, no wine. The nurse appeared, to expectation with the brewing of coffee. She and Imogen dealt with Ethel while the Smiths cleared the table, washed the dishes.

The nurse, a youngish forty, on only for this week, briefly offered her opinion: it was amazing that Ethel still lived. She recalled, in a blunt monotone, a few parallel cases, but soon progressed to more agreeable topics. They heard of the scattering of her grandmother's ashes; her neighbour's win on the pools, four pounds and some pence; her husband's attendance at violin-making classes; their walking holiday in the Highlands. She was a gasbag, used to entertaining the comfortless, and did not stint herself. She spoke, almost scandalously, of a man in the next street, a terminal cancer case in his late seventies, who still tried to grope her. "My husband said, 'Let the poor old sod have a feel. He deserves it.' I don't know if he meant it. He'd probably be furious if I let him." She had not smiled much, face square and stern, pronouns adrift. “You never know with men, do you?” she asked Imogen. “I don’t,” the headmistress replied. The nurse expressed surprise when told that Irène was French. “I wouldn’t have guessed from the way you talked.” This led to a disquisition on the accent of the old Ukrainian woman who lived next door to her, with her peasant headscarf and long, black clothes. “You’d think it was Vladivostok,” she said, with a fine disregard for geography, “not the middle of Manchester.” She was in no hurry to move, and they were glad of her company. When she’d gone Imogen confessed that she didn’t exactly understand the organization of the home-nursing service. She had thought that Mrs Jones, the usual district nurse, came in as a kind of private arrangement made possible because she lived only a few streets away. The replacement, here while Nurse Jones was on holiday, continued the practice, although evening attendance must cost the health service a pretty penny in overtime. “Perhaps they’ll send me a bill.”

Her mother, she said, was eating hardly

at all. They had tried her on some high-protein product, but she could not take it. Slops and intermittent sips of water or lemonade were her sole sustenance, so clearly she could not last long.

"She must have a strong constitution," Irène offered.

"Powerful. She was suffering from cancer for four years or so before Diddy Commons died, and that's eight years ago. She would not give in. She fought on and on, though the treatment she had must have made her feel wretched. She did not like to mention her weakness. I wormed the truth out of Diddy, but even then my mother gave me the impression that the cancer had been contained. After Diddy died she lived on her own, seemed better, had some casual help, until I bought this place and moved her in with me. She's been going down in these last two years."

"That's a sad end to life." Irène spoke softly.

"Look at her now. She's been near death for months. They've really tried hard at the hospital. I thought it would be nursing care only, that they'd let her slip away. She's not living now, not in any sense that she would have acknowledged. She's crippled with cancer, and strokes. She has no pleasure, and no understanding."

"No pain." Noel.

"Perhaps not. I hope she hasn't, though I'm not sure. She has such power of will that I wonder if sometimes she doesn't surface through all the drugs and disablement and recognize herself for what she is. Last time you were here, Noel, and that's only a few weeks ago, she knew you and remembered some things."

"If I were dying," said Irène, "I'd like to go in a second. Alive one minute, dead the next. Bad for those left behind, but . . . "

"Would you like to know that you were going to die?" Imogen asked.

"To be told, you mean, that the illness was terminal?" Irène. "I'm not sure."

"Wouldn't it depend on how you felt?" Noel straightened the crease of his slacks. "If you had been suffering painfully for a long time, it might come as a relief to be so informed, whereas if a burglar burst in with a gun this minute and said he was about to kill me, and I believed him, it would constitute a terrible shock."

"Constitute?" Irène repeated the word, laughing at it. Her husband, caught out, shook his head and stumbled on. "I look on it as the last exam. You do your best with it. Other people, more cowardly or unprepared, have managed it in the end."

"But it's so unfair, even as an exam," Imogen argued. "Some are carried off inside seconds with a heart attack while others have to endure wearing, degrading, killing pain over months. We don't know."

"Thank God." Noel.

"Personally," said Irène, "I don't fancy either."

"The first is preferable, surely?"

"I guess," Noel answered, "that most people would choose the second on the grounds that while there's life there's hope."

Noel Smith drew satisfaction from this conversation, since it prepared them not only for Ethel's imminent death, but also for a freer intercourse. They felt now that they had not ducked away from serious topics, and so could indulge themselves with the trivia of gossip. They had qualified for ordinary life.

Imogen, however, her mother's daughter, had not finished with them.

"In the last year or so," she began, "my mother has remembered, or rather liked to talk of nothing better than, her childhood. It's said to be so with old people."

"Is that right, Noel?" The ironic Irène. Her husband grimaced at her.

"I think she had a happy start to life?" Half-questioningly to Noel.

"Happy and successful. She and her brothers all did outstandingly well at school from the first day. My father worked his way up the corporation hierarchy. My mother moved the family into larger, more suitable homes. They all did well."

"Were you happy, Noel?" Irène asked. "In the same way?"

"Yes. I seemed to be in the middle of a house packed with grown-ups. By the time I started school, Tom was in his last year at the High, and Ethel and Joe at university. I was thinking on our way up here today, when we heard that man playing Handel on his cassette, how I was edged into my line of business mainly by chapels and schools. The hymns we sang, for instance."

"Like D. H. Lawrence?" Irène asked.

"Yes. Exactly. His mind opened to 'the golden corn / In Canaan's pleasant land.' Though he misquoted one hymn. But that was literature to us, a use of language outside ordinary life and allied to music. Hymns and Bible."

"Which one hymn would you particularly choose, Noel?"

He considered his wife's question.

"By cool Siloam's shady rill
How sweet the lily grows,
How sweet the breath beneath the
  hill
Of Sharon's dewy rose."

"Ummh." Irène murmured Gallic doubts, rising and musically falling. Imogen stood bemused.

Noel shook a warning finger at his wife.

"It's not the world's greatest poetry, I'll admit. But these hymns were written by literary men who'd studied Latin and Greek, had Oxbridge educations, and they squared us up, if we were so minded, though we didn't realize it, for the Palgrave we were offered at the grammar school. It was poetry of exactly the right level for ignorant but sharp young urchins like me."

"You were never that," Irène smiled.

"You think not? I wasn't ready for Mozart, though the choir at Starr Street used to roar through that Twelfth Mass Gloria. It's not even considered Mozart now."

"Did it, these hymns and services," Imogen asked, "affect my mother in the same way?"

"Yes, but not so powerfully. She and my brothers were mathematically minded. They took after my father. I had this interest in words. More so than Ethel, though she was a linguist."

"What if you had been part of a very literary family?" Irène.

"That's impossible to say. There were some books about the house. A complete

Shakespeare, I remember. Not that I made much use of it. But I was suited. Their prizes."

"You took after my grandmother?" Imogen asked.

"I guess so. Though she had no higher education really, grammar school to sixteen, training college. She learned to speak well because it suited the family's upward progress, but she was too busy until we were off her hands for much serious reading."

"Were you poor?" Irène took advantage of the conversation. It was her habit.

"Not really. But nothing like rich. Putting children, four children, through university cost money, even if we all won scholarships. But my parents were careful and by the time the Depression arrived my father held a well-paid job as transport manager."

"You were lucky?" Imogen.

"In many ways, yes. Not ideally so. But parents like ours reverenced education, and I had three first-rate examples."

"That might have put you off?" Irène.

"But it didn't. I took the humanities rather than the sciences, but I don't think that was a reaction against my brothcrs."

Imogen had walked across to the french windows and stood staring out to the still brilliant garden. She turned, and addressed them from a distance, causing Irène to twist in her chair.

"I've been thinking about what we said about dying." The voice lacked certainty; this had nothing of the headmistress, the administrator about it. Her body seemed too robust for the diffident delivery. "That one can perhaps find comfort at the end from one's achievements. If, if one was strong enough to recall and assess one wouldn't want to die."

"My father didn't," Irène said. "I think he was angry rather than anything else when he found out. Not frightened, angry."

"I suppose the recall could be sporadic, or bedside visitors could praise what you had done, for them or other people, and so remind you." Noel spoke easily enough. "My experience has been that those who have achieved anything on our side, that is, artistically, are mainly introverts and have this enormous sense of, well, if not failure, of so little accomplished compared with the wealth of opportunity. And the greater the talent the greater the understanding that so much more remains untouched. That's one of the crucial human drives towards wider, higher goals. And even with people one could consider extroverts, surgeons or athletes, some painters, and I may be wrong in my choice of category, even they often consider that they have managed too little."

"So the deathbed's a comfortless place?" Irène, smiling, pointing two fingers, revolver-like at her husband. "For us, nowadays, without the consolation of religion."

"Even with it," Imogen, a dark shape, sharply.

"Because we don't like change?" Irène.

"It's a good literary convention, though," Noel's voice had taken on a more emollient, didactic tone. "To have a person dying and to recall, in his, her mind or that of the narrator, the high points of the life."

"But it's no great use in real experience?" Imogen asked. "Real dying?"

"No. I've told Irène often enough that I'm proud of belonging to the human race. We may be damned for selfishness; we may destroy our world through carelessness with the environment; we may blow ourselves to blazes, but we've discovered the size of the universe, and some of the great laws which appear to govern it. We've built temples and palaces that give satisfaction over hundreds of years. Or written bars of music or lines of verse or painted pictures that uplift, revivify the living. And I've hardly started to list our achievements. But it's with the living that we must look for our success: those in the full rush and energy of life can best assess, or be moved by, or be improved by what we do."

"You're telling us this too late," Irène said, twinkling, not put out. "We're getting near the end. Why didn't you tell me this when we first met?"

"What difference would it have made?" he grumbled.

"Not a blind bit." The phrase rang oddly, deadly in a Frenchwoman's mouth. "I expect I should have gone on washing nappies or cooking meals."

APS.

"We had only one child. I was often at home."

"Would you have liked a bigger family?" Imogen demanded of Irène "It's a question I often debate with myself. I think now that I would. It might suit me to have a dozen grandchildren scattered about the globe. But I didn't want more children when I was younger, or I would have had them."

"Didn't Noel have a say?"

"No. He left the decision to me. He often did."

They stayed up late in constant talk. Just before they went to bed, they filed in to see Ethel. Having dismissed Noel, Imogen one-handedly tested and then with Irène rapidly changed her mother's soiled sheets and nightwear. Ethel lay momentarily naked, big boned, smooth, pitifully thin, scarred, starved, ugly, already laid out.

"It's all very easy with washing machines," Imogen said, and kissing her mother, gathered the bundle.

Irène, safe with her husband, could barely bring herself to speak.

15

IN the next forty-eight hours the Smiths learnt how far Imogen involved herself in looking after the motionless, undemanding patient. The daughter constantly traipsed in and out of the room, encouraging her mother to sip, to suck, to open her eyes, to attempt to recognize.

"I blame myself," she confessed to her visitors. "It's doing something. I can't bear to be helpless."

Irène, alone with her husband, expressed her angry pity.

"It would be better if Ethel died. Or if the doctors put her to sleep. She is not a person any longer. Why don't they?"

"There are dangers."

"That wicked people would take advantage of their opportunities?"

Noel, listening, was reminded of the student he had first met nearly forty years ago. She, much slighter then but with the same brown, dancing eyes, had expressed this sharp indignation about politicians and the cold war, about the failure of the British to try to understand, let alone become part of, continental Europe, of the haphazard methods of her English teachers. The smiling, shy, youthful French miss would fly off the handle, bridle, stand stiff with vexation. Noel had attributed these bouts of fury to the polemics in her family; with the Dalsaux one fought one's corner or one went unheard. Life in the more tolerant house of Smith had not exactly quenched the fire.

"I know what you're going to say," Irène declared. "'Don't get your hair off.'"

"Exactly."

"It isn't right. Imogen should not be called on to do these menial chores."

"Why not?"

"You English are all sado-masochists."

Noel shook a finger at his wife; he liked nothing better than to play the mock schoolmaster.

"Somebody has to look after the dying. And in Immy's case it will only be for a week or two at the outside. Not like some daughters who've spent years on end, the best part of their lives, caring for ageing or incapacitated parents. And that's not confined to us; in France I guess it's just as common."

"Such people should be looked after by professionals who can go off to something else once their eight hours are over."

"Too expensive."

The argument, if that's what it could be designated, soon blew over. Noel felt that his wife, if not exactly despairing of him, tended to classify him as unserious about anything but a few literary topics or cruxes.

Noel sent the two women out for a shopping expedition and lunch while he watched over his sister. He assisted the nurse and when she had gone spoke, without answer, to Ethel, held the glass to her dry, bloodless lips. Then he felt affection as he held the warm body upright, but this soon died as water drops spilled and the half-opened eyes closed, the head lolled.

A telephone call from Leslie French interrupted Noel's lunch of home-made soup and new bread. French gave an account of his visit with Imogen to Kay-Shuttleworth College; he was ringing from Glasgow, and wondered if he could call on his way back.

"How long will Dr Wagstaffe last?" The crudity of the question seemed forced out of him, as if Noel's noncommittal answers had screwed his moderation beyond common politeness.

"Nobody knows. The doctors are amazed."

"It's hard on Imogen."

"Yes."

"You don't think so?"

"She is very capable."

"Why has she never married?" French's impertinent question flew from the phone. Noel waited, expecting an apology or expression of embarrassment, but none was forthcoming.

"I hardly knew Imogen before this final phase of her mother's illness. I met her, of course, from time to time; we exchanged Christmas cards: I distributed her prizes once; Ethel kept me informed of her daughter's progress."

Noel amazed himself by the stiffness of his answer.

"Yes," French mused. "She knows her mind."

After a few questions Leslie French began to talk about the Englishness of England. Noel listened wondering what sort of paradoxes the man would dredge up to prolong the conversation. He compared the fields, hills, mountains and towns, spread himself on the 'sick hurry and divided aims' of Britain and Japan, enlarged on working practices, means of motivation, leisure, religion. This emerged interestingly enough with each point prepared for and delivered, as if for a lecture. That seemed likely. Then French swerved into Shakespeare. Of all the teaching in Japan he had most enjoyed his classes on Shakespeare, but only since his return here had he realized how 'foreign' his exposition had become. Of course he spent a great deal of his time explaining the language; it was absolutely necessary even with the most advanced students using the best annotated texts. Here followed a disquisition about how vaguely English students understood the Bard; they thought they did until they were asked to paraphrase, a despised exercise but one which revealed the crassest ignorance. He recalled how Dr Wagstaffe had supported him in this years ago against the arty 'let the words speak for themselves' faction.

Since his return to England he had come to understand that the universality of Shakespeare, that which he shared with Africans or Japanese, depended on its English nature. Shakespeare had no anthropological interest in the beliefs of society in the time of Lear or Cleopatra or Richard II, or rather only a secondary acknowledgement of such, his real power lay in his brilliant exposition of the beliefs of a Jacobean middle-class intellectual conservative. This was clearly a new conception to French, not yet clearly worked out, emotionally accepted but not yet backed by argument. Dogberry and Verges, it seemed, loomed as importantly as Hamlet or Henry V.

Noel listened with interest.

The thesis was not altogether new to him: the Englishness of Shakespeare. But this exposition had sprung from French's long term abroad and the unexpected rediscovery of his roots. Perhaps the death of his wife had severed foreign ties. But he had Japanese sons. French seemed to Noel not unlike a certain class of students, young people who became suddenly alight with new ideas, or ideas new to them, because they found themselves emotionally stirred. Here was Leslie French at sixty acting like a naive, clever nineteen-year-old, and Noel found himself both delighted and touched. It was possible, probable that French had been this sort of man all his life, an enthusiast, a seeker after unknown gods. Noel felt cheered, as if a message had been brought from on high by the archangel to announce to Ethel Wagstaffe that her life had not been wasted, that the jumpy liveliness applied to the wodges of knowledge she demanded from her staff and students lived still.

Behold it was very good.

He responded drily enough to French's roulades of sentences, but this in no way checked the man's vigour or excitability. Words tumbled; he lost himself more than once; he apologized and celebrated, scintillated into jubilee, came to himself in darkness, yomped on.

Noel knew delight.

"I'm pleased," he admitted. "And does this mean you've made up your mind to stay in England?"

"No. I'm not taking decisions yet. This has all come as such a surprise I want to savour it."

"I see." Noel did not. Leslie French the actor, the impresario was too much in evidence.

"It's a kind of epiphany. This sudden revelation of something that was already there, but until the moment unrecognized. No, that's not quite right. This patriotism," he coughed on his word, "did not exist until I returned. All these years abroad, three in Africa, nineteen in Japan have made me what I am, made me capable of recognizing my own country and nation."

"But didn't you feel foreign in Tokyo?"

"Of course. In spite of a Japanese wife and children whose first language was Japanese. I was European, an Englishman. But, and this is what amazes me, I only felt the foreignness of my position. It was negative. Since I've been back I've learnt the positive side, and its strength."

"It's not connected with people, with a person?"

"You mean have I fallen in love with an Englishwoman? No, I haven't. It's mad to say it, but I've fallen for a whole race." He laughed nervously. "What's your comment on that?"

"I'm pleased."

"Very tight-lipped, Professor. It wouldn't happen to you, eh? I thought you might understand, having married a foreigner."

"Well, you've given me something to think about, something I've missed, or only half caught. I'm fascinated, but now you must continue to test and expand your ideas here amongst your own people in your own language."

"Yes." The short word breathed half-satisfaction. "Thank you."

"Give Imogen a call later in the day when she's back. Talk to her if you will about what you're discovering. She's had a scientific training, and might throw a different light on it."

"Or cold water."

"I don't think so. I . . . you've discovered something about yourself, and that's always interesting. In any case, at the present time it's important that somebody should remind Imogen that there's a world outside her mother's bedroom."

"How long are you staying?"

"No more than a day or two. I've a lecture to complete for a literary society, and Irène has a thousand and one plans. Call in and see us when you come back to Beechnall, will you?"

"Thank you. I'll take you up on that. With pleasure. And I'll report further on my conversion to Englishness. Many thanks for bearing with me."

Noel walked smiling from the telephone. He'd have an interesting topic for the women when they reappeared. Irène would have something to say for sure. He wondered, in his slow English way, in which direction Leslie French's volatile mind would jump next and what form the new enthusiasm would take.

"You've something to answer for," he told the supine body of his sister, and was glad about that. Ethel stirred, groaned without force. He asked if she would like a drink, edged her upwards, held the glass to the cracked lips without much response. The eyelids urged themselves an eighth of an inch apart. He put her back, and covered her, stared at the Blessed Pre-Raphaelite, inquiring of himself if the brotherhood, or their feeble followers, were English with their oddnesses and despairing. He walked round the bungalow's neat garden paths in the warmth of the sunshine, and decided against wasting time on the Test Match. He could fall asleep without the help of the television set.

The doctor called in, his last morning visit. A smartly dressed young man with a red face and a quiff of black hair.

They walked into the bedroom together. The doctor touched, looked, touched again, made some slight adjustment to the patient's position, consulted the record and spoke, half-heartedly trying to rouse the patient. Nothing. The doctor hummed, made a note on his pad, checked the time.

"Yes," he said, motioning Noel forward. The brightness of the corridor revealed the cleanliness of the doctor's hands, as if he'd scrubbed them hard after examining each patient. "Yes."

"I'm her brother," Noel explained. "Her daughter is out."

"Nothing much you can do. Does she drink or eat? A little? Does she seem unduly uncomfortable?"

Noel made his report. The doctor played with a button on his open jacket.

"This nurse is coming in?"

"Twice a day."

"Good. Don't be afraid to get in touch with the surgery if anything happens."

"How long will she last?"

"Impossible to say. She's . . . We did not expect her to live for this length of time."

"Would it have made any difference? To the treatment?"

"No. I don't think she's suffered much pain. Her daughter, I understand, came down against the idea of a hospice."

"Do you find this sad?" Noel asked. The doctor looked momentarily surprised.

"We all have to die. Mrs Wagstaffe's had a long life, and from what I gather a very successful one. If she can die now without discomfort then we are all doing our jobs properly." He relented, turned to Noel. "Don't be afraid to let us know if there is any problem."

He was gone, leaving a faint aroma of disinfectant.

Ethel had not moved. Noel spoke to her, but came out unanswered.

Irène and Imogen returned at about three in the afternoon, talking volubly still, glad to pull shoes off tired feet. They had made some good purchases; the hall was cluttered with elegantly designed carrier bags. The lunch, which took an age to serve, had not been worth waiting for, but it had given them a rest and time for ample talk. It had been agreed that Imogen would accompany Irène on her next trip to France at Christmas or before.

"I shall be there then," Noel said.

"That will only add to the gaiety of nations."

"You've never seen Noel amongst the French."

The two drank tea gratefully, still talking. Some barrier had been broken for Imogen; she had been allowed to enjoy herself for an hour or two. That night, after dinner and the nurse's visit, the three opened a bottle of champagne.

"I shall have a hangover," Imogen told her uncle.

"I was trying to think of that word." Irène.

"It won't affect you in that way. Not champagne."

Leslie French rang and Imogen talked to him. Afterwards Noel expounded the man's reconversion to Englishness, and this led to untoward hilarity. They went to bed, all three, slightly ashamed of themselves. The day had passed in accordance with Noel's wishes; Imogen had been taken out of herself and during their evening's conversation they had almost forgotten the dying Ethel until the women changed her bed linen and nightgown.

Imogen did not need such pampering. She knew her duty and was capable of carrying it out. Noel wondered why he had thought otherwise. He did not underestimate his niece. He and Irène, both sleepless, whispered together in bed idly until midnight.

They left Manchester after lunch, having extracted from Imogen the promise that once the funeral was over she would come back to Beechnall with them for a short break.

"We don't know," she had argued, "how long it will be. My mother might hang on for weeks, and then it might be utterly inconvenient for you to have to entertain me."

"I've only just got to know you," Irène said. "I can't miss any opportunities."

"Does Noel visit his French relatives?"

"Noel is a law unto himself, for one thing. And for another I've no family anywhere near as interesting as you."

"I think you're flattering me."

The two women kissed, hugged. It seemed exciting to the husband.

"Imogen's a remarkable woman," she said in the car.

"Yes. Made a career right away from her mother's influence. That couldn't have been easy."

"No. Ethel was overpowering, I guess."

"But she came back in the end."

"Was that because she felt guilty, do you think?" Noel asked.

"No. I don't know any more about it than you do. Imogen's the sort of woman who's always on the lookout for challenges. This one presented itself, and she rose to it." Irène, driving, giggled to herself. "Sometimes I think I talk rubbish. How can I know why she did what she did? Codswallop? Is that a word?"

"It's dropped out of fashion. I haven't heard it for long enough."

"I like it," Irène beamed, accelerating. "It's nourishing to me."

16

NOEL spent the first morning back writing his lecture.

Once he'd started he felt instant relief, and, once half-a-dozen sides of foolscap were filled, careful pride. He had doubted, in his prime, his ability to draw conclusions from his reading, and now wrote even more cautiously. Though he knew he'd make constant changes, might even reverse the main direction, at least he was putting pen to paper so that he would, in due course, give a reasoned account of the very wide reading he had done, even if he offered no equivalently large interpretations. He wrote with a Biro; Irène had pressed him to invest in a word processor, but he'd resisted her instruction. He gathered the morning's sheets, reread them, made alterations, realized that he had left his work where he could easily pick it up next day, considered tomorrow's opening sentence, composed it, wrote it down on the back of one of the dozen envelopes littering his desk. Why he did not write it straight on to his first draft he did not know, but that was his superstitious method. He straightened his papers, books, pens, ready for the morrow, and smiling went downstairs.

"Lunch in about ten minutes," Irène announced.

"What is it?"

"Salad."

His wife had been out in the car to the supermarket, and had helped the cleaning woman to square up the drawing room. She had a look of determination about her.

"What are your plans for this afternoon?"

"More cleaning up. And a thorough examination of the garden."

"Anything you want me to do?"

"No. You go out for a walk and think about your lecture. I hate it when you're . . . "

" 'In vacant or in pensive mood.' "

She said no more. It had been her common complaint all through their married life that once he was preoccupied with a project he was fit company for no one. At one time she used to hope that his temporary removal from the niceties of social intercourse would be worth the implied indignity to her; now, she merely ordered him to get on with it, at his desk, on his feet, in his chair with a tome on his knee and a pencil in hand. She made no comment on the resultant books or articles, not even on the critics' praises or misunderstandings. That was one of her burdens: to see he had the leisure and the goad to complete his academic tasks.

He washed the dishes while she occupied an armchair in front of an Australian soap opera on television. When he questioned her about this, she replied with care, pointing out how they had failed to treat an interesting relationship seriously, or more often had discarded either humanity or consistency merely to rouse momentary interest in an audience presumably held to be paying only half attention.

"Why do you watch it then?" he had mocked.

"A topic of conversation with the rest of the world, and an attempt at creative criticism. I rewrite the scenarios in my head. Properly. That's the sort of exercise university English departments should set their pupils."

He hardly believed her; more likely she listlessly followed the protean domestic adventures of these familiar faces and voices, as Wittgenstein his 'mags'. It cleared her mind.

Noel set out along the road towards the park, sauntering. He thought of nothing: it was too hot for speed. His gentle, casual observation of front gardens or lawns affected by drought was interrupted by a purity of whistling from somewhere along the avenue.

It was his notion, suddenly crystallized by the clear sound, that nowadays the art of whistling had died. He attributed this to the lack of melody in pop music where rhythm or violence of noise took precedence over either tune or harmony. Or perhaps modern technology, the Sony Walkman (odd Nipponese English that, conjured up with those naively poetic but crippled car names by some of Leslie French's ex-pupils), provided the brain with the full sound of a group rather than the old fashioned crudity of a whistle, one note at a time, and the rest, harmony, orchestration, words even, provided adequately or feebly according to talent, but silently inside the head.

The whistler was walking towards him, in paint-splashed dungarees and carrying a short ladder. The intonation and rhythm were so accurate, and the sound so large, that they seemed almost instrumental. Noel recognized the swaying tune, an Irish air, arranged by Sir Arthur Somervell. 'Oh, she was as fair as an angel.' He could visualize the copy with Somervell's name, and 'Irish translation by Dr Douglas Hyde' that had puzzled him. Had Hyde translated the undistinguished English lyric back into Irish?

The man with the ladder passed him, continuing with his performance, disregarding his one-man audience, unaware of quality or purity.

Noel remembered being asked to accompany the singing of this song at a party at Ethel Wagstaffe's house while, at twenty, he was a student, fifty-odd years ago. He had been invited to Manchester for a few days to report on his progress at Oxford. He recalled Ethel's sons as charming, tumbling bundles of energy; about this time Imogen would have been born, or her mother carrying her. No, not sure. His sister had laid on a function in his honour, half-a-dozen Mancunians nearer the Wagstaffes' age than his, and after a meal, a baldish young man from William's office had sung, accompanied by Noel. Quilter, Ireland, Vaughan Williams and this. Noel could see the copy but not the name of the author of the words. Was it Molloy? But Hyde's name stuck. Had he read Yeats at that period? He doubted it.

> 'There Hyde before he had beaten
>   into prose
> That noble blade the Muses buckled
>   on.'

'Coole Park, 1929.' Not too long before their performance. Four or five years.

The guests had sat in the large drawing room, grander than anything the Smiths boasted in Beechnall. Noel at the piano had his back towards the audience as the bald man, Jimson, Johnson, Gemson? had sung. The singer had flung back his head, and his fine tenor voice had soared, so that Noel, nervous for the first few bars, had gained confidence and made much of the tall, black, German upright. The tenor, in proper concert fashion, insisted that his pianist shared the applause, and the boy had bowed awkwardly at a beautiful woman, wearing a hat indoors — was that possible? — a portrait painter's wife, languidly clapping.

In the brightness of August Yeats troubled Noel's mind again.

'Beautiful and gentle in her Venetian
  way.
I met her all but fifty years ago
For twenty minutes in some studio.'

Now Noel could not recall the woman's name, Pendleton perhaps, but she had spoken to him, and he had fallen in love with her for a few days. Perhaps that was Ethel's idea. The Smiths never held parties at their Beechnall house: meetings for good causes, but nothing for pleasure, not even at Christmas. But here was his sister, with her friends, who talked of Italy and Greece, and came prepared to sing. Noel had never met Mrs Pendleton, if that was her name, again, but he felt this hot morning for a few seconds the breathless embarrassment of a young provincial in love receiving the undivided attention of a beautiful woman. He would ask Imogen if she knew anything about her. Dead, he supposed. She'd be younger than Ethel. And suddenly overwhelming him again because a man with a ladder had walked past in the street whistling.

Noel looked about the dry avenue.

The whistling had died and the whistler was not to be seen. Noel hummed the tune. Irène often accused him of being a romantic, and here was her evidence. He'd tell her over tea and listen to her laugh and begin to exaggerate so that the party in a Manchester suburb matched some ball in Vienna at Prince Metternich's. He remembered the meal, not what they had eaten, but a frank discussion, into which he had been drawn, of the jilting of the daughter of the lady on his left by an MP's son. The guests at his end of the table talked with a harshncss that the Smiths would have shied from; they might have used coarser expression but they would not thus have damned the man's character. Later they had dissected the hypocrises of some parson caught out in sexual peccadilloes, described with some frankness. He supposed now that the men were solicitors or barristers and used to straight language in court or between themselves. The women had shown no sign of disapproval or shock, had smiled, even laughed outright. His lady in the hat had sat, to his disappointment, at the far end of the table and he had not had the chance to observe her reaction to the outspoken ribaldry. These were people of the world, he had decided, who had no truck with the constrictions of nonconformist and mealy mouthed conversation. 'Our conversation is in heaven.' He remembered some begowned, visiting celebrity preacher explaining in his sermon, which demanded awe of scholarship and gales of laughter for quips, that the Greek meant 'citizenship'. Why had he remembered that? He saw again the large teeth and wave of black hair and the white hands mesmerizing the crowded pews. The man had stayed overnight with the Smiths; in private he had been rather shy, the organ voice tuned down to a dry whisper. He had enjoyed his food, especially Mrs Smith's suet pudding, and had gone to his bedroom to lie down before his evening's ordeal. The boy had been instructed to black his shoes on both Sunday and Monday mornings.

Now Noel crossed the main road, hovering between the dual carriageways, and entered the park, still pleasantly occupied with memories. He walked up an avenue of lime trees, closely planted so that the road beneath was cool, and out into fierce brightness where he stood by a shrubbery of laurels and rhododendrons. He turned and looked back towards the wrought-iron gates trying to whistle the Irish tune, but managing only a breathy caricature. He had recently read in one of the facetious articles without which no quality newspaper was nowadays complete, that homosexuals were poor at whistling. That was on a par with other rules on guidance to the good life that these columns offered: never trust a man who wears a V-neck pullover or a woman who drives a Volvo. He had seen neither humour nor even a glimmer of sense there. Who wasted time on such items with pleasure? He did not; early nonconformity had done for him. He blew the lilting melody tunelessly towards the lime trees.

Suddenly he was surrounded by children.

Their unexpected arrival slightly frightened him; there'd be perhaps twenty who fluttered about him like butterflies, except these were noisy. Eight or nine years old, boys and girls, they moved round him, each holding a piece of paper which seemed, in their minds, to have some connection with him. They dodged and stood, never jostling him, the nearest a yard away, spelling out to themselves from their lists. One boy, rather fat, with hair clipped short, now stood exactly in front. The child's eyes were crafty.

"What letter does your name begin with?" That boy would make a police constable.

"Christian or sur?" asked Noel. All

were listening, consulting their papers, mostly silent.

"Both; it don't matter." Fatty, for all.

"N or S," Noel answered.

The children cheered and ticked, but no one thanked him.

"Three at one go," a girl said.

"What's these trees?" another asked, not directly to Noel, but loudly enough to include him among possible listeners who could answer.

"Lime trees," he said.

Eyes went down to papers again; a finger pointed; subdued chat changed to cheering.

"An avenue of lime trees."

Now the children began to drift off, though some seemed loth to leave Noel, this source of treasure.

A bearded young man and a young woman in spectacles both wearing scruffy jeans strode up smiling.

"I hope they haven't been a nuisance," the young man said. "They're on an observational jaunt. Teaches them to read as well as keep their eyes open. But they will do it all in a bunch. They're supposed to work in pairs."

"How do I qualify for three in one?" Noel asked.

The man looked at his list.

"Stranger with brown-laced shoes. Man with buttonhole." Noel wore a freshly cut Frensham bloom. "The third? I don't know."

"Does your name begin with S?" The girl. "Smith. That's it then. And I told them these were lime trees."

"They struck oil with you. There are only twenty to tick altogether."

"Many thanks," the young man looked about him. "We must keep an eye on them these days. Kids find trouble themselves, but there are oddities about." Noel felt accused. "We keep them in a certain area, and blow the whistle after a set time. Those not back don't qualify for marks and prizes."

He chased off after the girl; the children were now whooping and scattering, shouting advice and abuse.

Noel remembered that Ethel had said years ago that the most beautiful sound on earth to her ears was the squealing of children let out to play in a junior school-yard. 'There you grasp all the energy that we have to harness,' she had said. Noel watched the children still running up the road, combining their search with aeroplane flights or cowboy swoops or thumps.

He remembered, not for the first time this week, his own days in the infant school, how one day three or four of his friends had lined up behind him, holding on to jacket or jersey, and chuffed round the yard. Within seconds the train had been joined by dozens, scores and for a short time had snaked dragon-like round the empty yard. He had felt the heaviness of the weight behind him, seen the emptying of the play space as children rushed to join, the cautious enjoyment on the face of the teacher on duty, before the long line broke and the hundred children returned to their own concerns.

Then he recalled his grammar school, seven hundred boys crammed into the hall for morning assembly, lined up by houses, and the head boy, school captain they called him, striking a thick hanging Burmese gong as the headmaster entered. Sometimes the head had to turn and grip the still humming metal between fingers and thumb before he could announce the hymn.

The staff sat in a long line under the windows at either side of the head's dais. He could name them now; he had peered at them as a small boy at this north end of the hall. They stood, gowned and grand, some singing the hymn and the day's canticle (Magnificat Monday to Nunc Dimittis on Friday), learned men, fetched from the ancient universities and far corners of the country to educate the likes of him. Old Baines-Smith, he'd be all of thirty, sang heartily under his black moustache shaking his gold-rimmed spectacles while Lowther stared aristocratically forward, gently superior to such hocus-pocus. All dead now, he supposed. He wondered what they had thought about as they stood there: they had ambitions and troubles, Ned Soames had a baby daughter who died, expectations and joys. Tom Gott, 'Gobby' Gott, would be waiting to rush out for a cigarette, or an inch of it, cork-tipped, before the desperation of first period.

'And if I tempted am to sin
And outward things are strong . . . '

The boys sang, six-footers at the back and eleven-year-olds in new blazers. It was an ordered existence, with scholarship divided into forty-five-minute periods; success was paramount, competition keenly encouraged with little time for the stupid and the slacker. They were the chosen, the eminent-to-be, the knights of industry, the scientists, the next generation of educators, future lord mayors, men of power and influence, the great-and-the-good-to-come. Herbert Whittle, heavily prognathous, announced the sale of tickets for the school play and said that girls would be allowed in. The boys had cheered, sheepishly, as the master expected; the unmentionable had been hinted at. The captain called them to order once the master had stepped down. One of the mathematics staff, a doctor of philosophy, had told him years later, that what he remembered most vividly about the school was the light dancing on the hair of the pupils as they stood in their lines in assembly.

Noel could remember the way some of the staff walked: one had a stick and a reputed war wound; one crouched behind his desk to dodge shrapnel; one rolled like a sailor. He would recognize the voices, the handwriting, the laughs of these men. Now they were dead, forgotten, unless some contemporary had made a note, kept a journal. Noel dismissed his fellow pupils for the moment, except bitterly to remember that many were to die young in the next war, most as air crew.

His sister Ethel had been large in this service.

None of his teachers had personally known her; she was at that time a young teacher of modern languages in a mixed grammar school, doubtless standing gowned in morning assembly, eyed with admiration. And Ethel had fought to stay in schools and colleges; at a time when even childless married women were excluded from teaching she made her way upwards. He himself, Noel mused, had taught. A wry smile twisted his mouth. He wondered if his pupils had regarded him as set apart, unusual, eccentric. He had married a

French woman, for a start. Nowadays he heard from relatively few of his ex-students, attended no reunions, spoke when he met any by chance only of the present. He had inspired, he concluded, no affection from these young people. But then he had not written to them except by way of formal notes enclosed with testimonials. And yet, somewhere, occasionally, some middle aged men or women recalled him. Or so he hoped.

'Do you remember that time we took Dr Smith down to the Clinton Arms in honour of Samuel Butler?'

Noel could not think why they had decided to celebrate the author of *The Way of All Flesh*, and in this manner, and why he had accepted the invitation. He had sat in a corner squashed between two girls who had not known what to say to him, while the young men had waved their arms, lifted their half-pints, and shouted toasts. It made no sense now, was not to be compared with the orderly line of singing schoolmasters and the tall windows behind them and the corner where the PT teacher kept the box, the benches, the vaulting horse, the mats, and above in the ceiling the looped climbing ropes.

Ethel had said sadly to him once that she and he came too late on the pedagogic scene to make much difference.

"Eight to twelve is the age," she had claimed. "They're keen and capable of learning anything."

He had doubted whether many of his students who went into teaching dealt with children so young.

"We're on the margins," he had said.

"Not you. You have your research."

He did not consider, then or now, that his publications had changed the world overmuch.

Out in sunshine he was stepping briskly along the avenue. In the distance he could hear the shouts of children and as soon as he found himself completely beyond the limes and the shrubberies he could see the group, now much broken, about its energetic business in the distance.

The road bent and he caught sight of two of the youngsters, a boy and a girl, standing on the lower spar of the wooden fence which had replaced the rhododendrons as a boundary.

Noel waved to them, and shouted. "Have you answered all your questions?"

"Nearly."

The two clambered down and ran towards him.

"Do you know what this is?" The girl demanded, tapping her paper.

He took it from her.

The questions were photocopied from a handwritten page, and were nearly illegible. Frequent foldings had not Improved matters.

"Number six," she said.

'What is a ha-ha, and is there one in this park?'

"Is it a mistake?" the girl pressed. "Ha-ha?"

"It's daft." The boy backed her.

Noel explained how this ditch acted as a cattle barrier without spoiling the view over the park for the aristocrats, and that it was originally a French word.

"Sounds more like somebody laughing," the boy grumbled.

"That's it. Up at the top there," the girl said.

"That's right." Noel drew a diagram

on the back of their paper to show them the sloping turfed side and the perpendicular wall. "Ingenious, really."

The children thanked him and ran off at full tilt to examine the phenomenon for themselves. They would be at the bottom end of Ethel's ideal age for learning, eight or nine.

In his own childhood, if he was to trust his memory, the world had been a larger, and certainly an emptier place. Fewer people disturbed his consciousness; this hardly seemed likely but that was his recollection. The roads were not so thronged with vehicles then, but he had lived in a house with a family of six, a daily maid and a washerwoman.

He moved up the hill, whistling the tune of the hymn he had recalled from assembly, 'Abridge'. The headmaster had favoured it, though he seemed little in need of God's guardian-ship or guidance as he trod corridors, mortar-board on his bald pate, or in the full glory of his doctoral scarlet on speech day. He had aped the ways of the public schools to the advantage of his pupils, introduced rugby football at the expense of plebeian soccer, acted the martinet, disregarded the director of education, thundered from his rostrum about that Serbonian bog 'where armies whole had sunk' and into which some of them courted the danger of floundering, or so it had appeared to him.

Noel wondered now whether this superior being had been tempted to sin, and in what form. He laughed at his blasphemy, but the old man had married, for the first time, in his fifties. The lady, widow of a world traveller, had provided the school with that Burmese gong, shaped like a priest's hat, on which the captain celebrated the headmaster's majestic advent.

The children were congregating now, cavorting together, some hundreds of yards away down the hill. He could hear the shrillness of their voices. On this day of August heat, Noel tried to remember those foggy evenings when his father's trams and buses had ceased to run, and he had walked home from school with friends, in small gangs, in the choking, cold darkness. He failed, smiled again, walked harder. The 'ha-ha couple' ran past him, late for their rendezvous.

By the time he reached the park gates on the far side, he limped wearily and his hipbones ached. Rather shamefacedly he caught a bus home, sat down immediately, dozed. Irène mocked him, telling him not to forget that he was an old man now. He claimed that he had played that day his small part in the educational advancement of the younger generation, and told her about the 'ha-ha'.

Irène looked pleased, thought it probably was a French word, though her father had called such a ditch *un saut de loup*. "You've enjoyed yourself, haven't you?" she asked, serving tea.

"Well, yes."

"Somebody should force you old teachers back into business."

"But it wouldn't be for long."

They laughed and examined his ambiguity. Irène seemed happy to be back amongst the English.

17

ETHEL WAGSTAFFE died on the first day of September.

Noel and Irène were finishing breakfast, toying with newspapers when Imogen telephoned. She had found her mother dead in the early hours; each night she crept in two or three times. Ethel had gone without struggle, curled in exactly the same position as when her daughter had last soothed her. The doctor had now called and the undertaker, who had removed the body.

"Would you like us to come up?" Noel asked, prompted by his wife.

"There's no need really. I'm perfectly all right. Relieved, if anything. Of course, if you want to see the body at the chapel of rest you can come. Do you?"

"I don't think so."

He consulted Irène, who shook her head.

"No. You're right. She didn't look anything like herself. Such a small, drawn face. That's not how I shall want to remember her." Imogen sounded matter-of-fact.

"Is there anything we can do?" he asked.

"I don't think so. I'll let you know when the funeral is once the undertaker has arranged it. It will be about a week, he said. Have you any ideas about the form of service? I don't think my mother had any fixed or strict ideas about religion. I'll ask Canon Tom Wilkinson to lead it. He's known her for a long time. He was Anglican chaplain of Kay-Shuttleworth when he was a young man."

"He's the man who wrote a book on Christ's sayings, isn't he? I can't remember its title. And something on George Herbert. Wasn't he connected with the university up there?"

"Probably." Imogen sighed. "Think about the order of service, will you? Do you want to say something, or read something? I guess Ethel would have liked that, but don't upset yourself. No, I'm perfectly all right. That's not quite true. I guess I'm in shock. In spite of waiting so long. And its present form is that I don't feel anything, or perhaps a slight exhilaration. I'm making lists now. Those I have to write to, the newspapers I want to announce her death."

"The undertakers will do all that for you."

"When I've decided which, and what to say."

"Are you sure you don't want us to come up?"

"No, Noel. I shall manage."

"But you'll let us know if . . ."

"You fuss more than my mother. But thanks, Noel, really. I could hear her voice then, when you were speaking."

Imogen seemed in no hurry, and talked easily about her mother, asking his advice about which of Ethel's distinctions should be mentioned in the death notices. She recalled her father's funeral, and her mother's concern for the observance of strict proprieties.

"My father wouldn't have minded," Imogen continued. "In fact he had ordered a case of Moët and Chandon to be drunk in his office the day afterwards. He said we should all be encouraged to laugh."

"We did laugh at his funeral if I remember rightly. Or at the meal. I was surprised how cheerful Ethel appeared. She depended on Will, you know."

"Yes and no. He was shrewd, but too conservative for her. She wanted changes, if changes were to be made, to be done at once. He hung about. They weren't at all alike. It's amazing that they had such a good relationship."

"You don't remember any quarrels?"

"You didn't live with Ethel long without dust-ups, but he was a marvellous quiet arguer. To give her credit she always said that if she'd thrashed a point out with Will she knew every quibble her opponents would raise. They were a good pair."

"And clever."

"Oh, yes."

Assured that Imogen needed no immediate assistance, he put his wife on the phone to her. After Irène's rather French formalities of condolence the pair were soon talking with animation, even laughing. Noel cleared the breakfast table to give his wife a few minutes' privacy. From the sink he could hear both voices.

"No, no," Irène pronounced. "We know you won't need our help with the arrangements. That's not it. But you might need a couple of familiar old faces or a cup of tea in between."

Without making out the exact words he could understand Imogen's thanks and refusal.

The women talked on. About suitable clothes. About Ethel. Imogen must have embarked on some anecdote, for Irène uttered small ejaculations of disbelief or delighted expostulation. The call lasted a further fifteen minutes.

Irène came out into the kitchen, sighing.

"Will she be all right?" he asked.

"I think so. I like her, Noel."

"So do I."

"And I told her not to be afraid to change her mind. She'll ring later in the day when she's seen the undertaker again, and give us the time of the funeral. She's an independent sort of woman. Sturdy. Very English."

"What was the yarn she was pitching to you?"

"Oh! Yarn? Yes. That was when

she and Leslie French went to Kay-Shuttleworth College. He burst into tears."

"And she didn't approve?"

"She's like the rest of your family, except Ethel, ambivalent. She was surprised, didn't expect it, doesn't think men should act that way, but, yes, she was pleased."

"Is she attracted to him?"

"The subject never came up. You're an old gossip. Or a fiction-monger."

They held hands for a few minutes, unusually. They thought, separately, of families, then broke away.

Ethel Wagstaffe's funeral followed expectations.

Educationalists, back from their holidays abroad, attended in large numbers. The impressive Canon Wilkinson's service rang velvet-voiced, old-and-well-fashioned. The address by a writer, once on her staff, struck Noel as short, oddly noncommittal. He had no idea at the end of the speech whether the man, who had long greasy hair, liked her, but guessed he did not, or he would have sounded more pleased with himself. Leslie French read from Corinthians, quite beautifully, every word perfect, like an actor, while Noel recited the Twenty-third Psalm. Many hands were shaken; Imogen's bungalow was jam-packed, so that even the garden seemed noisily crowded, but her caterers managed.

Noel sat down several times, half hoping to be left alone, disappointed when it happened.

Imogen and Irène moved round, polite bundles of energy, everybody's favourites. Even pessimists enjoyed the occasion. Optimists argued amongst themselves that the best in education was over, and cheerfully prepared for a new dark age. Very few young people attended the meal, or the church for that matter. One of these turned out to be the son of a now-dead mathematics lecturer, whose widow, incapacitated, had ordered him along. A law don, he said that his parents often spoke of Dr Wagstaffe, but he remembered only vaguely what they had said. That seemed typical, though it could not have been so. People who were elderly and learned and arthritic confined themselves to trivial talk; they were out of the battle. When they spoke of bright young hopefuls, you found they were discussing professors in their fifties and sixties. Noel thought dismally of an anteroom to hell.

When by evening the bungalow had cleared, a long campaign, the funeral had been at noon, Imogen with her uncle and aunt drank whisky. All three sprawled, exhausted with hospitality but not uncheerful.

Imogen, draining her modest glass, asked Noel to sum it all up. Embarrassed, he crossed and uncrossed his legs.

"I think the same thing of all funerals, especially those on bright days, that is, er, well, that the dead person would have enjoyed it."

"Would Ethel?" Irène, plaintively.

"All those old friends she hasn't seen for years, all there, proud of themselves for making the effort. Or outlasting her. There ought to have been a party for her while she was still alive."

"She's not been much of a social being since Deirdre died."

"How long's that?" Irène, again.

"Eight years."

"God." The tired Noel found himself appalled. "Time."

Next morning they shut the house up, Imogen had completed all arrangements, and set off in two cars for Beechnall. They stopped several times; Noel and his wife each rode with Imogen part of the way.

Back in Beechnall they ate little at dinner but finished a bottle of claret between them. They hardly knew what to say, as if the serious part of the death was just beginning, and the wine did little to open their lips. They stayed up late watching a television programme about a policeman who listened to Mozart quartets on his car cassette player and spoke in gruff riddles. Alien and homely it suited their quietness.

Next morning Noel woke cheerfully, went about the house singing hymns as his father might have done. Irène busy with breakfast laughed at him. Imogen wore a white dress.

"It's so quiet here," she said.

"This is a back street."

"So's mine, but cars and lorries rattle up and down it all day. And night."

"Some public-spirited rate payers had bollards put in to prevent people using this as a short cut."

"Isn't that inconvenient? For you?"

"No, we soon got used to the idea of coming in at one end only."

Imogen nodded, bemused, unlike her brisk self. She ate slowly. Irène talked about the house, which her niece had not visited before, explaining why they had not moved to a smaller, more convenient place.

"Isn't the garden too big for Noel?"

"It always has been. But we have a man in two days a week and he keeps it neat." Irène laughed, curling a finger at her husband. "As long as it's full of greenery, we don't mind."

"Including weeds," Noel coughed.

"Will you stay in your Manchester place?" Irène asked Imogen. "Or your mother's?"

"For the present. I haven't thought about it. It's convenient, I suppose."

On this first day Imogen seemed content to moon about their rooms. Irène refused to let her help so that the guest spent an hour in the hot afternoon walking the streets. At dinner Irène outlined her plans.

"This first day, you've done nothing, or I hope you have. That's good for everybody, especially energetic people like you. From tomorrow you can tell us what you want to do. Noel has been digging out pamphlets. You can see the town first. Is somebody sending your post on? They are. Well, that will alter matters, won't it. You'll want to sit down and reply."

"Shall I?"

"It's entirely up to you. We'll rush you around or give you a rest. At least I shall. Noel will talk philosophically to you. He's a decent old stick."

"Thank you, dear wife."

Next day the two women made an excursion, lunched out, toured the city's shopping areas. From Irènes bedroom account to her husband Imogen had spoken more of her last years as a headmistress than of her mother's slow death.

"She was pleased to give up school, and go back to Manchester." Falling rolls, staffing difficulties, the constant nag of administrative duties, most of which were in her eyes unnecessary, and the threat of further responsibilities had left her with the conviction that she was running a small department in a branch of the civil service and that the education of children only marginally entered into consideration. "And she said hers was a good school, with a good reputation, in a good catchment area."

"Does she seem happy now," Noel asked, "that she's finally free?"

"She doesn't seem depressed. She only tells me things obliquely, if that's the right word, odd sentences here and there amongst all the olla podrida about window displays and prices, and litter and motorists and architecture."

"She talks a lot, then?"

"Oh, yes. And you can see she's not used to being contradicted."

"Like her mother."

"That's another thing. I formed the impression that she didn't see a great deal of her mother. Nor altogether eye to eye. Most of her teaching was done in London or the Home Counties, and she'd pay Manchester a couple of cursory visits at most during the year."

"Did she phone regularly?"

"I don't know. I'll ask. She can talk easily enough about it all, without any sense of guilt that I've noticed."

The next morning's post brought a great number of letters which had been forwarded by her neighbour. Imogen grumbled cheerfully, and said she'd better spend the day answering these.

"There's no hurry, is there?" Irène objected.

"I've a puritan conscience. If I have a job to do I have to get it out of the way first off, or otherwise I'm worrying myself silly about it. It has its advantages."

"Is that your mother's example?"

"Yes, and my father's and my uncles'. All the lot. I guess my grandparents were just the same. Isn't that so, Noel?"

"Yes, yes. I'm a bit like that."

Imogen, however, offered to cook lunch, but was led to the large dining-room table and instructed to begin her replies to the letters of condolence. Irène drew the curtains, so that the room swam in a delicately green, aqueous light. Imogen sat down with her pens and Biros, her notepaper, her mouth pursed like an examination candidate.

"Let me know if there's anything you want."

When Noel went in to call his niece for coffee at eleven, she had completed a pile of answers and had drawn one of the curtains. She sat straight, almost aggressively, as if any moment this chore would be interrupted by a call for summary justice on some ill-behaved child or comment on the scheme of some senior member of staff. During coffee she seemed exceptionally preoccupied so that Noel guessed her to be immersed still in choosing suitable phrases to answer the letters about Ethel. A printed card would be better. She returned to her task grimly smiling.

Lunch was early, soup and salad, and once more Imogen took to her table. About three she and Irène went off to the post office together. From his study window Noel admired the brightly coloured starchiness of their summer dresses. When soon after four Noel crept down for a cup of tea, the women were together on the garden seat which they had moved into the shade. They talked only listlessly, almost as if they had quarrelled. The sun shone powerfully still. Imogen said to Noel that she had finished all the writing she intended for that day, but she'd have to settle to it again tomorrow.

"I thought we might have a day out," he said.

"Let me break the back of this, please." She spoke mischievously, deepening her voice. "Sir."

In the bedroom that night Noel asked his wife how Imogen seemed.

"She's here. She has someone to chat to. She likes the house and the garden. And us, I think. She's not talking about going home yet."

"Oh, good. These last months with her mother must have been a strain."

"She hasn't said much about it."

Irène, perfumed from her bath, brushed her hair vigorously.

Outside it was daylight still.

"Amongst those letters this morning was something like a proposal of marriage from your friend, Leslie French." Irène spoke to her mirror.

"He hasn't told me."

"Don't for God's sake mention to her that I've said anything."

"No."

"It was a queer sort of letter. You couldn't exactly make out what he was getting at."

"What do you mean?"

"It was very long, page after page. The story of his life, and the conclusions he drew from it all. And then these remarks about their getting together, their suitability, his diffidence — about writing in these terms to so remarkable a woman. But it wasn't written as clearly as I'm putting it to you."

"How was it put, then?"

"Well, I, as an outsider, had no difficulty in reading it as a proposal of marriage, but if it had been addressed to me I wouldn't have been altogether sure."

"He was deliberately vague?"

"Vague was not the word," Irène answered. "Convoluted. I wasn't very impressed. It could have been that he felt really shy, nervous about making such a proposal. On the other hand he might have been preparing himself for a rebuff, so that he could have told himself in time that he hadn't really meant any such thing."

"Good God. And what did she say?"

"She asked me what I thought, and I said my piece. Much as I've told you. But I didn't know the man so I was in no position to judge. I asked her if he had given her any hint of this before."

"And had he?" Noel was forced to these questions by Irène's silence as she concentrated on face and mirror.

"Not really. In many ways he seemed a confident, outgoing type. An actor. A show off. Trying to impress. Dressed to kill. You know the sort of thing."

"I see. Was she pleased?"

"I couldn't tell. She seemed greatly amused, and yet distant. Like a headmistress, putting it back into the in-tray for further consideration. She wasn't upset at all. Or vexed. But on the other hand she was more thoughtful than I'd expected. I advised her to consult you."

"Thanks."

"That's why I'm giving you a warning. What do you think about this Leslie? Were you favourably impressed?"

"Not my cup of tea. A bit of a showman."

"So he won't suit her?" Irène pressed.

"I'm not prepared to pronounce on that. They'd make quite an attractive pair. They don't look their age, but . . ."

"You mean they've fixed habits?"

"I'm sure that's so. But both have had their crises. Imogen and Ethel, that's obvious. But French has just returned to England, after a bereavement, and it's excited him."

"So your advice would be to delay a decision?"

"I suppose so."

Noel glumly opened his book; Irène still at the dressing table scrutinized her skin for faults.

18

THE following afternoon Noel accompanied his niece to the pillar box with her handful of letters; the pair strolled further along the tree-lined avenues.

"Do you know Leslie French very well?" Her question fell naturally amongst others about neighbours and architecture and front-garden designs.

"Not really. He called in on me since he came back from the East. He was staying with the Lukes. Tom was a colleague of mine early in our careers."

"Did you like him?"

"Yes. I'm old and selfish now, and I resent people telephoning out of the blue and inviting themselves here, but, yes, I quite took to him. And then you told me about Ethel's infatuation with him. It must run in the family."

"Is he a scholarly man?"

"I shouldn't think so. I've never heard of anything he's written. He'd be practical, actually producing plays, getting up on the stage. And he's spent a great deal of his working life abroad."

"Do you know anything about that?"

"No, not much." Noel walking the streets suddenly clasped his fingers together on the top of his head. "He married a Japanese lady who died, and he has two sons out there. But you know all that better than I do. When I last spoke to him, well, apart from a few words at the funeral, he seemed very excited to be back in England."

"Wouldn't anybody be so?" she asked.

"I see what you mean. No, some might be disappointed, thinking we had changed for the worse. His views were tied up with Shakespeare, and the Englishness of the man, and how those insular, provincial views made him universal."

"That doesn't sound very sensible," Imogen said.

"Well, he'd claim that Shakespeare's personality allied to his particular provenance would lead to a tremendous power of language which is the main cause of his universality."

"Not what he said, but how he said it?"

"They can't be separated altogether. But the poetry moves one, catches at the emotions because one realizes, consciously or not, one is being guided, worked over, roughed up, elevated, you name it, by unusually magnificent verbal music."

"That wouldn't apply to foreigners, would it? They wouldn't understand the nuances."

"Neither do a lot of English people for that matter. I see Shakespeare as an immensely sophisticated writer, inside a great tradition of English writing, and a new knowledge of Greek and Latin and Italian at his beck and call, but at other periods critics have taken a different view, of a naive artist 'warbling his native woodnotes wild'."

"Shakespeare never meant a great deal to me," Imogen confessed. "I quite enjoyed occasional trips to the theatre to see the plays, but I couldn't say what made them so marvellous. Except that everybody said so. All the experts on literature. I took their word for it, but it didn't mean too much. I'm trying to read a bit more now I've retired. But Leslie French made a good case out, did he?"

"I'm not so sure of his logic, but he was excited, moved, as far as I could see, in a way he didn't expect, by England and Englishness."

"He was unbalanced?"

"That's just about the right word," Noel answered, smiling, fingers clasped powerfully in front of his chest, "as long as you don't interpret it as 'mad'. But knocked off balance, askew is just about right."

"Did Irène tell you he wrote proposing marriage? Or that's what I took it to be."

"Didn't you know?"

"It was wrapped up. Well, slightly. I suppose it was clear enough. Do you think he was afraid of me?"

"You're successful. Yes. I shouldn't be surprised."

"And unmarried. For all he knew I might not have been attracted to men."

"Yes."

"What do you think, Noel?"

They had reached a main road, wide,

noisy with traffic, edged with sooty lime trees. Leaves hung faintly yellow. Lorries shook the ground, thrashed grates.

"You need my advice, do you? I don't know either of you well enough. The first question I have to ask is whether you were at all attracted to him." He thumped a blunt question when she did not immediately reply. "Are you?"

"He's interesting. I quite like him. Like you. But I'm not bowled over. I've never thought seriously in that way about him."

"I see. He's not completely ruled out, then."

"No." She drawled the word, breathed in and squinted at him, screwing her eyes attractively. So, he decided, she might have received a suggestion from some bright young man on her staff. She'd turn him down because she could see all the snags as he could not, but she'd be pleased he'd had the courage to speak out.

"Next." He'd reward her with the dry-as-dust professor. "You're both at stages in your life that involve considerable change."

"You sound like a newspaper astrologer," she mocked.

"And that means you should be careful." He waited for a further barb, and receiving none cleared his throat to continue. "He'll have to go back to Japan. That's where his sons are. Both in full-time education. It involves difficulties. It must. I don't know how you see yourself as stepmother to two foreign boys, brought up in an alien culture. With Japanese grandparents rightly wanting their say because they've taken over the care of the children while their father's gallivanting round England." He'd used one of Joseph's, his own father's old verbs. "You might relish challenges of that sort. I've no idea what it's like to live in Japan. Irène took to England easily enough, because she knew the language well, but I think she really looks forward to her month or two's escape into France."

"Go on." She sounded grimly amused as they turned into a side street.

"You'll also both be set in your ways, so that you'd have to be prepared to make considerable adjustments, reciprocally agreed. That won't be easy. But you'll understand all this without my assistance. The real test is whether you're attracted sufficiently to the man."

"Oh, yes?"

"Only you can answer that. And it means you'll have to get to know him. If you want to."

"So I should give some noncommittal, neutral answer for the present? And make him woo me, while I poke round into his character? I suppose that's sensible." She sounded amused.

"I'm a dull man."

"What would happen if Irène said she wanted to live permanently in France?"

"If there were good reasons I'd go. But we've been married nearly forty years."

"And you know each other inside out?"

"I'd hardly say that. She constantly surprises me. Perhaps that's because I'm a poor observer. Besides I'm seventy-five. I shan't live for ever. With a few of my books I'd be happy enough pottering about there."

"But it's not likely to happen?" she asked.

"Not as things are now. One never knows."

"You don't feel guilty having taken Irène away from her own country and language and relatives?"

"No. She was interested in all things English. It was her own choice."

"She must have been very young."

"Nineteen. I was thirty-six. It's a biggish difference, but in many ways she was more self-sufficient than ever I was. On the face of it, our marriage didn't seem a very good bet, but it's turned out decently."

"Decently?" Imogen was mocking again.

"All marriages have their drawbacks. You must have seen it with your staff. Irène made a good job of bringing up our son. And she did some academic study as well as teaching and good works. Looked after me."

"Not easy?"

"None of it's easy." Noel took the question seriously. "We were lucky. One in three marriages ends in divorce these days. And I wouldn't be prepared to say that people rush into wedlock without thought. There are what they call 'viable alternatives'. But come to grief many do." He smiled at his sentence order.

"Look at your father and mother now. Who was stronger?"

"My mother was the more forceful, but that's not quite the same thing. Ethel brought us up, but by dint of forays parallel with her educational work. At a period when married women didn't teach. She did part-time, worked for the WEA, the private sector and so on. It couldn't have been easy. I suppose she was determined."

"And Willy had pull. And money. He used his influence in her favour. Your father was by no means a nonentity."

"I know that."

"You didn't ever think your mother neglected you?"

"Do a Mrs Jellyby on me?" She laughed out loud in delight. "I'm trying to read *Bleak House*. No, I don't. I came late. A bit out of the blue, four years after Ray. Nobody ever said anything to me, but that wasn't surprising in those days. I put back her chance of full employment. It didn't stop her. We had a nanny who lived in. But Mother spent time on us. Taught me to read. Took us out on Sundays. Gave us an hour or two every day. Arranged good holidays. She had a great deal of energy, and I guess she didn't feel frustrated as many ambitious women must have done cooped up at home. By the time I was in school, she'd be about forty, the war was on, and there were all sorts of opportunities open to her, with the men away. But even then, she gave us attention."

"Well done, Ethel."

"She'd plenty of drive. And a servant or two. And determination. She made her way. You Smiths knew how to get on."

"But like my father, she did it against the run of circumstance."

They walked faster, and silently, until they reached the avenue were Noel lived.

"Slow up," he said. "I'm out of breath."

She stopped altogether.

"What am I to do?"

"As you suggested. Get to know him." He touched her arm. "That's what you'd do, anyway."

"I'll write tomorrow. There's no bursting hurry."

Two days later at lunch Irène asked him if he would be at home the following

Monday. She had consulted his calendar, found it free of engagements.

"Leslie French proposes to stay the day with us."

"With us? With Imogen, you mean."

Both women pulled comical faces, as if he didn't know half. He made a few inquiries, learnt that Imogen had written to French, who had already telephoned three times.

"Sounds serious," Noel countered. "I'll dress for the occasion."

Leslie French arrived on Monday soon after ten. Carefully groomed, he wore sports jacket, neckerchief, open silk shirt, check trousers, multicoloured golfing socks and polished brogues, and yet his face seemed anxious, arid. They sat in the garden while he recalled his travels in Britain. Certainly the man spoke well, put himself out to entertain; he told how one landlady's daughter had found a pearl in a Loch Ness oyster. At no time did he seem in a hurry to have Imogen on her own, but Irène insisted that her husband go indoors to help with the lunch. They saw their niece walking the garden with Leslie, but when Noel went to call them in the pair were sitting as they had been earlier on rustic seats three yards apart on either side of the table on the patio. French seemed to be describing some first night in London. He broke off as if it were unimportant so that Noel could neither name the play nor guess the date. There was no air of celebration, but none of awkwardness. French knew how to catch the interest.

Inside Noel poured chilled white wine into large, tall glasses. The suitor had been given long enough in sobriety. They laughed a great deal, and at one stage Irène, very unusually, dropped into her own language to flavour some anecdote; Noel did not know whether the visitors understood, but it did not matter. As of right, French capped the story with some account of a Nipponese fracas. He made them laugh, Irène especially.

The 'lovebirds', Irène's word, were allowed to wash the dishes together. They talked freely, he dropped a plate, but their spirits were not dashed. The Smiths pottered in the garden; the other two remained indoors, then on the patio. Behind the cotoneaster hedge

Noel asked his wife how the campaign progressed; she smiled, pleased with herself. At four-fifteen tea was served outside in the best china with two sorts of cake. Leslie and Imogen sat apart, but talked freely, like old friends or recently reunited colleagues. Noel asked French about Ethel.

"The best principal I ever had," he answered.

"She was a woman." Irène, mischievously.

"And I was a young man." French was determined to answer seriously. "And therefore more impressionable, I suppose. But she knew what she wanted: high standards and a good admixture of knowledge. Her examination papers compared, I thought, very favourably with those of the English tripos, at least as questions. You needed to know something to score with Ethel, but once that was understood she was willing to grant a wide variation of choice, of personal freedom."

"Did that go down well with her staff?" Noel.

"Speaking under threat of correction, I've never seen any educational body agreed about anything. Some said she was too academic for the type of students we had; others that she wouldn't allow them to be creative enough. Everybody had to do some science just as everybody had to do some essay work. My guess is that the students did better in English; the science staff felt they were at a disadvantage. Their two or three hours a week didn't give them time, they said, to do anything for pupils ignorant of basic scientific concepts and of mathematics. Whereas, everybody had, they argued, some experience of English language."

"Did they drag their feet?"

"Not altogether. There were several very good people, one biologist especially. Franks. L. J. Franks. He wrote a book on the teaching of science, and he rose very high in the inspectorate. Of course by the time I arrived at Kay-Shuttleworth Ethel was something of a national figure. She appeared on radio and television, was quoted occasionally by newspapers, was one of the great and the good, at least in the north-west."

"The govermnent never honoured her." Irène.

"My impression is," French broke off, looked at Imogen and Noel, "that she turned down any approaches." Daughter and brother said nothing; they did not know. "And it was said that your father refused a knighthood."

Imogen shook her head. "I think he would have told me. My mother might well have kept quiet, but he liked to poke fun at the vagaries of human pretension and vanity. Ethel, though she might well have refused to be honoured, would be more impressed."

"And what's your view?" to Noel.

"You need friends or sponsors to get on to these lists. She realized that backers and supporters are necessary everywhere, especially in education. Ethel was a politician, I guess, in the old sense. Not crafty, exactly, but knowing her way about. She had to fight and wriggle her way upward. She needed friends."

"And your father?"

"Clever. Level-headed. Principal of a well-established firm. Had a head start."

"How did they meet?" French asked.

"At some music club. My mother taught at the local grammar school."

"I didn't know they were particularly musical?" Noel.

"They weren't. But the music club was the right place to be seen. Where lawyers and bright schoolmarms could meet."

"Ethel didn't waste her life," Irène pronounced, in the end.

That stopped their talking so that they sat awkwardly.

"Three children, head of two large training colleges, some influence in educational practice, a book, dozens of grateful pupils. Yes." Imogen.

"What remains?" Irène pressed.

"I do." Imogen laughed at her. "Education's like science. You make your bit of progress, and then it's superseded in time."

"Except in schools and universities where theories come round and round." Noel.

"Noel, you're a cynic." Imogen.

"When, that afternoon, we visited Kay-Shuttleworth," French began, and it seemed like a sermon, demanding unquestioning silence, "the thing that struck me most was how little of Ethel was left there. Her room was unrecognizable. They'd altered the places where she reigned. I bet if we'd managed to get into the library they wouldn't have had her book on the shelves. I couldn't help thinking that the groundsman — little chap, what was his name? — had left more of a mark with the trees he planted and the paths he'd marked out."

"Would Ethel have minded?" Irène.

"I don't think so," French answered. "As long as her principles remained: hard work, dispelling of ignorance, intelligent questioning."

"She'd have hated it." Imogen. "She was as vain as the rest of us. More so, perhaps, because she'd more to be proud of. She, in her view, had it right."

"Is that good? Or bad?" French, almost sarcastically.

"It's the way to get on — to believe in yourself."

"Is that the secret of your success?"

"That and other things."

This short exchange quietened the party again. These two had temporarily dispensed with politeness.

The rest of French's visit passed

pleasantly. He stayed to dinner, and another longish conversation with Imogen, punctuated with his laughter. He left by taxi soon after eleven when the three made straight for bed.

19

OVER their morning tea in bed Irène and Noel dissected Leslie French's visit.

Irène expressed disappointment that Imogen had said nothing the previous night, for though apparently relaxed, their guest had gone upstairs with brief, meaningless pleasantries exchanged.

"Perhaps she had nothing to report," Noel answered.

"They had a few hours together. At least we organized that properly."

"You were ideal. Tactful." With irony.

At breakfast, Imogen appearing on time, crisply dressed and smiling, talked to them. She gave some account of her conversation with French, repeated one or two of his anecdotes, but said nothing about offers of marriage, or preliminary approaches.

"Are you seeing him today?" Irène asked. She rarely hid her meaning.

"No. He's going to a solicitor's. About

a house he owns in Cheshire."

She seemed to know no more; nor showed much interest.

"What would you like to do?" Irène again.

"Is there a picture gallery in the city?"

"At the Castle. I don't think it's very good."

"That doesn't matter. I'm no judge. But I think it's a sound idea to teach myself to look at paintings, even at something not very distinguished."

"Why is that?" Irène.

"Ethel. Her influence and say-so. Pictures ranked with plays and music and poetry and novels with her. They were high points of human achievement, and we should profit from them."

"Did she?" Noel, this time.

"I'm not so sure about that. Her training was literary, and she always read a bit. But it was a nook and cranny business. In spare minutes. She was so busy organizing and lecturing and administrating and travelling here, there and everywhere that she hadn't the time, the long hours necessary for anything outside educational study. She'd go to occasional concerts and plays, but it was all by chance. When the college did something interesting, she'd invariably turn up, and to give her her due she'd understand what they were about, and what their difficulties were, but she didn't make her own way. She didn't choose for herself which writers or composers or painters to follow."

"How many of us do?" Irène.

"That's so. But with reproductions and records and CDs now it's much easier to make your own choice."

"But what about when she retired?" Noel, now interested.

"From what she said, I think she'd intended to remedy the deficiencies, but she'd left it late. She and my father travelled about a bit, and she'd give a few lectures. And then he became ill, and had to be looked after. And Deirdre Commons had joined them."

"And she wasn't a culture vulture?" Irène laughed at her own words.

"She was an intelligent woman who'd worked her way up to be head of the domestic science department at Kay Shuttleworth, and done it the hard way. My guess is that they talked and watched telly more than they'd let on. My mother was pretty shattered by the time Father died, what with the nursing and then the blank. I mean she was, what, seventy-four and had been retired for eight years so that she felt right out of the important world. She was tired, I guess. And a little later she started to be ill, and then Diddy."

"And when Miss Commons died?" Noel asked.

"My mother, oddly enough — but she was in more ways than one an odd woman — rallied quite considerably. There was a remission of her cancer, and she didn't seem lost any more in that great barn of a house. But she didn't go out much, especially at night. She wrote an enormous number of letters to friends and old colleagues, and had a dog to talk to. She'd never had a pet before."

"Did she have any distinguished pupils?" Irène.

"Yes. Teachers and heads and administrators, as you'd expect. Some even did well in business. A textile millionaire.

John Tate, the architect, did a post-graduate certificate, and then changed careers. And people on the stage. Sheila Stone, Freda Temple, Tom Kendrick. And TV, radio, the newspapers. They didn't all stay in teaching."

"And Edmund Hughes?" Noel interrupted.

"Yes. Though I don't suppose she wrote to him."

"Did she ever speak about him?"

"I once heard a visitor question her, and she answered easily enough. As far as I remember he'd been at Manchester where he was an outstanding student, and he published his first book of poems when he was doing his year at Kay-Shuttleworth."

"Yes. *Wind Invitations*."

"My mother said they had considered offering him a job at the college he was so gifted. But they decided against it. He wouldn't have fitted in. And he went to London and taught for a time and became a journalist."

"This is the drunk?" Irène asked. "The man who wrote the play about alcoholism."

"*Toss-pots to Tipperary*. We saw it, if you remember, at the Cambridge. It was crude and very funny."

"It upset me," Irène answered. "As a play shouldn't."

"They didn't put it on at the college?"

Imogen looked at him with some disdain, headmistress to urchin. "I don't know. But I guess his books were in the library."

"Is he any good?" Irène asked her husband.

"Yes. Especially his first two. He was tortured even then. But the poems have a magnificent finality about them."

"And he declined?" Imogen.

"The third book came years later. He began to drink heavily, and dropped out. His friends arranged for *Toss-pots* to be put on, and an earlier play called *In the Wilderness of Sin*."

"Was that good?" Irène.

"I've read it, but it's left hardly any trace. It was about a family split up in Eastern Europe during the war."

"And?"

"Some of them came together . . . But . . . " Noel threw out his hands.

"It's not like you to forget, Noel."

He pulled a rubbery face at his wife. "Draw your own conclusions," he said.

"Is he still alive?"

"No. He died about four years ago. I saw the obits."

"I seem to remember my mother complaining that journalists had been ringing her up about him. I think she liked it really, though she wasn't well."

"But she wouldn't approve of him?" Irène.

"It's hard to say. He was only at the college for one year, and I don't know whether she had personal contact with him."

"Not many training colleges have students who publish books. Not many lecturers for that matter. And this had a tremendous reception. Properly, in my view. And you said they considered taking him on the staff."

"Yes. But she wouldn't feel responsible for him."

"Do you think she read any of his poems?" Irène.

"Knowing Ethel, yes. She would have had a look. And at the reviews. And she'd have asked the English department what they thought."

"It would have been in Leslie French's time, wouldn't it?"

"We must ask him."

"Is he the most famous person Kay-Shuttleworth College ever turned out?" Irène demanded.

"I've no idea." Imogen, stone-faced with thinking.

"Edmund Hughes is certainly in favour these days. When a man dies there's usually a period when he loses position, when critics attack him. But I suppose Hughes never had any sort of high ranking while he was alive. There have always been people who admired him. One young man on my staff used to speak highly of him, said if his name had been anything but Hughes he would have been much more regarded. And some firm brought out a book of collected pieces last year, with another to follow."

"Were they any good?" Imogen.

"I'd guess not. From reviews. I've not read them yet. But all the reviewers greatly praised his earlier work, and condemned his neglect, and pressed for a complete poems, properly edited. So he is well known now, amongst those who read poetry. Though that's a small minority. I believe they've announced a programme or two on telly. Radio Three is already drumming up enthusiasm for him. That's mainly Everard Peters, that young man of mine, he's professor now, in Wales. And one of the posh Sunday mags did him, Peters again, and to their credit, quoted good pieces."

"So he is famous." Irène.

Noel laughed.

"Not as soap-opera actors who are on the box two or three times a week. But inside his narrow circle, yes. And I believe his reputation's enormous in America. So, yes, he is well known."

"What would Ethel have thought?" Irène asked Imogen.

"I doubt if she ever did. About Edmund. My mother worked more like a scientist than a poet." She raised eyebrows at her uncle. "If that makes sense. But there were many things outside her ken. I can remember her telling me about the cinema club at college. Another of her bright young men ran it. And she went along because it was her duty, and she approved of the organizer, and took Father with her. She saw nothing in these films, though Daddy greatly enjoyed them. They used to argue, he told me. Once when I was there they had a set-to. Ethel laid it down that films were popular entertainment, and could in no way equal the great poems or novels of English. My father said that was like arguing that because the tabloid newspapers were bad there could be no masterpieces written in the language. He also took the line that it was a new art, and that some people responded more freely to visual rather than verbal stimuli. I don't think he knew much about it, and would never have considered going to the pictures, as he called it, except at the college club. But he liked to keep my mother up to scratch."

"Was she pleased?"

"In a way. Or puzzled. I think my father said she sent for this young man and asked him if the motion-picture industry had produced anything to equal the great works of Sophocles or Shakespeare."

"And what answer did he give?"

"I don't honestly know. But Ethel would trouble herself about it. That was her line. That's what education is about."

Imogen's face was stern, as she must have looked when about to deliver a rebuke in morning assembly.

"It seems incredible to us now, but intellectuals like my mother honestly believed that they could set the world to rights. She in her provincial training college. And dozens of other principals and head teachers in their little tin-pot establishments. Just look. At the end of the First World War Ethel was nineteen and at university. Never again would a slaughter of innocents like that be allowed. There must be general access to education, to learning and literature and philosophy, to the ancient languages and above all to the expanding sciences. Bright working-class children would be given their chance to share these advantages. Of course many weren't. Too many parents couldn't or wouldn't afford the money to be spent on fares, or blazers, or sports kit. And even some of those who were admitted weren't treated properly, and left early. But, it didn't kill the enthusiasm. Neither did the Slump. Nor the Second World War. That, unlike the first, was a just war, against evil. It also, incidentally, gave Ethel her opportunity. But in spite of the Holocaust, Stalinist atrocities, bombing cities flat and the rest Ethel still thought she and her like held the key to civilization."

Imogen paused. She had spoken without force, almost whispering.

"After the Second War people like Mother felt that everything, personal relationships, nutrition, trades union conflicts, care of the environment, could be catered for by people of education and understanding. Ethel didn't mind nationalization of coal and steel and so forth; it seemed sensible. The fact that we and America were at loggerheads with Eastern Europe didn't seem to deter her and her like. I don't think Mother had much use for communism, but it seemed a necessary social experiment in backward places like Russia. Oh, the world was going to be right."

"And nobody believes all this now?" Noel asked.

"I suppose," Imogen replied coolly, "this makes a mockery of your beliefs. You thought literature could shape better humans out of us, could replace the religion or religions that people could no longer believe in?"

"I still think that a knowledge of great art can improve an individual's quality of life."

"For everybody?"

"To some extent. Some because of genetic endowment or upbringing or circumstances will profit more than others. Wouldn't you agree with that?"

"Yes," Imogen smiled. "But literature's marginal."

"What's important, then?"

"Human nature and economic laws." She spoke laughingly now.

"Expand. Expound." He caught her mood.

"Human beings are almost invariably self-regarding; that is, selfish. Their own status or comfort is what counts. They might set off with all the goodwill in the world to establish equality or just laws but before long they're feathering their own nests."

"Does this apply to your mother?" Noel.

"You must remember she always lived comfortably. Your father had a good job; she went to university when it was unusual for a girl. My father was well-to-do. Ethel's fight was for woman's place, her own you could say cynically, and then for educational advantages for all. She was genuinely concerned about unemployment, about the Jews in Germany and Austria. We often had foreign children in our house when I was young. There was a biggish Jewish community in Manchester, and she joined societies concerned with the care of refugees from Hitler." Imogen smiled at them. "She wasn't just chalk and talk."

"How should we govern the world, then," Irène asked, "if we're all so awful?"

"Pragmatic laws, which will change from time to time, to keep the selfishness of most of us within bounds. They'll never be exactly right; some few will always get away with it, while others will suffer, and not always through their own fault. But this country, even at its present level of volatility, seems capable of making and amending such acceptable rules. Some countries aren't perhaps so capable. It might be that we shall slip into revolutionary wildness if we're not careful."

"And what will cause us to do that?" Irène again.

"If we get the economy wrong. And food becomes short. Even consumer goods."

Imogen waved her hands vaguely, as if she were tired of argument, or found their inability to grasp such obviousness tiresome.

"And how does education fit in to all this?" Noel.

"Preparation for life. Preparing people to do jobs. This is a technological society." She smiled wanly.

"It doesn't need much schooling to sweep the streets or the factory floor, does it?"

"You said it. Perhaps some would do well to leave school early."

"Ethel would hate that," he said.

"So she might. And even I would demand basic standards for all, so that they who drop out early can come back later if they so wish."

"Who would decide what those basic standards were?"

"You. Me. The government. The education committee. There's always been an elite to lay down the law. But schools are full, I'm told, of children who don't want to be there."

"Was yours?" Irène.

"No. But mine was a middle-class district with children on their way to the professions or the managerial roles. Of course, some rebelled, kicked over the traces, but the large majority knew why they were there, approved of our methods of drilling them through exams, and enjoyed the games and social activities. But we were not an average school."

"Is there nothing we can do for, let's say, children from rundown, inner-city housing estates?"

"I suppose there must be. But we don't seem to have it right yet. If there were jobs for everybody, then I think those schools would do better. That's what I mean by getting the economy right. It can cure a multitude of sins."

"And the cultural factor?" Noel, annoyed into jargon.

"Certainly I would encourage people to use their language properly. And give them guidance while they are in school. Even if it turns out they'd sooner sit in front of a television screen than read a book. You think I'm cynical, don't you?"

"Well . . . " Noel drawled his uncertainty.

"It's only because I try to work to advantage inside the limits of what I can manage. Education is like politics: the art of the possible. This may seem little enough with things as they are, a mere holding operation. But nowadays, to people like me, who began their careers at the end of the great age of the grammar school, educationists such as my mother seem to suffer from delusions of grandeur. They had had this great reservoir of lower-middle and working-class children, who knew quite well that a good matric exemption would mean a white collar, permanent job five days of the week unlike the part-time slavery and unemployment their fathers suffered. That made them sharp at school. And their capability of tremendous academic achievements led Ethel and her colleagues to think that everything they wished was possible. The Twenties, Thirties and Forties for all their economic stagnation, for all the political failure and the war, made its secondary teachers, its training college lecturers believe that education, the small field they knew, could provide any miracle they asked of it."

"And it can't?"

"Can't and couldn't. Ethel did marvellous things. She combined her ideals with practical schemes of acquiring knowledge, and I wouldn't want to take any of the credit away from her, but she couldn't change the world. If that was done, it was done elsewhere, by power-mongering politicians, arms manufacturers, warlords, paranoid mega-criminals."

"Is that so now?" Irène, getting in before her husband.

“Possible. Though the pendulum might swing.”

“Ethel sounds a very great lady,” Irène pronounced.

Imogen rubbed her hand on the surface of the table, pleased. “She was that,” she admitted. “And she lived at a time when her sort of planning seemed not only right but had the possibility of fulfilment. It must have been bliss. Teaching has always been hard work, but her underlings, and hundreds like them, achieved their little miracles. They affected a minority only, but the effect was not negligible. It looked like the emergence of meritocracy. But . . . ”

Imogen now drew circles on the table top with the tips of her fingers. She watched her hands as if they worked in dependently.

“She made the most of her opportunities,” Noel admitted.

“I think that’s so. And it left her with a sense of optimism. Or perhaps it was the other way about.” Imogen considered her doubts. “Her optimism enabled her to make something of the chances she was given.”

"Unlike some of us," Noel said.

"I remember just a couple of years ago." Imogen ignored her uncle. "She'd been quite ill, but had come out of hospital. I began to drive up nearly every weekend. And I remember her sitting there in the dining room looking out on to the garden. The sun shone, but it was cold, with north-west winds, the sky clear blue, and white cherry trees in blossom. And she sat there in a wheelchair. I thought she'd nodded off, but she suddenly said, 'Do you know, as I look out at that sunshine I suddenly feel glad that when I've died it all will still be there, the walls, the birds, shadows and flowers.' And she smiled, radiantly, as she could. I thought about that long enough; she must have felt better, ready to live again, and her excitement took this peculiar form of words. Her cheerfulness broke through. She knew that she hadn't too long to live, but she didn't say, 'I'm glad I've got another year or two and feel well enough this morning to enjoy life with all its drawbacks,' she came out with this other sentence."

"Was she deceiving herself?" Irène.

"I'm not sure. She'd accepted her death, but wanted to make that part of the momentary euphoria. She probably really felt what she actually said. Her temperament had translated the situation into these words." Imogen looked from one to the other. "Is that possible?"

They gave no answer.

"If only she could have died then," Imogen continued, "that would have been perfect. But she had another two years to come, growing weaker and more dependent and without any enjoyment of any sort."

"Your father went quickly, didn't he?" Noel rather curtly, clearing his throat.

"He was ill for some time, but the end was short. He died one afternoon, when nobody was with him, in his sleep, they said, and quite unexpectedly. Typically. Getting it over without fuss. He'd hated the time when he was bedridden."

"That seems very like him," Noel said. "But we can't usually choose the way we die."

"Ethel's was a great life. And I hope she thought so. That's what I mean by her optimism. Towards the end she wasn't there, really. But I think she knew before that what she had accomplished, unlike you, unlike me."

"Oh dear, oh dear." Irène pulled comical long faces at them, and all three trooped out to the kitchen to continue over the washing-up of a few pieces of crockery. The two women cheerfully chattered off for the town, the picture-gallery, a pub lunch. Noel, uplifted, promised to make dinner.

"Light. Not too much. Nothing fattening."

"I'll rack my brains."

They set off, dressed to the nines, to catch the bus.

20

LESLIE FRENCH telephoned three days later. His silence had surprised Irène and Noel, even if Imogen made no comment.

"She's a stoic," Irène had said.

"Or doesn't expect much?"

This time French wanted to take them all out to Derbyshire for lunch.

"I'll have to inquire of the ladies."

"So you must."

Again in private Irène voiced her doubts.

"That's not hopeful," she said. "why does he ask us, and not just Immy on her own?"

"He's perhaps not made up his mind yet."

"Then it's time he had."

The date was arranged, two days ahead. Imogen had said nothing about a return to Manchester. She spent a good part of each morning replying to the many letters her neighbour had sent on, and appeared greatly to enjoy Irène's company.

"This is a peaceful house," she told her uncle.

"Nothing happens very much, that's true. But I think Irène will go over to France next month for a week or two. Her mother's not been too well. She's said nothing yet because she thinks it's unfair to me to keep leaving me behind. But if I suggested that you'd go with her, would you?"

Imogen was willing.

"You'll really enjoy seeing Irène as a Frenchwoman. They claim she's become very English. But I think, for all her time here, and she's spent nearly twice as long in England as she has in France, that she hasn't changed at all, basically."

"She must have."

"In a thousand and one small ways, I'm sure. But she's like your mother, you know. Ethel, for all her time away, headmistressing-it over this place or those people, was always the Midlands Methodist she was at eighteen."

"I don't think she'd any, or many, religious beliefs."

"That's unimportant. If she'd become

a militant atheist, it would have been in a Methodistical way."

"Have you left such a mark on your child?"

"Irène insisted on speaking French to him at home so that he could chat away to her family when we went to France. But he's in Australia most of the time now, and I doubt if he ever speaks a word of the language."

"He's a scientist, isn't he?"

"A mathematician. He teaches some higher form of economics." Noel smiled. "And runs his own business on the side. He's doing well for himself."

"Who's he like?"

"Irène's side in business. Though perhaps he takes after my father, your grandfather, in some ways. And he has our ambitious streak, isn't afraid to try something out of his class."

"That's Ethel. I guess in her younger days she thought nothing was beyond her."

"Within reason," he said.

"Within reason," Imogen agreed.

Outside it was raining, the tropical summer over. When Leslie French hooted his arrival, it still poured and his windscreen wipers furiously laboured. Irène fetched him inside, made him sit down to coffee, telling him it was no use driving off in a hurry when they wouldn't be able to get out of the car. Noel helped his wife in the kitchen, giving the visitor ten minutes on his own with Imogen. There was no rush. He had ordered lunch for one-fifteen at the King William the Fourth, less than an hour's drive away.

"At least we're all dry here," Irène said, wheeling in the trolley.

"And the forecast is promising for this afternoon," her husband spoke from behind, like a butler.

"So we won't rush things." Noel still stood formally at his wife's elbow as she poured coffee. He handed out small gold-rimmed plates, home-made biscuits.

"This is perfect," French said, lifting scalding coffee near to his lips and down again. He added, after a question from Noel, sombre sentences about tea ceremonies in Japan, and the effort seemed to knock the spirit out of him. The three listened, put courteous, brief inquiries.

"How much longer will you stay here?" Noel.

"Another month at most."

"Have you decided to sign on again?"

"The university wrote to me, I received their letter only yesterday, offering a new, less confining contract. I was touched. They must think more highly of me than I had guessed. I can hardly refuse it. It surprised me. The Japanese are tremendous workers. Without work their life appears pointless. And yet they have offered me this light timetable. With excellent pay. I don't quite understand it. I certainly did not expect it."

"So you'll accept?" Irène, finally seated with her guests.

"Very likely. But I've not quite decided."

"You don't feel like retiring?" Noel.

"My forte is teaching. I'm only just coming to see that. I'd be lost if I hadn't a class to instruct."

"You could lecture," Noel answered, "and produce amateur drama."

"And perhaps write a book." Irène, excited. "About life in Tokyo."

"I shall have to go back to Japan in any case because of my sons. Until they finish their formal education."

"Do you think they'll work in Europe? Or America?"

"Or Australia," French admitted. "It's possible. But they are more Japanese than English. When I phoned them last week my younger son's accent was so, so oriental I could barely understand him."

"Perhaps that was the telephone." Irène, sympathetically.

"No. Reception was as clear as a bell. He hadn't spoken English outside the classroom for two months."

Imogen listened to this without comment, above the battle. She sat straight-backed, cup and saucer solidly held. French did not look at her, nor address his remarks to her. She sat politely acknowledging by smiles or nods the interest she had in French's talk. Now he delivered a lecture on the learning of Japanese, the differences between an Eastern language and our own. He explained well, never allowed their interest to flag.

"Can you speak it fluently?" Irène asked.

"I can make my way, yes. Of course, I look like a foreigner. So they expect errors and mispronunciations. Nobody could tell from your appearance whether you were English or French."

"You are both," said Irène, without guile.

The schoolgirl's joke seemed to jerk Leslie French from his momentary introversion. He barked a laugh, sat upright, twitching the sharply creased trousers an inch.

"I have a week or two to make my mind up," he said in a different, almost military voice. "And I shall do it." He coughed. "Some of us have had it too easy. I had supportive parents, went to a good school where they trained me properly for university. All the jobs I really wanted fell into my hands. I didn't do national service. I've enjoyed a whole series of interesting posts. My employers in Japan have just expressed their highest confidence in me, and in a practical way."

"What's the snag, then?" Noel spoke gruffly, setting the man to rights.

"There is no snag. I've always intended

to work until I was sixty-five, if not beyond. And this I shall do. I've temporarily been seduced by England. I came out into the rain this morning, and it was like a benediction."

"Doesn't it rain in Japan?" Irène.

"Of course it does. But here it rains on the houses and plants and the language I've known since I was a boy. I heard a man in the street shout out that it was 'siling down'."

"An Old Norse word, I believe." Noel.

"I am English." He suddenly trumpeted a line or two of Gilbert and Sullivan, conducting without embarrassment, "'For he might have been a Rooshan. / A French or Turk, or Prooshun, / Or perhaps Italian; But in spite of all temptations / To belong to other nations / He remains an Englishman, ta-da, he remains an Englishman.' That's made it rain again, hasn't it?" His voice, in fact, was a pleasantly tuneful baritone.

The Smiths collected the crockery and together wheeled the trolley into the kitchen. Irène instructed her visitors that they had better get themselves ready for Derbyshire.

"I'm ready now," French said. "I travel light."

"'A wand'ring minstrel, I,'" Imogen carolled, contralto.

It rained all the way there, through the mining towns and hilltop villages where people shuffled under umbrellas, bored, outside shop windows that were faintly lighted. The four scrambled out in the King William car park, French ushering them forward. He had donned an ankle-length foreign-looking black rain cloak that gave him the appearance of a crow as he batted his arms up and down to make sure that his charges did not stand too long in the wet. Inside he inquired efficiently after their table, sat them down in the bar with sherry or mineral water against the dark panels and hanging strings of horse brasses and prints of huntsmen. The two women talked animatedly as if the race across the car park had awakened them. Through the small diamond panes of the windows they could see wetly shining concrete, cars, a wall and a stretch of hawthorn hedge. Beyond that grey skies, mist, no hills. Rain splashed into deep puddles.

They were summoned to the dining hall, shown their table, which stood in an alcove by a window. The waiter murmured. French expressed his, their satisfaction.

"Well," Noel began, "what do you make of this as a bit of England?"

French considered, then misunderstood, perhaps deliberately.

"I like the formality, even though it must mean delays."

"You prefer McDonald's speed, do you?" Irène asked. "Do they have Big Macs in Japan?"

"I guess so. Without my patronage."

"You never took your children there?"

"No. Nor did my wife or her parents. At least, I don't think so."

The women giggled at his disingenuous ignorance. The waiter appeared with foot-square menus, silently took orders. French next negotiated over, then nominated their wine. For the moment his public behaviour, rather good, unostentatious, at ease, made Noel suspicious. Was the man always like this? Was he acting the part? Was he trying to make a good impression on Imogen? Or himself even?

"I tell you something," Imogen said, seriously.

"Go on." Noel was pleased.

"I don't often go out to lunch or dinner, but whenever I do I am amazed at the numbers of people who can afford to take their food in these places. The country is supposed to be running down, but here they are with their bottles of wine and the time to waste . . . "

"Here *we* are," Irène interrupted.

"We're retired. We have savings. We've paid off our mortgages."

"Aren't these people actually doing business with each other?" Noel asked.

"I doubt it. They may be giving a *quid pro quo*. But business is surely arranged over a desk, with figures to hand, and machines and secretaries, not in a place with muzak and waiters and an alcoholic fug."

"You're a puritan," French told Imogen.

All this sounded naive to Noel.

They had begun on the rather watery soup when a man walked across, confronting them.

"Professor Smith," he said. "Alan Faulkner."

"Yes. We met on the station platform. In Manchester."

They exchanged a few words, Smith briefly introduced his companions, Imogen last.

"My wife was at your mother's college," Faulkner said. "We're flying out to the Canadian Rockies next week."

"On business?"

"No. A fortnight's holiday, before the winter."

"You're keeping busy?"

"Run off my feet."

Faulkner said he'd detain them no longer. Noel watched him rejoin three other middle-aged men in good suits who were soon engaged in cheerful conversation. Faulkner's wife must have returned to him. Noel remembered the furious sentence about the wife's desertion as Faulkner flounced off for his train. Some compromise had been reached. Or some lies told. A burst of laughter exploded at Faulkner's table. Noel told his party what little he knew about the man. This led French into an anecdote about a senior colleague at his first school whose wife had run off with a junior member of staff, had had a child by him, and then eight years later she returned to her first husband.

"I paid them a visit while I was at Kay-Shuttleworth," French said, "and they were just like any other married couple. The little boy was nine and treated like the rest of their family. He had changed his name. They were older."

"Were they divorced?"

"They had been, but they remarried."

"And what happened to them?"

"The usual. I lost touch. If they're still alive, they'll be very nearly eighty. But they seemed a perfectly normal, affectionate couple with no sign of trauma. I'd met him at a conference, and he invited me to call in some time."

"You knew his wife?" Noel.

"Yes. There was a fearful rumpus at the school when she disappeared. In the Christmas holidays. We knew the young man was leaving; he was a physicist and had found a job in London. She went with him."

"And on this visit did your friend say anything about his wife's elopement?" Noel, again.

"Not a word. Nor did I. But what has stuck in my mind was the ordinariness of their life."

"Had he taken a new job?"

"Yes. While his wife was away, he'd been appointed second-master of a large school near Doncaster. That's where I paid the visit, immediately after the conference. I wrote to thank him, of course, for his, their hospitality, but we never kept the correspondence up. And I think, we're always willing to make excuses for ourselves, that it was he who let the acquaintanceship lapse. He was no letter writer. Neither was I, for that matter. Now, your mother," to Imogen, "was meticulous."

"Is that a happy story?" Noel asked. "Or a sad?"

"In a book it would have been happy," Irène said, "because the ending is happy. But in real life, I don't know."

"Would you have taken Irène back in such circumstances?" Imogen, uninterested.

"I don't know what it would have felt like after eight years without her. It's impossible to judge."

"He wouldn't have taken me back,"

Irène replied. "And I couldn't have brought myself to ask him."

The exchange had made them uncomfortable, as if they all hugged secret faults they'd be forced to confess. Outside it rained just as sullenly. Imogen asked French about his work in the theatre. Again a dull answer; he'd done less and less in the last two years. No, even if he settled in England again he did not think he would take it up.

"Why not?" Irène.

"I'm getting old. Virtue has gone out of me."

"You're sixty," said Imogen. "And that's not old."

French told how he'd done a Byron play at Kay-Shuttleworth. It had not been a great success, but he'd worked like a dog to make his actors understand the fashion, the code of the piece, and then to speak the verse effectively, dramatically, with music. "They weren't mad keen, even in those days when students did as they were told: it was biblical; it lacked big crowd scenes. But I wouldn't give up. I slaved away, and in the end we managed it. I wasn't sure myself whether

I'd be right to try to mount it. The short preface, showing how lively Byron was, caught my interest."

"But it didn't work?" Imogen.

"As a bit of theatre put on for three nights, no. But people remembered it years afterwards. That's the beauty. And the oddity. Nobody else knew it. They could boast. Or quote. Or baffle examiners. It made its point as perhaps some of the other more popular plays didn't. The Shakespeare productions ran longer, a whole week with three matinees, so that the schools could come in and see them."

"Can you remember any of the verse?" Noel challenged.

French gently touched his forehead with the tips of the fingers of his left hand.

"Yes. Lucifer:

Did'st thou not require
Knowledge? And have I not, in what I show'd,
Taught thee to know thyself?

Cain replies:

Alas I seem
Nothing.

and is answered:

And this should be the human sum
Of knowledge, to know moral nature's nothingness;
Bequeath that science to thy children, and
'Twill spare them many tortures."

French did not raise his voice, did not attract the attention of the other diners, but spoke with a luminous intensity, differentiating between the parts, making certain each word carried an appropriate emotional weight and discharge. The three were impressed. French had shown no embarrassment, had exactly suited his delivery to the situation, had quoted the blank verse as a master. They sat in silent admiration.

"What did Ethel think?" Noel, in the end.

"She saw it. I think she liked it. You had a religious home background, didn't you? And she wanted the college to be different. But she was worried that the society would run its funds down. She was a bit of a small shopkeeper in some ways."

"She'd invite the right people." Imogen, very quietly.

"Yes. Not the director of education, I remember. He'd be bored, she said. But the bishop, some theologians, a professor or two of English. I think she hoped they'd be shocked."

"Were they?" Irène.

"Not at all. That parson who took her funeral — Wilkinson, is it? — was a young member of the staff, and he said Byron would have made a good clergyman."

They talked about the theatre, plays they had enjoyed, and became animated. French gave an imitation of Donald Wolfit's world-weary curtain speech after playing Lear and compared it with the sprightly equivalent after Benedick. Noel recalled a performance in London during the war of *Heartbreak House* with Robert Donat as Captain Shotover, with Felix Aylmer and Deborah Kerr. They discussed Shaw and musicals, Shakespeare and opera. French became expansive, a brilliant mimic. With a sentence and a few gestures he'd suggest a whole scene, an actor's character, a role, a real person, and yet this was done without exaggeration.

They talked with zest, prolonging the meal.

When they finally made their way to the car it was raining still.

"So much for the forecast." Noel, gloomily.

"We'll go down into the town, park there and look at the river in the rain." French sounded enthusiastic. They splashed together through the streets, French leading with Imogen under his red, blue and yellow golf umbrella. Noel wondered where he'd acquired this, or if it was part of the equipment that came with the hired car. They called in at a bookshop, where French questioned the owner about Bernard Malamud. Noel saw a paperback of his book on Shakespeare's late plays on the shelves, while the women gloated over a magnificent manual of gardening which Imogen bought. They left their purchases, at the shopkeeper's suggestion, to be collected on the way back and cheerfully talking made for the stone bridge.

There as they watched the brown water, fast running among the grey boulders, rain pelted. A few cars swished by, but the sky over the blackened hills was uniformly grey. The sound of the river, its constant heaviness of energy, kept them occupied.

"People will think we're fools standing out here in the rain," French laughed.

"So we are," Irène answered. "It's great."

"All the stream that's roaring by
Came out of a needle's eye," French shouted.

"Who said that?" Irène.

"Don't know. Yeats, I'd guess. Is that right, Noel?"

"I think so."

"It doesn't make much sense to me," Imogen said, pleasantly.

"You men are not to explain, even if you can, or think you can," Irène ordered.

"I think there's a brightness in the sky over there." French cheered them. "Is it coming this way?"

"We stood here early this summer, and the river was so shallow, you wouldn't believe it," Irène lectured them. "Now look at it."

They watched the quick, dully flashing waves, the ripples, cleavages, ravelling; tangles of twisting debris swirled past.

"You could almost have walked across," Irène said.

"'All things are flowing; nothing waits.'" Noel, lowering his umbrella, to test the rain. "Heraclitus."

"Could you say it in Greek?" French demanded.

"Yes."

"Don't." Irène laughed out loud.

"I don't know about you," Imogen spoke for the first time, "but I'm getting wet."

"I beg your pardon." French sheltered her more comprehensively with his umbrella.

"Our best plan," Irène said, "is to get back home before we're soaked. "We'll be there by about four-thirty and tea. It's not going to stop."

Again they marched off over the puddling pavements. In front French bent in earnest conversation with Imogen. They collected their books, and were glad to settle in the car, although the weather was not cold.

Back at the Smiths' home, they pulled off their shoes, hung up macs, opened out the umbrellas to dry. Imogen and French were settled before a gas fire, instructed not to move. Noel followed his wife to the kitchen.

"We're giving them a few minutes to themselves, are we?" he queried.

"Of course. Did you enjoy the outing?"

"Very much. And you?" Irène beamed as she donned a frilled apron.

"Yes. Our Mr French excelled himself. He's very entertaining, isn't he? I wonder what Imogen thought? She might not like men to show off. She's very quiet in some ways, don't you think?"

"She's not altogether like her mother. Ethel wanted to be in charge, even of social intercourse. She'd switch the topic to something she knew about to achieve her end. Imogen just cocks her ear. It's more frightening. She's rather like Willy Wagstaffe. He'd listen long enough and say not a word until you began to wonder what sort of fool you were making of yourself."

"She is formidable."

"She's a successful woman. Yes. Not so much so as her mother, but she's never let her mother's reputation overawe her. And I guess she's never traded on it."

When the tea trolley was laden Irène asked a mischievous question.

"Who'll be doing the talking when we open the door?"

"French."

"What will he be talking about?"

"Oh," Noel answered, catching the mood, "Bernard Malamud."

"What did you say?"

"He's an American Jewish author. He was asking the man in the bookshop about him. You've read *Dubin's Lives*."

"So I have."

Outside the drawing-room door Irène pulled faces, in anticipation. They could hear nothing through the solid door. She signalled him to fling the door wide, but he responded gently.

"It makes a perfect match." Imogen's voice.

"What does?" Irène.

"Your carpet and your wallpaper."

French, springing to his feet.

"Yes. They're both very faded."

"Like the owners," Noel said, gesturing with the milk.

"I've brought cake only," said Irène, "but we have crumpets if you'd like them."

"Pyclets," Noel translated into demotic.

Imogen and Leslie French declined the offer, looking with approval on their thick slabs of Genoa cake.

"Home-made?" French asked Irène.

"I'm afraid not. Supermarket. Don't tell them in Japan, but it's delicious."

French now recalled a visit to the Wagstaffe house in Manchester when Ethel had boasted that she had made the cake.

"What sort was it?" Imogen.

"Was it good?"

"I can't remember. It wasn't awful. What surprised me was that she, the principal, the All-Highest, had stooped so near humanity as to bake a cake. I was new to Kay-Shuttleworth, and she seemed ancient and eminent. I am older now than she was then, but one has no idea at that age. I was impressed, and honoured that I'd been asked."

"Who else was there?"

"A scientist called Franks. Ethel wanted us to get together on some project, but it came to nothing. In fact, he left almost immediately. I'm not so sure that he didn't go to be an HMI. His wife was present, and said nothing. And Miss Commons."

"Did she comment on the cake?"

"Who?"

"Diddy. Deirdre Commons."

"Not that I remember. That was her line, wasn't it? No, no, she didn't. Nor did we use Christian names in those days. Dr Wagstaffe, Dr Franks, Miss Commons."

"That was better," Noel said. "Nowadays every woman you know is Gill or Sue." He frowned. "I can't distinguish. I can't remember names anyway."

"Ethel was meticulous about that. Don't make errors over people's names. Take trouble. Learn them."

"It's cosy in here," French said.

"It wasn't cold outside." Irène.

"No. But this is a most comfortable house. It feels lived-in. And welcoming."

"Would you have said that about my mother's house in Manchester?" Imogen asked.

French frowned slightly, as if the question disturbed him.

"It was well looked after, and tasteful. With large, old-fashioned furniture."

"It's still there. That was from my father's family."

"And plenty of pictures. And bright cloths and covers. I think your mother had picked up tips, ideas from some of the infant schools she visited. She always praised them to us for their drapes and bold colours. But in some ways, perhaps this is unfair, it was a bit like a school, either an odd mixture or regimented uniformity. Not quite human, if you know what I mean."

"Is that true, Imogen?" Irène gently.

"I never noticed. I was brought up there." Humouring them.

"Your house is harmonious and heart-warming. It is very slightly surprising and typically English."

"Well, Irène is responsible for it," Noel argued. He found French pretentious in this vein.

"Then you've become an Englishwoman."

"That's what my family say."

"And do they approve?" French pressed her.

"I don't know what it means. Neither do they. I expect I've changed some of my habits. I speak English all the time. I think in English, though sometimes I dream in French. Did you think in Japanese?"

"Not really. I taught English. And my colleagues were, at first at least, mostly English or American, so that we spoke English at work. I suppose I did occasionally use Japanese in my head, to myself, but rarely. I guess I felt that I must keep my English up-to-date and pristinely native, especially when as lately they tended to appoint more Japanese-born instructors."

"Will you be pleased to go back?"

"Yes, in a way, but . . . I shall be glad to see the boys, and my wife's parents. They have been very good to us. But I see the end of my time coming. I shan't do more than another three years of work there."

"And you'll come home?"

"I think so."
"Even if your sons stay?"
"Well. Yes. They'll be seventeen and nineteen then and won't have completed their education. It's tricky. Circumstances might alter. I could change my mind."
"You always had the idea of coming back?" Noel asked. "Even when your wife was alive?"
"I think so. I kept my house . . . I'm not sure. Her death changed everything. It was so unexpected. She was only forty-two. It came suddenly. It knocked me flat. We were coming over to Europe this year for a holiday at the end of my present contract."
"But you had no idea of settling?" Noel continued.
"No. Not really. Especially if I was offered another spell out there, which seemed likely. At the end of that we'd have had to think again. Because of the boys. But her end came so quickly, with three months warning, less than eighteen months ago. A brain tumour."
He shook his head to discourage further questions.
"I was lost."

"Did your wife speak English?" Irène brightening him.

"Fluently. We spoke it often at home."

The man looked thin, bloodless, raddled, his body made shabby by the smartness of his clothes. He sat, hands clasped together below his knees as he leaned forward. His high colour had disappeared; his hair lacked life; the veins in his grey hands swelled purplish, large.

Noel who a few moments ago had despised French for his conversation and its literary trivialities was shaken. Three or four sentences about his wife's death had changed Leslie French from a spruce, well-preserved, rather vain, loquacious sixty-year-old to an invalid, a frightened wreck.

Both women remained quiet, sympathetically so. Noel stood, walked over to the window to announce after scrutiny that the rain had stopped. Imogen came to be with him. Behind him he could hear Irène fiddling with the teapot. Imogen asked him a whispered question about a rose bush, which she named, *Gallica complicata*; she had no need of his answer. Noel hummed, conducting 'The

Gentle Maiden'. Imogen now inquired what the tune was. He meandered on about Somervell's arrangement and Hyde's translation into Irish. She murmured encouragement. They gave French time to recover.

When Noel turned round French sat as before, hands clasped, but without the disfiguring rigidity.

"Can I pour you another cup of tea?" Irène asked him.

"No, thank you, m'dear." French's voice had regained its strength.

"You've only had one. I shall be offended."

"All right. You've argued me into it."

He pushed himself up to pass cup and saucer, and stood, quite still, hand held out in anticipation. He took his cup without tremor, replaced it on his table, sat down and straightened the creases in his admirable slacks.

"You're very kind to me, Irène." His voice was deep, strongly produced, almost theatrical. "I shan't forget my visits to this house."

"Aren't you paying any more then?"

"I hope so. But we often fail to give

proper recognition of kindness rendered." Noel saw French as translating some flowery Japanese expression into a Victorian equivalent. It seemed unnecessary, forced.

The Smiths persuaded their guest to stay for the evening meal, when they talked with inordinate cheerfulness over their wine. Imogen and French were left together, with large gins while the hosts cleared up. Conversation in the sitting room appeared muted as though the meal-time joviality had dispersed itself. Imogen might well have been a headmistress offering hospitality to a distinguised visitor who would later distribute prizes. Formality ruled; friendliness came second. Each knew her or his place, acknowledged and respected it.

The evening grew more cheerful, but to Noel it seemed as if they had somewhere missed an opportunity to enjoy themselves. They talked, but at random, never revealed secrets, never laughed outright, tiptoed away from the serious. It was a pity.

When French left early, before ten o'clock, claiming he had to be up with the lark to visit a Japanese acquaintance in London, Noel felt tired, his shoulders and hips aching. Imogen helped Irène with her end-of day chores, refused more alcohol, but sat until past eleven, stiff-backed on the settee. Noel excused himself, tottered upstairs, undressed with clumsy speed, turned the lights out and was asleep seconds after his head touched the pillow. He did not hear Irène come to bed, but at midnight, his first visit to the lavatory, she slept comfortably.

21

"I DON'T quite fathom Leslie," Irène interrupted her husband.

They were both reading in bed, having half-heard the six-thirty radio news. Noel obediently laid his book on the duvet.

"I thought he was going to faint," she continued, "after he'd spoken about his wife's death. I've never seen anybody change so quickly. It was as if he were acting it. I'm sure he wasn't. He went chalk-white. And yet he never calls her by her name, always 'my wife'."

"Out of respect to our foreign ignorance."

"What is her name," Irène asked, "Mr Clever?"

"I've no idea. Was it some name like Ikuko? That comes to mind."

Irène laughed. "Where on earth have you dragged that from?"

"I don't know. There are plenty of Japanese names in the newspapers these days and perhaps that one has stuck. For all I know it's a man's name. Or even a surname. The Japanese put back to front like Chinese or Hungarians, I think. It just shows how ignorant we are of that part of the globe."

"Would you call Leslie normal?" she asked.

"No, not really. He's an actor. What about you?"

"I hardly know him, but yesterday afternoon in the King William he was attractive. And out in the rain by the river utterly charming. But then back here after he'd mentioned his wife, he changed. It was as if he'd switched off. Oh, he tried to be nice, and put on the right voice, but he never said anything interesting again."

"Did he before?"

"Don't you like him, then, Noel?"

"He's not my type, no."

"I do. He's vulnerable, but valuable." She laughed at her word play, as she always did, proud to be so dextrous in a foreign language. "I agree with you that he's a show-off and the rest, but I guess he'd be a marvellous teacher. But yesterday, that worried me and made me wonder if he's the right man for Imogen."

"That's hardly a decision for us."

"None of your dry, stiff upper lip. I know that quite well, but we can show interest, surely." Irène frowned, patting the bedclothes. "We don't want her to do anything silly, now, do we?"

"Who's to say she's an exception to the rest of the human race?"

"You've got it on you this morning. At least it shows you're concerned."

"Or I've got, or am about to get, out of bed on the wrong side."

"I shall talk to her about it. Do you think that's wrong?"

"No. As long as she's willing. She's not a young girl, you know, Irène. She's in her fifties, has had a very successful career. She might not thank you for interfering."

"She'll think I'm patronizing her?"

"Something of the sort. But do as you like. I wouldn't know how to start."

That was wrong; he knew how he would approach Imogen, though he had no intention of making the move.

"Do you think," he continued, "that he's serious about getting married? Whcre's our evidence?"

"I wonder about that myself. There was that first letter."

"Has Imogen said anything? To you? Recently?"

"My impression now is that she has. Well, hinted. But perhaps Leslie for all his outgoing ways is one of these frustrated, hog-tied people.

"Good word," Noel mocked.

"You just listen to me, and don't go wandering off into etymological subtleties."

"Yes, ma'am." He took her hand.

"What I'm trying to say is that he can't clearly express the things he feels deeply, especially in public."

"Not many of us can. At least, without practice. But I see what you mean. I don't know. He's knocked about the world. I was as shaken as you were to see him in such a state. It was as if it had suddenly burst on him where he was, what he was doing, what had happened to him. I don't think I'm an imaginative man, but it seemed unusual."

"So you're as worried as I am?" Irène

asked, banging her held hand and his on the coverlet.

"Worried? It doesn't concern me closely enough, but yes, roughly. You have a word with Imogen. I shall feel more . . . well, less anxious."

"Are you intending to say anything to him, Noel?"

"No. What could I say?"

"You're a devil for worming things out of people. And you've this innocent look in your eye so you can ask blunt, quite rude questions and not cause offence."

"Has Imogen said anything about going back to Manchester?"

"Not yet. I'm pleased, really."

"You get on well. You don't mind taking her to France, do you?"

"I shall enjoy her company."

They left it there, returned to their books, he to a John McGahern novel, she to Ronald Gray's *Cambridge Gardens*.

They were pleased with each other. As often now.

At breakfast Imogen said she should be getting home to Manchester.

"There's no hurry," Noel said.

"I've enjoyed every minute here. You've

done me good, and I shall come again if you'll have me, and I shall be going off soon to France with Irène, but it's time I started clearing things up."

"There's no rush, Imogen."

"I've decided to sell both houses. My mother's and my own. The market's not too good, but the agent who lets my mother's place thinks he'll easily get rid of it at a reasonable price as a nursing home for the elderly. Billy and I will share the proceeds. And as to my place, well, it was a temporary arrangement. I wouldn't choose to live there for the rest of my life."

"Where will you settle?"

"I haven't thought about that."

"Have you just this minute decided to start clearing up?" Irène asked.

"No. I've known all along what I was going to do. I've talked to Billy about it, over the phone as well as at the funeral, and Tom Friend, our solicitor. But yesterday I told myself that I was quite myself again, that I'd recovered from my mother's death and dying as far as I ever should, and so there was no possible excuse for procrastination. So tomorrow I go back."

"We're enjoying your company."

"I'm enjoying living here, but that's no excuse. Tomorrow. My mind's made up. In fact, I've already packed this morning."

They did not argue. Imogen again wrote letters on the dining-room table, quite unperturbed. Irène could hardly wait to question Noel.

"Do you think she's going back because of the way Leslie acted?"

"I've no idea." Noel, jovially gruff, noted his wife's disappointed face and made an effort. "She'd made up her mind what to do, and decided that the sooner she carries her decision out the better. She's like her mother. She wants action. Especially when she has to do what isn't very pleasant."

"Clearing the house?"

"Both houses." He coughed. "She asked me if there was anything we particularly wanted."

"And is there?"

"No. I said I'd ask you."

"I don't know what's there."

In her will Ethel had left her brother

a Bonington watercolour which in her last years she had kept, surprisingly, in the bank. He had not yet collected it, and remembered it only vaguely She had bought it years ago, on the advice of a friend, and had always seemed a little ashamed of her extravagance. Willie Wagstaffe had shown no enthusiasm, pronouncing it 'good' with a straight face; Noel guessed that this dry brother-in-law had been intrigued by his wife's action. Perhaps Ethel had achieved her ambition: to impress her husband.

At lunch Imogen outlined her plans. She knew exactly what was required.

"Won't you be sorry not to be able to go into the house where you were brought up?" Irène asked.

"I couldn't go into it before. Until the occupants were out. I was quite happy there. But it's only bricks and mortar."

"I left home when I was nineteen, thirty-nine years ago, but it seems now, and to be growing more so, the most important place in my life."

Imogen nodded, unclear.

"Has Leslie French sold his house in Cheshire?" Irène lining the target up.

"I don't know. Sometimes he wants to keep it, sometimes not. I think that was the place he was going to retire to, with his wife."

"Is it let out?" Noel.

"Yes. It's a small, newish, detached house in a decent district; that's how he described it. Nothing distinguished. I've not seen it, but once he said to me that it just about summed his life up. After all his world travels, he's ended up like some retired small-town bank manager.

"He must own a house or flat in Tokyo?"

"I think his place there belongs to his parents-in-law. They're quite well-to-do, I gather."

"He's a strange man," Irène chanced it.

"You can say that again."

Imogen appeared to be willing to talk about Leslie, to mull over his character, to discuss his future, but she in no way concerned herself deeply.

"I can't make up my mind whether or not he's attractive." Irène did not give up easily.

"I think he would have been good-looking when he was younger, but now he's old he's drying up, withering away, but because he's not running to fat he dresses in smart clothes for the youthful figure, and that makes the whole thing wrong."

"That sounds pretty damning," Irène said.

"No, he should wear shabby grey suits," Imogen answered her, "like an old schoolmaster, which is what he is. It's only his appearance I'm talking about, not his character."

"You'd give a favourable report there?" Noel, quizzically.

"I don't know him well enough. I'm suspicious of these actors. He has a beautiful voice, certainly. And he can use it. I guess that he's been pretty successful in his career, at least in so far as he's instructed his pupils outstandingly well, and had some influence on them."

"But he doesn't consider that's enough?" Noel.

"I guess again he wouldn't want to be an administrator. Perhaps he wanted one of his productions to do well in the outside world, to win some student competition, to be transferred to Edinburgh or the London stage."

"I see."

"He applied, he told me, to the BBC as a radio producer, but they wouldn't have him."

"Why was that? Did he say?"

"They liked someone else better. He mentioned one or two names, they meant nothing to me but were obviously highly regarded, who had been taken on at the same period that they refused him."

"Was he disappointed?"

"Yes. Who wouldn't be? He partly blamed my mother for giving him the wrong sort of testimonial. She praised him highly enough he said, but she should have asked him what it was the BBC wanted to hear. But Ethel thought she knew it all and wrote the wrong right things."

"Did he hold it against her?"

"It's a long time ago. I suppose he did. He didn't sound too vengeful, but he muttered on that it was typical. She always knew best, but in many ways she was a blinkered provincial who wrongly considered her opinions had universal validity."

"That sounds a thorough condemnation," Irène said.

"He didn't seem too hurt. Not now, anyway. And I guess he was probably right. 'Mother knows best.'" Irène mused on the judgement. Imogen made these confessions without emotion.

"One of my father's worst criticisms of a man," Noel said, "was: 'He's not to be told.'"

"You mean: he won't take advice."

"Yes. Even direct orders."

The three talked, worked in the garden together, sat unreading after dinner, discussed French and Ethel again, laughed a great deal, rather nervously, but enjoyed the, for them, noisy evening which ended soon after eleven.

When Imogen came down for breakfast she carried her cases with her, put them ready in the hall. She had, they found, stripped her bed, folded her bedclothes neatly enough, Noel said, for CO's inspection. The room was faintly redolent of her perfume. Imogen helped with the breakfast dishes, thanked them again with mathematical exactitude, loaded her car, hugged them warmly and was gone. She had a mournful expression, Noel commented, when she muttered her last words, "I shall miss you two."

"Do you think she meant it?" Irène asked him.

"Yes. For the moment."

"Do you wish she lived here, Noel? Permanently?"

"That's an odd question. I hadn't even considered it."

"Consider it now."

"Not really. I'm a conservative. I don't like change much. I've enjoyed her company, and you've helped her over a tricky period."

"Won't it be hard for her, clearing those houses?"

"No. She'll be efficient. Now that the tenants are out she'll have no trouble."

"Will there be a lot of stuff to be read? Ethel's correspondence and so forth?"

"Do you know I've no idea whether Ethel was a magpie or not. I have the vague notion that Ethel's study was kept locked so that the tenants couldn't get in.

Whether she had received letters that are interesting is another matter. Or whether she wrote anything."

"Do you think so?"

"I doubt it. Ethel will be, would have been one of your practical-advice-mongers. She wouldn't be so good at it as her husband; he had the advantage of appeal to the law books, but . . . I don't know, Irène. I'm making Ethel less interesting than she probably was."

"Did you think the obituaries in the newspapers got her right? I've just read your copies again."

"Yes and no. They listed her positions and committees, as they had to. But they didn't put their finger on her strength. She would have said that she was interested in the acquisition of wisdom or understanding through knowledge. There was this great, and ever-expanding corpus of knowledge, science, the arts, the newer social subjects. She even wrote to me about psychology and its relation to literary criticism years ago. So she made sure that her students knew a great deal, and just as crucially knew how to expand that knowledge.

It seems important to me. Even now. And right. She started when learning, the acquisition of knowledge was thought to be pre-eminent. Later, ideas changed. Liveliness of approach mattered. Not Gradgrindery. If one was mentally alert, then one could and would search out the information one needed. Or so the newer arguments went. Ethel wouldn't have it. 'Get used to acquiring the information' was her line. Feel guilty if you don't. I remember her quoting her brother Tom about modern mathematics, theory of sets, topology and so on being useless in junior schools. Not mathematics, he said. Mumbo jumbo for the majority of them. And he was a brilliant mathematician. And a terror."

"But Ethel and Tom would choose the knowledge to be acquired. They wouldn't allow, for instance, pop music on the curriculum."

"That's always the trouble with educationists. All of us. But Ethel's students left her college knowing a great deal more than they did when they entered. And that was no mean achievement on her part. She was, moreover, a good picker. She chose excellent staff."

"Leslie French?"

"Yes. He'd be marvellous as a young man. That's why she'd fall in love with him. Not only for his good looks, and her frustrations, but because he could and did carry out her will."

"You make her sound almost human," Irène ventured.

"And successful. She affected the way dozens of influential people thought."

"But not those from the top drawer? Wouldn't she have done better in a university with really bright pupils? Even in politics?"

"No." Noel considered his wife, who sat elegantly dressed, pretty still at the age of fifty-eight, her eyes wide, her mouth curled with mischief. "No, schools, grammar schools, training colleges were her place. There was no emphasis on research. Teachers were praised for their ability to teach, to enlarge their pupils' skills and learning. She could do that, and could organize it. And it's a fairly rare gift. When I consider what she managed and compare it with what I did, there's no doubt at all who was more successful. She was. Of course, I'm terribly out of date now, as I expected. Nobody takes my books very seriously. Oddly, Ethel's methods seem, if I am to understand the newspapers, to be coming back into favour."

They talked on, glad to be together, but missing Imogen.

"Was Ethel pleased with her achievement?" Irène asked suddenly as they were preparing to go upstairs to bed.

"To some extent. Yes, she was. Those who are going to shine have to look on themselves with favour a good part of their time. It's a necessity in the recipe for success. I expect she had moments of discouragement, or doubt. I'm sure she did. But, by and large, she was certain that what she was doing was right, and that she did it well."

"And when she retired?"

"She'd be lost. The likes of me can potter on with research. And I don't think for one minute I was as immersed in my job as she was. It was her life, as my work never was. I thought a large lot of my committee meetings were a waste of time."

Irène made for the door, looked round the room.

"Noel," she said, "Ethel thought you had done better; you were a professor."

"Yes, she would have liked a chair." His wife crossed in front of him, and he switched out the lights, closed up the sitting room. "That makes no difference. We can't always judge how well we're doing. She lived and took a leading part in the great age of the school; she was a teacher, a head, a college principal who helped shape, crystallize the thinking of that period. She was a leader. Among dozens or hundreds, yes. But amongst them she stood out. No, Irène, I can't see Ethel as anything but a success, however it may have appeared to her at the time."

"Even though her ideas have gone by the board?"

He smiled gently at the expression, which she had picked up from him as he had from his father. He wondered vaguely about its provenance. Marine? Over the side of the ship? Or the banquet table? He must look it up; he owed it to his sister.

"That happens to everybody, even though some of hers are creeping back into favour in one form or another, probably in ways she'd dislike."

"You admired your sister, Noel?"

"Yes. And feared her. She was energetic, bent on getting her own way. That's why she did so well. You get nowhere sitting about waiting for something favourable to happen to you. It rarely does. You have to make your own fate. Work for it."

"Did you?"

"In small ways."

They stood for a few moments in the quietness of the hallway, an elderly man and a middle-aged woman, before they toiled upstairs. Noel's hips ached as he dragged himself by the stair-rail, but he felt a solid, if momentary, satisfaction at a society which had produced his sister. Irène had reached the landing.

"Was she lovable?" she called down. He paused, painfully.

"You'd be surprised what and whom people choose to love. But, no, I don't suppose it was an outstanding characteristic."

"Did you love her, Noel?"

"Yes. She looked after me when I was young. We met only occasionally after she had left home, but, yes, she didn't mind showing overt affection for me. I was one of the few. Yes, I loved her."

He creaked up the rest of the treads, not certain that he had done justice to a notable woman.

Three days into the week Leslie French telephoned to thank them, belatedly, for their hospitality. He apologized profusely, if vaguely. He had been busy and preoccupied.

"I never visit your house without coming away alive with something to think about."

"Um." Noel did not intend to encourage French in this kind of talk. Downstairs, on the second telephone, Irène chattered, friendly, mocking, questioning.

"No. I shan't bother you with my problems. Even if I thought you could solve them." That's ambiguous enough, Noel decided. "Is it impossible to speak to Imogen?" He asked at length.

"She's gone back to Manchester?" Irène.

"Oh, I imagined she was staying longer. I must have misunderstood."

"She made her mind up suddenly." Irène explained Imogen's intention to empty and sell the two houses.

"I see." French sounded deflated. "I'll ring her there."

Again Irène flashed into detail, describing Imogen's phone calls to her. Noel, silent at his end, compared the bright speed of her voice with the glum, laconic rejoinders. It was French who rang off, rather rudely, saying he had to catch the next post. Noel waited for Irène to spin upstairs to ask for his opinion. She did not, and he was disappointed, returning to his reading. Literature, not life. Downstairs she sang cheerfully an Elgar song about a poet speaking to God in grief and thus finding fame. He despised words and setting, and in any case Irène needn't sound so damnably bucked about it.

At lunch Noel raised the question of French's call.

"What are these problems?" he asked.

"Raised by visits here?" He tried to sound exasperated, and failed.

"Imogen," she answered, "and Imogen again."

Leslie, she had decided, could not make up his mind. He saw the advantages of marriage to a woman of Imogen's achievements and attractions, but was doubtful of his reception from sons and ex-parents-in-law if he returned for his last three years in Japan with a new, foreign bride on his arm.

They discussed the issue, Noel unwillingly and shortly, but thrice. The last burst came at bedtime.

Irène thought, it appeared, that there would be little difficulty. If the Japanese parents were reasonable, all would be well. The boys would soon be used to a new foreign mother. Children, in her view, were tougher than adults. The difficulties existed only in Leslie's inadequacy, his lack of confidence, his proneness to invent nonexistent obstacles.

"You've got it all worked out," he chaffed her.

"Somebody has to. I'll ring her tonight to tell her he called. Noel, why didn't

Imogen tell him she was going back?"

"None of his business. Imogen wouldn't put off what she'd decided to do just because somebody else might have other ideas."

"Would she marry him, Noel, if he asked her?"

"I haven't the foggiest notion."

"What a ridiculous expression. I want her to be happy."

"What advice, then," Noel spoke slowly, one word detached from the next, "would you give her if she asked you whether or not she should marry?"

"She wouldn't do it; ask, I mean."

"But if she did?" Noel laughed at his own childish obstinacy.

"I wouldn't consider him. Not in a million years."

"Oh, dear." He coughed ironically. "He'd be disappointed. He likes you." Noel stroked his chin. "He really set his stall out to impress you."

"Imogen. Not me."

"I don't think so."

"You don't like him very much, do you?"

"I keep telling you he's not my type.

He's his own worst enemy."

The conversation was broken, between visits to the bathroom, the struggle out of clothes, Irène's brief attention to her face. Noel, if he admitted it to himself, was slightly jealous of French, but on Imogen's account, not his wife's. He did not want French to carry his niece off, to Japan, Cheshire, anywhere. That seemed unnecessary. Immy was her own woman, with a career behind her, and a strong retirement to follow. She should not (Noel mocked his own certainties) lumber herself with French, who'd demand much and give little in return.

In bed Irène said she'd telephone Imogen who had not been at home earlier in the evening. Noel closed his book, finger-marking the place, to listen. No one answered; Irène allowed the phone to ring on.

"She may be at the other house," Noel said, "still working."

He went downstairs quite sprightly for the telephone book, read out the number. Irène pressed buttons, repeating, copying his voice, disturbing the air in the wide hall of William Wagstaffe's villa. No reply.

"She's out." Irène voiced the obvious.

Disappointed they settled to their books.

"We should have a television set up here," Irène said.

Noel groaned, comically, read a sentence of Paul Theroux.

"Yes, dear."

22

IRENE finally spoke to Imogen after two days of failure; the niece had been away at a friend's in Derbyshire, and now she had started her clearance of the two Manchester houses.

"Will it be a big job?"

"Yes. My mother's place will. Though it was to some extent cleared up first after my father died and then again when we let the house. Of course, there's my mother's study which we kept locked."

"Did your father not work there?"

"No, he had his own place downstairs. The house is really huge. A warren."

"And his is tidied up?"

"Yes, my mother and Diddy saw to that after he died."

Irène let on that Leslie French had been round asking for Imogen. "He threatened to get in touch with you."

"He hasn't succeeded yet. But that's not surprising."

"Noel and I keep discussing him, and

whether we like him or not. What do you think?"

"He's decent enough. A bit fond of himself, perhaps."

"I thought he was what Noel calls rather sweet on you."

"He's what I'd call susceptible. But he'll change his mind, I expect."

Irène left it at that, reporting the conversation to Noel, but as they were preparing for bed, Imogen rang again to say that French had caught up with her.

"And do you know what he wanted?" Imogen sounded amused.

"To marry you."

"Oh, Irène. You're incorrigible. No, he wants to write a biography of my mother."

"Is that a good idea?"

"Well, I didn't encourage him. He's the sort of man who'd need help and comfort all the time. And moreover, he put it in a way that I didn't take kindly to. He said he'd worked it out that he'd now have sufficient money to retire, but he didn't want to give up regular work unless he had some quite substantial substitute. And this the biography would provide. He'd have to work on it in England."

"What did you say?"

"Say? Very little. But I thought the more. What about his boys? Isn't he responsible for their education and keep? He appeared quite content to leave that to his wife's parents."

"They're rich, aren't they? And perhaps they're pressing him."

"It all seems feeble to me. Not that I raised the matter. I merely asked him if he'd done any preliminary work on the book, or if it was just an inspirational moment." The sarcasm cut.

"And?"

"Oh, a great torrent. He'd been considering it on and off for years, but now with Ethel's death and his opportunity to settle down full time to write it, the idea seemed particularly apposite. He talked all right. A great deal too much for me. He doesn't realize, in the slightest, when he's overdoing it. He's no real judgement. Especially of his effect on people. Or, at least, on me." Imogen sounded tart.

"And what was your answer?"

"I said I couldn't prevent it, if that's what he wanted to do. But I also said that I'd consult Noel; if he gave a favourable answer then I'd seriously think about it myself. It would hold me up. He'd want access to Ethel's papers, whereas I'd just shovel them away and burn them."

"That would be a pity."

"Irène, you're as sentimental as he is. You see, I wonder who'd want to read a book about my mother? I doubt if she was as important as all that."

"But if he wrote it really well, it wouldn't much matter about Ethel's relative place in the world. The book itself would be the attraction."

"I don't see that, any more than I see him producing a classic. He'd make a fair job, that is if he didn't cave in, but it would need to be about somebody in the public eye for a publisher to look at it. Anyway, ask Noel, will you?"

"Would you like to speak to him? He's right here now."

"There's no need. And no rush. Just invite him to think about it. At his leisure. It will do friend French no harm to wait a day or two. If he's serious about this project, a few obstacles in his way will be an advantage."

"You're a hard woman."

"All my life, Irène, I've been plagued by people with stupid bright ideas."

They left it there.

Over drinking-chocolate Irène put the question to her husband, and watched as he assumed the role of a stuttering professor thinking. He stroked his chin, rolled his head about, plastered down his thinning hair with flat fingers. She enjoyed the performance, encouraged him, telling him not to hurry, to deliberate.

"Ethel was never quite a national figure," he pronounced.

"And is that the criterion?"

"Well. These days. Cartoon characters, puppets, television readers and actors and comics and sportsmen are all enormously well known. And therefore, they or their creators are deemed worthy of biography."

"Only because the quick sale of these books will make money for publishers," she argued.

"Hasn't that always been the case?"

he returned. "With a few honourable exceptions? Now Ethel was known in limited circles. She managed *Who's Who*. But."

He began to nod, almost violently, as if he were qualifying himself for fame as a television puppet. She wondered if he had deliberately veered from the subject.

"Would Ethel's life be interesting?" Irène pressed.

"To whom? That's the snag. Let me try to put it clearly. Ethel was the head of several, three, successful educational institutions. But they were provincial. All propounded methods that are now regarded as old hat. All depended too much on the printed or written word. She wrote one book, which is again not only out-of-date but has been long out of print. She was a member of a national committee responsible for an influential report, which will be mentioned in the histories of education, but has little to recommend it to modern theorists or classroom practitioners. She had no pupils who are considered distinguished by our society. No well-regarded ideas can be directly attributed to her. Most of her contemporaries are dead."

"So she might as well, according to you, not have lived?"

"I don't say that. She was influential, but in rather out-of-the-way places."

"Like some provincial town clerk or backbench MP?"

"Yes. Especially if such have done their work well. Some of the fine boulevards in this city are the work of, to us, an early, unknown town planner. Most can't name him, but we can enjoy his skill, his foresight, his choice."

"Do you know his name?"

"Brown."

She laughed, wondering if he had made this up.

"Let's just think," Noel began again, "about Ethel, because I'm in no position to judge French's qualifications as a biographer. Ethel had considerable influence, though not as much as she would have wanted. She fought, for instance, hard for the academic content of the B. Ed. and used to claim that her students would know more at the end of her old course at Kay-Shuttleworth about their own subject than they would at the end of that degree. She lost. It's interesting now that right-wing groups are taking exactly her line. It's a fascinating bit of social history, but it would hardly make a book. Perhaps an article or two.

"What about her effect on students? Individually?"

"She belonged to the period of the Great-I-Am heads of institutions."

"Like you?"

"Yes. Though she did it better than I did. She was a powerful figure. If you were called in front of Ethel it was a bit like appearing before a high-court judge. Signs of kindness might well appear, but they'd tend to be lost in the pomp and ceremony. And Ethel could be a bully."

"That's not too good?"

"Oh, I don't know. I don't suppose that girls who became pregnant at Kay-Shuttleworth would run to her to confide. But Ethel would have some member of staff or matron who'd know how to deal with the situation sympathetically. She was a first-rate organizer in that way. In public she was a decent speaker, clear, always had things to say, even if she was never a spellbinder. But she looked the part. She was a success, though she felt in her last years that the education system was slipping sadly, but she was only known inside very limited circles. If she appeared on radio or television, it was on programmes of minority interest. The national newspapers rarely made even small headlines of her pronouncements."

"It could still be interesting, though." Irène waited for his answer. "Couldn't it?"

"I can see it as a little book produced for ex-students of the college. With lists of sponsors at the front. See your name in print. Or a longish biographical essay on the KS centenary magazine in due course. Ethel did remarkably well, make no mistake. *Si monumentum requiris, circumspice*. There'll still be students of hers in the schools from thirty years ago who may have clung on to one or two of her ideas. And I'd have to agree with you if you told me that her life would be just as readable as that of television cooks or games and quiz-panel players or politicians or footballers or even actors, but their names are known and that is what sells the book."

"There's not much hope, then?"

"Not as a commercial proposition, no." Noel scratched his head. "I'd like to read it. Her struggles with some awkward director of education, her attempts to convince her staff that they should make timetable or curriculum changes would interest me more than any accounts of cup finals or Broadway first nights, but then I'm not your usual reader. Teacher-training colleges are inherently as fascinating to me as big-game hunts in Kenya, or foreign cities, or contacts with royalty or appearances at the Scala, Milan. Even the darker corners of MI5. But there's no supporting cast in Ethel. The people she worked with were clever, well-intentioned people who were interested in seeing that working and lower-middle-class children had a fair start in life and that clever and assiduous pupils were encouraged, and so her acquaintances were prepared to go out and teach in colleges and schools to see that these ideas were realized. But such people don't run across the duke of this or that in places where notables eat, or exchange banalities with well-known Autocue readers, or share a speed-boat or a ski slope or a howdah with a personality. They merely go to work five days a week, and give up some of their evenings and Saturdays and holidays to make sure they're doing their job to their own satisfaction."

"You sound cynical?" Irène's voice was tender.

"I don't understand our society."

"Was Ethel very unusual?"

"I speak without my book, but I suppose she'd be amongst the best six heads of training colleges since 1918. It's impossible to know how to judge such matters. But she made Kay-Shuttleworth a known and respected name amongst those who were interested in such things. And, moreover, she was a woman. She had to be better than the men to be given a chance. But whether she'll appear in the textbooks of the history of education like Arnold or Thring or Sanderson or even James Kay-Shuttleworth, I don't know. Survival, in literary terms, is a very odd business."

"If Leslie wrote a really detailed

account, let's say of life on the staff at Kay-Shuttleworth thirty-odd years ago, wouldn't that be of interest to historians in the future?"

"Only if education in the Fifties was, for some personal or contemporary reason, in fashion with them. Why should, let's say, an account of a Wimbledon final be more important than that of a student's first day at college or a squaddie's first day in the army. I can see that the battles of Ypres, or Passchendaele, or Stalingrad, or the dropping of the atom bomb on Hiroshima or Nagasaki could be regarded as world-shaking events, and that eye-witness accounts by individuals, especially if they were perceptive, would somehow carry more weight because of the importance of the event. But I don't know. I read a fascinating account by a very intelligent man of his recovery from schizophrenia but neither agents nor publishers would touch it. No popular appeal."

"No sex and violence."

"Something of the sort. The reader would have to work too hard. But in any case Ethel's battles would be dull and long-drawn-out. She'd perhaps lose sleep over them, but no reader would. Like the selling-off of a piece of college land to build houses. Much said on both sides. Serious committees. Official advice and conviction and pride in status all there, but most readers want something more gripping. My father went to what he called class meetings and prayer meetings when I was a boy and at these people 'gave their testimony', that is, told how they were converted and what the effect on their lives had been. As far as I can make out these were delivered in set terms, were dull as the speakers were dull, but were heard because everyone at the meeting accepted the importance of conversion, the changed life on earth and the eternal life hereafter. They needed to be reminded, even in this boring, formalized way of the importance of their accepted forms of evangelical religion."

"And?"

"So with French's account of Ethel. If, for some reason, God knows what it might be, the educational system from the Twenties to the Sixties becomes seemingly significant," Noel leaned on the word with heavy, breathy irony, "then Ethel will be worth reading about."

"But that's unlikely?"

"Yes. And there's one other thing. Just warn Imogen that French will want to poke into her private affairs. What sort of mother was she? Had she time to spend on her children? Did she rule the roost at home? Did she provide nourishing or exotic meals for the family? He'll be digging for anecdotes. She might not be pleased."

"So you're against the biography?"

"Again, yes, but my opinion's of no account. These objections should be bluntly put to French, and then if he's still determined, he should be allowed to get on with it. He may be wasting months, years of his life to no end. He must want to do the job, be determined to do it for its own sake."

"Nobody wants to write unless there's a chance of readers."

"I agree."

Irène gave her account of the conversation to Imogen and then made her husband repeat it for himself. When he had finished, and Imogen had questioned him, she said solemnly, "Your wife did justice to you. She reported you really accurately."

"She's clever. She probably made my point of view clearer than I did." Imogen didn't deny it. "Have you decided what you'll say to French?"

"Get on with it. I'll tell him what you say, and what I think, and I'll give him all the help I can. Then it's up to him."

"Has he written anything before?"

"Some English course for the Japanese, and articles in various journals. So he said. But not a book. Do you think he's capable, Noel?"

"How can I know? When I watch modern biographers at work I'm baffled. They write at inordinate length, quoting great swathes of letters and documents. Of course, they are omitting the larger proportion, but not enough for me."

"Didn't Victorian biographers write in this lengthy way?"

"Oh, yes. But they were writing for an audience which was used to length, had the leisure to read properly. And they concentrated on the public life, be it politics or poetry. Since Freud, it's all been different. We need our scandals and dark sides. Now I know you said Ethel fell in love, if only temporarily, with French, and perhaps with other young men on her staff. But there was no word of this to these favourites. Only when it seemed overwhelming was it mentioned to your father, perhaps with the object of killing or containing the desire. Such matters ought to be dealt with, but it will need a delicate touch."

"You mean," Imogen asked, "that my mother never committed adultery?"

"I guess that she never even considered it."

"Why was that?"

"Ah, now you're trying to make a biographer of me. Asking me to guess. Well, pressures of society, for a start. There was adultery, I don't doubt, even in Manchester and Kay-Shuttleworth, but in Ethel's case she didn't put passion before her ambitions. Perhaps she wasn't highly sexed, or had a perfectly satisfactory sexual relationship with your father. I'd need further evidence."

"That of your own eyes wasn't good enough?"

"It was not. We hardly met. We were all too busy furthering our careers. I guess I wasn't much good as an observer of that sort. Do you remember that man who came over when we were having lunch at the King William the Fourth? Some time ago he sent his wife, a really beautiful woman and an old student of Ethel's, to consult me about their marital difficulties."

"And?"

"We talked. She said it had helped clear her mind. She spoke of further meetings or invitations to visit, but nothing came of it. She wrote me one card of thanks, an Anthony Green painting of an ugly woman with her legs apart, drinking tea, showing her knickers on a balcony high over a garden. Beyond that, nothing."

"What do you conclude?"

"That I'd been no help. Or she'd become too busy or immersed elsewhere to want to continue the acquaintanceship."

"Did you, do you feel disappointed?"

"We all like to think we have power.

So, yes. And she was good to look at, though I'm an old man."

"No deficiency of sex urge there?" Did she resent his slur on her mother's libido?

"If only you knew." He shook his head helplessly at the phone. "This biography business has been worrying me. There's a man living in this street who is said to have served in one of the German death camps. He's a Balt of some kind. Though I'm not sure that the word hasn't connotations of landowning, the squirearchy. He'd be, at the best, an NCO. But corporals would be something, in a position of influence, lance-jacks organizing the death squads. Now for years he's worked in this town in the ironworks, a quiet, dull man, a good worker, a father and grandfather. He waddles down the street as I do."

"You don't waddle."

"Thanks. He's my age. If it's true about his service with the SS or whatever, that would have lasted perhaps four-five years at most. Now what sort of biography would he deserve?"

"What's worrying you, Noel?"

"I wonder how many of us, given that man's circumstances, would have acted in the same way. In our armed forces NCOs were taught to bawl at their recruits. I remember A. J. Ayer in his autobiography recalling in a shocked way how somebody had slanged him about untidiness in a way that wouldn't have been tolerated in his sort of civilian life. And so I don't think most men would have taken long to get used to killing Jews or 'inferior' races by the hundred when they were ordered to."

"What's this to do with Ethel?"

"Old age, stupidity, the meandering mind. Odd thoughts about biography. I apologize."

"Sometimes, Noel, you frighten me. You make ordinary life sound seriously flawed. I don't mean minor faults. You're not completely pessimistic, are you?"

"No. There are balancing good things. Music, painting, verse which are as outstanding, heartening and human, as these atrocities are bad."

"Yes."

They rang off, she subdued. Noel felt

that he had allowed his own foolishness, his propensities to darkness, to dominate the conversation. He said as much to his wife.

"Oh, Imogen will make allowances for you. She knows you."

"Do you think I'm pessimistic?"

"Not really. Only old."

Irène laughed, callously, he thought, and walked out to her kitchen where she was baking. Her gas stove cheered. He could not understand why he felt depressed, but surprisingly found himself less gloomy by the next morning.

For more than a week they heard nothing from either Imogen or Leslie French. Irène was now beginning to consider her Christmas shopping having convinced her husband that they should both spend that holiday with her mother. Imogen had suddenly decided that she was too busy to accompany her aunt to France for a week at the end of October, and perhaps on this account considered herself in Irène's bad books. Irène certainly had not been pleased, had put herself out to make sure that the short holiday would be interesting, and so perhaps her brief, rattled reply to Imogen's letter had been taken amiss.

"I wonder if Leslie has started the biography," Irène asked her husband.

"I think about it pretty well every day." He sounded sarcastic.

"Do you come to any conclusions?" Irène, disingenuous.

"That Ethel was an elitist."

"And dull?"

"Probably. She picked out people by examination. She saw her teachers as an elite corps, but they had to win and deserve their places. And they would influence others who were not so gifted, who would slave at factory benches, but would have learnt something in school about science and poetry and the distant world." Noel stroked his face. His wife smiled at him.

"It sounds good," Irène answered. "Did it work out?"

"I doubt it."

"Why not?"

"Not enough Ethels about. And people lost their belief in the importance of the subject matter they taught."

"It's sad. It's so even in France now."

"'These be your Gods.'"

They wandered away from each other, dissatisfied with Beechnall and themselves.

"I hope he writes it," Irène called back, fresh-voiced.

23

AT the end of October Irène went on her own to France and family.

They had heard twice from Imogen who gave dry-as-dust accounts of the clearing of her mother's house which would be sold in due course, very profitably, as a nursing home for the elderly. Now it was almost empty. The first letter mentioned Leslie French who had made a start on the biography by spending a week in the Kay-Shuttleworth building, and examining polytechnic and education authority records. She made no attempt to evaluate his success. The papers from Ethel's study had been stowed for sorting in one wicker basket he had provided and had already been stored in the spare room of the Lukes' house in Beechnall. Imogen wasn't too sure where Leslie was or what exactly he was doing. The second letter did not mention him at all. Noel had already drawn Irène's attention to advertisements in the

Times Literary Supplement and *Times Higher Educational Supplement* asking for information about Ethel Wagstaffe.

"He's serious then?" Irène.

"He always gives that appearance. I suppose he's announced his project to his boys and the grandparents."

"Why do you say that, Noel?"

"I wonder if he'll get an answer from them that will change his mind, have him haring off back to Japan."

While Irène chivvied her family in France and reported the results by phone, Noel tidied the garden, read a little, listened to Radio Three and felt mildly off colour. He was pleased to hear Imogen's voice on the telephone, cheerful and brisk.

She had finally cleared her mother's house, had put into store such furniture as she wanted for herself, had tried to rouse the interest of her brother, William, but had failed and therefore ignored him.

"You surprise me," Noel answered. "I've found that when wills are in question people, even the kindest, become predatory. And those who already have, plenty want their full share, pressed down and running over.

"I did get Shirley, his wife, up here."

"And?"

"She's a reasonable woman. She said what she'd like. Not too much. Now I've taken my dip, and the rest will be sold. There'll be some valuable things, silver, pictures and furniture. They're all in at the auctioneer's. Your Bonington's been valued; I had to arrange that with the bank, and I'll have it delivered to you inside the next few weeks. And would you care for that print from my mother's bedroom, the soulful lady? I hardly like offering it to you, because if you don't want it it'll go straight into the dustbin. It's a cheap affair. You remember it, don't you? Ethel said you admired it when you were young."

"It was the nearest thing in the Smith household to a sex object. Bare shoulders."

"Would you like it?"

"Yes, please."

Imogen laughed. "You're always too diplomatic, Noel. It doesn't please me that you take it."

"Ethel valued that picture because some young man once told her it resembled her."

"That shows how we can deceive ourselves." Imogen slowly sucked in breath. He heard the sound clearly, could identify it. "My mother looked like one of those huge fierce ladies with henpecked husbands on old seaside postcards."

"I didn't think you knew about such things."

"Now you know."

Noel chuckled. He remembered the occasion when a fellow scientist had sent just such a card to Tom; his brother and his mother and father had failed to hide their shock from their youngest son. A small man peered owlishly over the fence to where a stout woman squatted with a trowel in the border at the corner of her garden, her face scarlet with outrage. The dialogue ran: 'I see, madam, you've weed in your garden.' 'HOW DARE YOU!!!' J. T. Smith had sniffed his disapproval. His wife had been pale, having taken a first glimpse, perhaps in anticipation of his displeasure. The card had arrived while the family were still at breakfast. Joseph had guffawed, then blushed beetroot. Thomas abroad, missed the effect on the family. The Smith parents, sensibly, limited the length of their strictures, so that the keen-eared Noel learned nothing he should not. Ethel picked up the card, raised her eyebrows, returned it to the tray, did not laugh. Father Smith could not resist a final word of disapprobation.

"A waste of money," he pronounced, "and vulgar." Nobody spoke. Perhaps encouraged by the silence, he proceeded. "It seems a pity that a man with a first-class honours degree should choose to send this to another similarly qualified. And both, I ask you, almost doctors of philosophy." He seemed strangely agitated. "Doctors indeed. Utterly childish." The subject was dropped, but ten minutes later when Father Smith donned his raincoat and bowler hat in the hall the subject was playing obviously on his mind still.

Ethel passed.

"Childish," her father growled. "I cannot understand such infantile . . . " He broke off.

"'Unless ye be converted, and become as little children, ye shall not enter into the kingdom of heaven.'"

She spoke as if to herself, but ethereally, and passed through the hall, stately as Maud. Noel coming down the stairs with a satchel looked, not without fear, at his father's glaring eyes. The old man's face was flushed. Ethel had disappeared.

"There's a great deal of difference between 'childish' and 'childlike'," his father instructed him. Smith senior opened the front door, kissed his wife who had kept away until the right moment and walked the length of the street with his son, face clear, mind now occupied elsewhere.

In later years Noel had tried to interpret this memory.

Ethel would not have seen much advantage in the card itself. Had she noticed that her father appeared ill-tempered or off colour that morning, and taken her opportunity to rile him? He could not guess. Ethel was not a vindictive woman. The oblique attack, making a merely verbal point by quoting a sacred text, was more like Noel's style than his sister's. Ethel preferred to be straightforward, directly blunt. But why had she raised the matter at all? A blow for feminism? A woman demonstrating to men how unimportant were many of the matters on which they chose to lay down the law? A plea to her father to be more liberal, to think again. A joke about cheating or stealing or over-eating would have been acceptable, but not one about excretory or sexual functions. Smith was an intelligent man; his defence would have been that polite society had decreed some subjects taboo, and it was therefore sensible to observe the prohibition, unless there was great advantage to be gained. He was a serious man, had mildly complained once to a notable visiting preacher for repeating in the pulpit a story about some American frontiersman who had defended his deception of an east coast rube with the text: 'I was a stranger, and ye took me in.'

Noel, later in life cherished the innocence of these remembered certainties; found substance in his father's refusal to say 'damn' however great the provocation, in the old man's strict prohibition of alcohol lest his example tempt some weaker brother into sin. Ethel, Tom and Noel were freer, though oddly, Joe had retained much of his father's back-street-chapel primness of mouth. Old J.T. would have demanded of his free-thinking children if they were the better for drinking wine or swearing and might mischievously have asked if adultery was now numbered amongst their new-found freedoms. Tom, always extrovert, would cheerfully have claimed it as a favourite pastime merely to show disapproval of puritan dogma, but Ethel would have agreed with her father about drawing the line though with a more liberal interpretation of liability.

Thinking of his sister, Noel Smith wondered how he would have interpreted this incident to a biographer. He himself would have drawn his own line, would not have mentioned the postcard to French. It appeared too trivial. Ethel needed something more serious than a poor music-hall joke to defend. Would she have approved of his censorship? He could not say. Ethel could compromise as well as she could hector. Leslie French would have his work cut out.

Imogen telephoned to inquire how Irène was enjoying France. She expressed her regrets that she had withdrawn from the expedition, but said there had been no chance of holidays while she had to clear her mother's house.

"It's upbringing," she said, cheerfully. "Eat your bread and butter first, then you can have your cake."

"I've reached an age where I prefer bread and butter."

"I've been thinking about these things. Leslie French sent me a huge questionnaire on my mother over a week ago. I've been thinking about it, and spent the whole of yesterday filling it in."

"Where is he?"

"Beechnall, c/o Professor Luke. Do you have difficulty answering these questions? I do. There were queries about Ethel's politics. She voted at every election as far as I know, but never joined a political party. We didn't discuss it much either when I was younger, or later. I remember her saying that, though she was an old-fashioned Liberal turned Labour, education did better in the Macmillan era because the country was more prosperous. Ethel would be a materialist. Mother knows best. The state, and its advisers, must make sure that excellence was always available to its citizens."

"She would have been disappointed recently?"

"I suppose so. We never spoke of education in these last months."

"No." Noel cleared his throat. "Was French's interrogation good?"

"Long. Repetitive." Imogen sounded dismissive. "He spattered the target. He could have covered the same amount of ground with about a quarter of the number of questions."

"But you filled them in?"

"Yes. With a bit of 'refer to my answers to question 23 and question 24', you know."

"You haven't seen him?"

"No. Except for half a day in the Kay-Shuttleworth period. He called in, at very short notice, and asked to be shown around my mother's house and garden. It was inconvenient, but I obliged him. He brought a camera, took a thousand and one photographs, made copious notes. It was sensible, I suppose."

"Had you cleared the place?"

"No, but I'd made a large start. It looked nothing like what it was in my father's day. He also borrowed some photographs of my mother from the albums. He'd only need them for a week, he said, but I've heard nothing of them since."

"It takes time to make copies. Commercially."

"I don't suppose he's lost them." Imogen didn't sound confident, he thought. "I'd never wondered before," she changed tack, "why my mother didn't stand for the council. Do you know?"

"I guess," Noel mumbled his answer, very slowly, "that she'd think she'd concentrate on what she did best. A council's job was to provide her with all the money she asked for, and hers to use it wisely. Fighting over priorities with transport or roads or housing or dustbins was important, but not important enough to rob her of the time she could spend on her real work. She served on the education committee and the university senate and so forth, but there she used her expertise. The sort of establishments she worked in were well regarded and, comparatively speaking, well funded. The larger side of politics — where does the money come from? how do we divide it? — never concerned her except perhaps at times of election or crisis. Another thing that has crossed my mind is that your father held a very low view of politicians, and this may have had its effect."

"I never noticed."

"No. You may be right. I can mention it to you but not to French."

Imogen thanked him for his tact, reflected sourly on French's shortcomings, then paused.

"I've been thinking, Noel, about my mother's life, almost as if I were going to write it myself."

"A good idea."

"No, thanks. But I wondered how I'd set about it. Just in case Leslie asked my advice. I take it he hasn't tried his questionnaire on you, has he?"

"Not yet."

"A pleasure to come. Do you know, I see her life as a series of heaps, almost randomly made up. That's my picture."

"How is one heap divided, distinguished from another, then?"

"Chronologically. Early life, school, university, first job, marriage, family, first headship. That sort of thing. But as you look at each pile, you can change one ingredient about with another without much overall effect."

"Wouldn't that be so for most of us?"

"I don't know. I've never thought about it before."

"Would it be so in your own case?" Noel asked.

"Very likely, but I don't consider myself nearly the success my mother was, and changes in society made my way that bit easier."

"Is there nothing common to your mother's heaps?"

"She was strongly competitive and ambitious. And clever."

"And these I take it," Noel pressed, "hardly seem suitable attributes of a modern saint?"

"She wanted to be outstanding, but for herself."

"Couldn't that still have valuable social results? I'd choose a headmaster or college principal every time if he was capable of brilliant ideas or practical schemes or of carrying his staff and students with him, and pay no attention at all to motive. God knows that would be hard enough to sort out in any case. I'd judge a life on what was achieved, not why. Ethel had a powerful if limited effect for good on hundreds of people, and that's what counts, not that she wanted to score off her father, or the male sex, or equal her brothers' successes."

"She was disappointed that she never became a professor, Noel."

"Yes. You always say so. It's sad. She would have done the university proud. But I guess she had a wider influence staying where she was at Kay-Shuttleworth."

"Why didn't the university appoint her?"

"I don't know. I never made inquiries either from her or from people I know there. At a guess I'd say they wanted some younger man. There'd be talk about the future, broader horizons, a modernistic outlook, importance of schemes of research. Ethel's old-fashioned corpus of knowledge to be acquired would be seen as a hindrance rather than as an advantage."

"And who was right?"

"Much to be said for both sides. Ethel thought one ought to know the rules before you broke them. Her opponents wouldn't see any sense in acquiring rules you were going to dispense with in any case."

"Where do your sympathies lie?"

"As usual, all over the place. The very large majority of people are not going to be original, break new ground. On the other hand, it doesn't do too much harm, especially with clever people, to make them consider that they are capable of thinking in new ways."

"Even when they're not."

"Even when they're not. It tends towards liveliness, and that's a virtue." He coughed. "All this shows how difficult a biography is. Would Ethel have done better to remain a classroom teacher, introducing individuals to new educational experiences, as she was originally, or did we all profit when she moved, like you, into administration?"

"There are fewer gifted administrators than teachers," Imogen said.

"I doubt that. Besides, consultant surgeons still perform in the operating theatre."

"You think I and my mother did the wrong thing?"

"Nothing of the kind."

They left it there.

As he was settling down to prepare his lunch next day Irène rang from France to say that her mother was in hospital. Mme Dalsaux had suffered a heart attack in the small hours, but had begged not to be taken to the city infirmary.

"Why was that?"

"She said she wanted to die at home. They're peasants, my family, even the educated ones."

"But?"

"We convinced her by the light of day. She needed treatment. She wasn't going to die. I went with her. We shall go again later this afternoon. She was comfortable enough."

Irène seemed much in control; she was

not averse to taking the lead, laying the law down, and her relatives found her sufficiently forceful, or foreign, to allow this. She spoke to her husband rapidly in English to keep her sisters in the dark. When he rang that evening she reported that her mother was still very ill.

"Are they hopeful?"

"Her age is against her. But, yes."

"Do you want me to come over?"

"There's no need. Just see to the cat. I shan't be home for a week or so, I expect. You can manage."

The postman delivered a large envelope from Leslie French. It held the questionnaire, a list of those to be interrogated together with a demand for further names, and a letter.

This opened with an account of French's qualifications to write Ethel Wagstaffe's life, and claimed that already 'new and fascinating' lines had presented themselves. 'I had expected that educational concerns would be the foundation on which I'd base Principal Wagstaffe's biography. This will not be altogether so. My few weeks of research, intense and intensive I must admit, have suggested otherwise. She is revealed as a much more complex and endearing human being than the public figure we observed gracing educational platforms.'

Noel sniffed.

He was as interested in muckraking as the next man, but wondered what secrets French had turned up. Very few, he suspected. The prose style reeked with exaggeration. Noel laughed to himself, dismissively.

The final paragraph offered news.

'This weekend I shall fly out to Tokyo. The writing of the biography will occupy two or three years at least and will require a constant sojourn in England. Now that I have made such rapid progress with the work in these past few weeks, advance far beyond my wildest expectations, it seems best for me to return to Japan on two grounds. First, I must amicably terminate my university contract as well as make provision for the education of my sons. There will be snags there. I had hoped to supervise their lives for the next three years, but I shall not be able to do that and (twice strongly, uselessly, underlined) work on the biography. If

I am satisfied that my sons are well looked after, and their futures assured, and my parents-in-law have so far been wise and generous benefactors to them, then I can return with a quiet mind to England to complete this book, which will, it is my earnest hope, crown my life's work. These few weeks which I shall spend in Japan will moreover give me the opportunity to look over my task from a distance, and this can only bring advantage. To see, to consider an English provincial project from the far side of the world must add further perspectives. I hope that when I have begun to write I shall be able to call upon your good offices to read and comment on the work in progress.'

Noel pulled a wry face. His sincerely. Leslie A. D. French. Les the Lad, and his constant sojourn. Poor Ethel. Lapped in the embalming bandages of French's slimy, deathless prose. He returned the letter to envelope, to rack.

There had been no mention of Imogen.

Early that evening Noel read the letter over the telephone to his niece. They laughed at the phraseology.

"He's a poor fish," she said.

"Oh, I thought you might be keen on him."

"No, thanks. Though he did suggest that I went to Japan with him. He'd be able to show me the ropes."

"No underlying motive?"

"I wouldn't think so. You've been living too long with Irène."

They chaffed each other.

"What do you think," he asked later, "of these fascinating lines French has discovered about your mother?"

"They don't exist outside his head. Ethel kept herself to herself. There were very few private letters. Notes on lectures about discipline, corporal punishment, curriculum reform and so on. And these hints, yours about the young man who thought the picture resembled her, and my father's tale that she had been in love with French, they all would have been tactfully forgotten, put aside, buried. Her life consisted of doing her work. You know what educational institutions are like. Long-drawn-out wars about next-to-nothing; same old problems, and solutions, coming up once every fifteen years, the everlasting argument about the curriculum, the drawing-up of timetables. I always did my own, as my mother did. She had the right sort of mathematical mind for it. When I telephoned her to let her know I'd got my first headship, that was the one bit of advice she gave me. 'Do your own timetable, and then you can be sure it will be fair. Or as fair as possible.' That was my mother, absorbed in what she was doing. I often found that important projects on which I wasted weeks of my thought and that of committees galore turned out to be nonstarters or perishable goods, whereas something I decided off the cuff, not bothering with, was the most crucial thing that year. But she was there, and knew what was going on, and could be encouraging to those she judged to be doing their jobs properly. On the other hand she enjoyed family holidays."

"Did she now?"

"Oh, yes. She organized us. Trips abroad. France, Italy, before the war when we were quite small. Giving the family a good start in life was one of her principles. And holidays counted. And she enjoyed being efficient in a different sphere. But if Leslie French comes all over dramatic and suggests that she had a secret life, of adultery, perversion or whatever, even dreams, he'll have his work cut out to convince me. I'd be just as likely to believe she indulged in bank robbery or tightrope walking."

Noel admired the power of the scorn in her voice.

"Why did your mother do so well, then, Imogen?"

"People accepted her leadership. That's not easy. And she filled up every day. Nobody could accuse her of slacking."

"Was she liked?"

"On the whole, yes, for a woman in her position. There are checks and balances to everything. Ups and downs. But the Zeitgeist coincided with her notions and so she succeeded. How about that for a sentence for Leslie French's book?"

"She didn't impose her ideas on the world? On her part of the world?"

"To some small extent. More than most of us."

Noel nodded at the resigned voice in the earpiece. Imogen continued equably.

"Who has had the greater effect on, let's say, Leslie French's two Japanese sons: Hitler, Tojo, Einstein, Henry Ford, T. S. Eliot or Ethel?"

"You're making fun of me."

"Uncle, I wouldn't dare." Imogen's voice was lively.

"Did she choose your name?" he asked, out of the blue.

"I expect so. She respected Shakespeare. He was part of that knowledge we were all heirs to. I believe, you'll know this, that now scholars aren't sure that Imogen was the name Shakespeare intended, or wrote."

"Imogen," he mused. "Yes. A splendid mistake." He repeated the two names. "Imogen, Innogen, Imogen. Yes. She made a good mother in your view?"

"Of course. Why do you ask that?"

"I was thinking of Irène's mother." They had spoken about her at the beginning of the conversation. "Farmer's daughter; lawyer's wife. She was nothing like Ethel. And yet they had France in common. '*France, mere des arts, des armes et des loix*.' I can't help thinking of your image of her life as disparate heaps of similar objects. That's beginning to trouble me."

"I can't come to terms with my mother's death. A poor, shrunken husk of a body when she had been so strong. Lying useless. It doesn't bear to think of. How old is Madame Dalsaux, Noel?"

"Seventy-nine. Four years older than I am."

"Oh, God."

"Is anything wrong?" The fright in her voice startled him.

Imogen took her time. He realized that each had wounded the other with mortality.

"I wish now I had gone with Irène. Ridding myself of the houses wasn't nearly the chore I expected."

"You'll be able to visit the old dear. She's a tough old stick." He failed as a prophet. Later that night Mme Dalsaux died, easy as a bird hitting a power cable. Her daughters were not with her. "I'll go and read French's questionnaire. He's put in quite a few blank sheets for my suggestions."

"*Tabula rasa? Tabulae?*"

"I'll say. I'm pleased, rather than

otherwise that French has appeared to smarten us up about Ethel."

"If he had not," Imogen said, "we should have had to invent him. Well, do your homework properly. Full answers in complete sentences."

"Will he understand them?" he asked.

"Oh, no."

The evening sun touched an empty stretch of wall. He'd hang the Blessed Beatrice, damsel Ethel there, he decided, to be caught only by red west light.

"Don't expect too much," Imogen warned him. "It'll be better than nothing."

She put down the phone before he could answer. He stared in surprised disappointment at the silent instrument. He returned to his study. An hour and a half later as he played evasively in his head with French's questions the telephone rang again to announce a death in France.

'*Did'st thou not require*
Knowledge?'

Other titles in the Ulverscroft Large Print Series:

TO FIGHT THE WILD
Rod Ansell and Rachel Percy

Lost in uncharted Australian bush, Rod Ansell survived by hunting and trapping wild animals, improvising shelter and using all the bushman's skills he knew.

COROMANDEL
Pat Barr

India in the 1830s is a hot, uncomfortable place, where the East India Company still rules. Amelia and her new husband find themselves caught up in the animosities which seethe between the old order and the new.

THE SMALL PARTY
Lillian Beckwith

A frightening journey to safety begins for Ruth and her small party as their island is caught up in the dangers of armed insurrection.

THE WILDERNESS WALK
Sheila Bishop

Stifling unpleasant memories of a misbegotten romance in Cleave with Lord Francis Aubrey, Lavinia goes on holiday there with her sister. The two women are thrust into a romantic intrigue involving none other than Lord Francis.

THE RELUCTANT GUEST
Rosalind Brett

Ann Calvert went to spend a month on a South African farm with Theo Borland and his sister. They both proved to be different from her first idea of them, and there was Storr Peterson — the most disturbing man she had ever met.

ONE ENCHANTED SUMMER
Anne Tedlock Brooks

A tale of mystery and romance and a girl who found both during one enchanted summer.

CLOUD OVER MALVERTON
Nancy Buckingham

Dulcie soon realises that something is seriously wrong at Malverton, and when violence strikes she is horrified to find herself under suspicion of murder.

AFTER THOUGHTS
Max Bygraves

The Cockney entertainer tells stories of his East End childhood, of his RAF days, and his post-war showbusiness successes and friendships with fellow comedians.

MOONLIGHT AND MARCH ROSES
D. Y. Cameron

Lynn's search to trace a missing girl takes her to Spain, where she meets Clive Hendon. While untangling the situation, she untangles her emotions and decides on her own future.

NURSE ALICE IN LOVE
Theresa Charles

Accepting the post of nurse to little Fernie Sherrod, Alice Everton could not guess at the romance, suspense and danger which lay ahead at the Sherrod's isolated estate.

POIROT INVESTIGATES
Agatha Christie

Two things bind these eleven stories together — the brilliance and uncanny skill of the diminutive Belgian detective, and the stupidity of his Watson-like partner, Captain Hastings.

LET LOOSE THE TIGERS
Josephine Cox

Queenie promised to find the long-lost son of the frail, elderly murderess, Hannah Jason. But her enquiries threatened to unlock the cage where crucial secrets had long been held captive.

THE TWILIGHT MAN
Frank Gruber

Jim Rand lives alone in the California desert awaiting death. Into his hermit existence comes a teenage girl who blows both his past and his brief future wide open.

DOG IN THE DARK
Gerald Hammond

Jim Cunningham breeds and trains gun dogs, and his antagonism towards the devotees of show spaniels earns him many enemies. So when one of them is found murdered, the police are on his doorstep within hours.

THE RED KNIGHT
Geoffrey Moxon

When he finds himself a pawn on the chessboard of international espionage with his family in constant danger, Guy Trent becomes embroiled in moves and countermoves which may mean life or death for Western scientists.